Jackie
Yo[illegible]
story teller. I can not
wait to hear/read
your stories
In friendship
Barb

Gatherings X

The En'owkin Journal of First North American Peoples

Fall 1999

Theytus Books Ltd.
Penticton, BC
Canada

Gatherings
The En'owkin Journal of First North American Peoples
Volume X 1999

Canadian Cataloguing in Publication Data
Main entry under title:

Gatherings

Annual.
ISSN 1180-0666 ISBN 0-919441-86-6
1. Canadian literature (English)--Indian authors--Periodicals.* 2. Canadian literature (English)--20th century--Periodicals.* 3. American literature--Indian authors--Periodicals. 4. American literature--20th century--Periodicals. I. En'owkin Centre. II. En'owkin International School of Writing.
PS8235.I6G35 C810.8'0897 C91-031483-7

Editors:	Greg Young-Ing, Jeannette Armstrong, Rasunah Marsden & Florene Belmore
Design & Layout:	Florene Belmore
Proof Reading:	Regina (Chick) Gabriel
Cover Design:	Florene Belmore
Cover Art:	Trauma Mama Inc.

Please send submissions and letter to Gatherings, c/o En'owkin Centre, RR #2, Site 50, Comp. 8, Penticton, BC, V2A 6J7 Canada All submissions must be accompanied by a self-addressed envelope (SASE). Manuscripts without SASE's may not be returned. We will not consider previously published manuscripts or visual art.

The publisher acknowledges the support of the Canada Council, Department of Canadian Heritage and the Cultural Services Branch of the Province of British Columbia in the publication of this book.

Printed in Canada

TABLE OF CONTENTS

FIRE

Editorial Note

Welcome to the tenth anniversary volume of *Gatherings: The En'owkin Journal of First North American Peoples.* The first annual volume of *Gatherings* was published by Theytus Books for the En'owkin International School of Writing in 1990. At that time there was an excitement running through the Aboriginal community about the first journal in North America that would publish a current sampling of Aboriginal literature each year. Over the years, after nine volumes of *Gatherings,* over three hundred Aboriginal authors have been published in the journal.

This special volume celebrates the first decade with a selection of some the most pertinent writing published throughout the first nine volumes. These volumes contain a wide sampling of works by most of the established Aboriginal authors in North America, other Indigenous authors from around the world, and some astonishing pieces by talented emerging writers. It was a difficult editorial task to choose a representative retrospective selection for this tenth volume. Indeed, a vast array of excellent authors and quality writing could not be included.

This commemorative volume is especially dedicated to four Gatherings contributors who have since passed on to the Spirit World: Colleen Fielder, Lorne Simon, E.K. (Kim) Caldwell and Arnie Louie. It has been an honour to publish these talented authors in the Gatherings journal and allow them to live on through their writing. Pieces by Colleen, Lorne, Kim and Arnie that symbolize what they stood for were chosen to be the final words in the closing Tribute section of this volume.

Much Respect,

The Editors

Guest Editorial

In the remaining years of this century, we must escape the ecologically destructive path we are on and begin to live in balance with the productive carrying capacity of the Earth.

The list of environmental dangers we face are familiar and indisputable: a human population that increases by three people a second; a decline in global food production since 1984 through topsoil loss of twenty-five billion tonnes a year; toxic chemical poisoning of air, water and soil; atmospheric change from acid rain, ozone depletion and accumulation of greenhouse gasses; destruction of tropical rainforest at the rate of one acre per second; species extinction at an estimated rate recently revised up to 50,000 species annually.

Human beings are now the deadliest predator in the history of life on Earth. We have reached this unprecedented state of urgency because we no longer remember that we are animals who retain an absolute need for air, water, soil and other life forms for our survival.

In the five hundred years since Columbus' arrival, the waves of immigrants to North America have lacked the respect for the Earth as a sacred place and the spiritual connection to the land that the Aboriginal people have. To the newcomers, land and its resources were merely "resources," "commodities," or "opportunities" to be exploited until exhausted and then abandoned. Today, transnational companies with head offices in other countries with even less attachment to the land, continue to accelerate the destructive process to maximize profit.

If we are to resolve our ecocrisis, we must achieve a new spiritual covenant with the land and with all of the other life forms with whom we share this planet. I have learned from my Aboriginal friends in Canada, the U.S.A., Brazil, Sarawak and Australia, that they understand to the very core of their being that the Earth is their Mother, the source of life itself, and this tinges their actions with respect and reverence. We, non-Aboriginal people, have much to learn spiritually from Aboriginal people and need to do so through dialogue based on mutual respect and dignity.

It would indeed be the greatest achievement to reach the

new millennium living in harmony with the planet.

It is high time we learned to listen and allow ourselves to benefit from the teachings and perspectives of Aboriginal people themselves. In the midst of all the misrepresentation, misinformation and propaganda that exits today, I consider it a blessing that my Aboriginal friends at the En'owkin Centre and Theytus Books have taken the responsibility of compiling and publishing this important annual journal of writing by Aboriginal people.

"ORATORY: Where We Come From"

Speech to the Unrepresented Nations and Peoples Organization

Hua Kola, my name is Arvol Looking Horse, my Lakota name is Horseman. I humbly stand before you as Keeper of the Sacred Pipe, which White Buffalo Calf Woman brought nineteen generations ago. *Wakan Tanka*, Great Spirit created everything upon mother earth. *Paha Sapa*, the Sacred Black Hills in South Dakota is where our spiritual power and identity flows, the heart of everything that is. Our stories tell us that our ancestor emerged from the place we know now as Wind Cave. Many of our stories and Star Knowledge informs our way of life.

After the Creation story a great race took place around the Sacred Black Hills in an area called the racetrack. The race was between the two-legged and the four-legged. The two-legged won the race. From that time on we used the Buffalo for ceremonies, for food, shelter and clothing. Our First People were the *pte oyate* (Buffalo People). The extinction of the Buffalo reflects the status of the Lakota people.

The victimization our people have experienced at the hands of government representatives over the last hundred years continues to this day, and it must stop. A hundred years ago the government ordered the slaughter of sixty million Buffalo, this constituted our main livelihood. The intention was to pacify and reduce our people to a state of dependence and poverty. Our Sacred Lands, the heart of our Nation, was guaranteed with the signing of the 1851 Treaty. At this time the representatives from the White House had the bible and our representatives had the Treaty Pipe. They prayed over this land. Over a hundred years ago, that was our way of life. We kept our word. Then, gold was discovered in our holy land. A Lakota Standing Rock Delegate, Goose, made this statement regarding the events that took place.

> General Custer and some soldiers came to me and asked me if I was able to go and show them where I found this gold... I told them I could, so we started for the Black Hills... Soon after our return, General Custer started for the Black Hills a second time, to keep the white prospectors out as the land belonged to the Indian. ... Sometime after, I and some oth-

> ers were called to council held at Red Cloud Agency, Nebraska to confer with some commissioners that were sent out by the government to cede the Black Hills to the United States... We refused on the ground that a majority of the Sioux were out on a hunting trip.

General George Custer tricked Goose into thinking they would protect the land; instead Custer ended up paving the unexpectant road for the white prospectors, the Fort Laramie Treaty. The invading settlers defaced our Sacred Black Hills and we have struggled for the return of our holy land to this day. Our leaders have always fought to protect the land and the people. Crazy Horse and Sitting Bull, two of the greatest Indigenous leaders in American history, never signed a treaty and never relinquished Aboriginal title to the land. Crazy Horse had the most followers and he refused to Treaty. They were both politically assassinated for their resistance to the U.S. subjugation. However, their blood relatives are alive and well today. They can kill our leaders but their visions will never die.

General Custer and General Ulysses Grant were under orders to "pacify" the "hostiles" using any means necessary. The United States government waged a genocide campaign against my ancestors. Our people endured unspeakable acts. One example of how they dealt with the "Indian problem" was the Massacre at Wounded Knee in 1890. Four hundred unarmed men, women and children were slaughtered. At the time of arrival there were over fifty million Native Americans. In one hundred years they decimated our populations to a mere million. Some tribes were slaughtered to extinction. There were more "casualties" in the so-called Indian wars in a fifty year period than there was with WWI and WWII combined. The holocaust of Native Americans has yet to be truthfully depicted. Our status is similar to that of the Buffalo. In fact, there are more of our ancestors remains in museums than there are living survivors. We seek to reclaim these sacred remains which were perversely displayed for all Americans to observe, further degrading our forefathers. It is time to restore the dignity of our People and Nations.

The survivors were forced on to concentration camps, the

United States government called reservations. Our children were taken to Christian run residential schools where they were physically, emotionally, sexually and spiritually abused, and severely punished if they spoke their language or practised their traditions. Our ceremonies were outlawed. Our ceremonies were forced underground for fear of persecution by the United States government until the 1978 Freedom of Religious Act. A country that was founded on the principles of democracy and religious freedoms did so with the blood and soul of my ancestors. The injustice continues. I am here to see it stop. We must correct the historical wrongs. We need your help to do this. Apartheid and genocide exist in America and will continue to exist unless the world pressures the United States to deal justly and honourably with the First Americans.

Today, with so few resources available, our people are at the mercy of government officials. These same government officials continue to take our sacred lands, livestock and horses. We have no avenue for due process or legal recourse. We are not protected by the U.S. constitution. That is why I address you today, to pursue our rights on behalf of the Sioux Nation. We are a resilient and spiritual people who know the time has come for prophesies to emerge from sacred places.

A prophecy which has great significance for us is the story of the Great Flood which came to this sacred island long before the contact with Europeans. A flood was sent to purify Mother Earth and our people were residing in an area we now call Pipestone, Minnesota. This sacred stone represents the blood of our ancestors. It was sometime after the flood that the Sacred Pipe was brought to our people by a spirit woman we now refer to as White Buffalo Calf Woman. She instructed our people in sacred ceremonies and how to live in balance with all life. The bowl of the pipe is made of the *Inyansa* (red stone of our mother) and it also represents the female. The stem of the pipe is made of wood and represents the Tree of Life and the male. The Tree of Life represents the root of our ancestors. As this tree grows, so does the spirit of the ancestors' people. The only time the pipe is put together is when you are in prayer. After she had given these instructions to our ancestors, she said she would return as a White Buffalo Calf.

Our prophet Black Elk said the Nations Sacred Hoop was broken at the Massacre of Wounded Knee in 1890. To begin mending the hoop we have led a spiritual ride to wipe the Tears of the Seventh Generation from 1986 to 1990. The Nations Hoop has begun to heal and mend. The prophecy tells us the White Buffalo Calf will return.

In August of 1994, a White Buffalo Female Calf was born. This tells us it is time to take our rightful place in leading the people towards Peace and Balance once again. We will be strong and the people will heal. Our healing is global.

On June 21st of 1996 we will return to the Sacred Black Hills to pray for world peace. We will pray for the return of our holy land. We will pray for the two-legged, four-legged, and winged ones and for Mother Earth. We ask you to pray with us. Indigenous Nations know our earth is suffering. Humanity is heading towards total chaos and destruction—that is both a scientific and spiritual fact. The new millennium will make harmony or the end of life as we know it. Starvation, war and toxic waste have been the mark of the Great Myth of Progress and Development. As caretakers of the heart of Mother Earth it is our responsibility to tell our brothers and sisters to seek Peace. We ask every Nation to declare June 21 World Peace and Prayer Day. Pray at this time with us from your sacred areas, churches, temples, mosques. Pray for the Seventh Generation to have World Peace and Harmony. This is the message I bring to you. May Peace be with you all.

Mitakuye Oyasin

Roots and Wings

There is nothing more that we parents can do than give our children roots and wings. We teach them all we can at home and the rest is entirely up to them to figure out.

One time when one of my sons was a child he said to me, "Mom, I think I know why they are taking down our forest and our totem poles, and disturbing our graves." And I said, "Why?" And he said, "So that we won't be able to tell that these are our homelands."

Back home we people of the Haida Nation have started calling our sacred islands "Haida-Gwai," because that's what we always called them. We don't call them "Queen Charlotte Islands" anymore, because that's what the whiteman called them. And so I urge all our First Nations to re-establish our own names for our homelands. Each of us has our own names for our mountains, our valleys, our lakes and rivers. Re-establish those names! Then we will always be reminded that those are our homelands, and that the Creator gave us the responsibility of looking after those homelands and governing ourselves in our own home.

The Creator did not put us here so that we would have to be subservient to somebody else's provincial or federal government, or somebody else's rules. We don't fit into their government and their laws and their ways, because many of their values are in direct conflict with ours. And so our First Nations must re-establish our own distinct governments too. That is the only way that there is hope for our people and our land.

This Sacred Land

The land on which we live is sacred. I know this because many many Native people lived here in Peace and Harmony with the Nature Spirits. The people did not have policemen, padlocks, prisons, penitentiaries or burglar alarms. Nor did they have the "book" (the Bible). But they knew about the Great Spirit, who created everything.

A great chief of the *Similaka-meugh* (Eagle People, now known as Similkameen) was born in this place, along with others of the People, before and after him. They all drank the crystal clear water of the valley's rivers and streams, grew their food on its unpoisoned soil, breathed its fresh, clean air, and worshipped the power of the Sun as it blessed them with life each morning.

Our Ancestors had a special respect for the Mother Earth and all it offered them. I'm told by Elders they built their shelters in the ground, which provided them with an insulated warmth in the winter and a cool dwelling in the summer. If one looks carefully around this area, one can see signs of this lifestyle.

Many of the valley people respected the wild creatures which walked the land, flew in its winds, and swam in its rivers. They took only that which they truly needed for food and gave thanks to the Creator for those provisions. Life was much less complex then, and the People of "The Ashnola, Similkameen and Okanagan Valleys" enjoyed life that way.

It makes my heart heavy when I see our Native people forgetting the true and good ways of our ancestors. It saddens me to see them come in with bulldozers, drive over, scrape off, and flatten out our sacred Mother Earth which housed, fed and buried the People. It is unfortunate to see the Red Man, slowly become a "brown" white man as he puts the value of money and material possessions above his oneness with the spirit in all living things. He has forgotten that Grandfather Sun, Mother Earth, Grandmother Moon and our Spirited Waters need to be honoured, respected, cared for, and shared with for their spiritual, emotional, mental, and physical powers. He has forgotten that those powers also lie within himself, waiting to be revealed and united with others in a positive way.

When a child does something very wrong, a good parent will take away a special privilege which the child is used to. When the child shows that he has learned something positive by making his mistake, then he is allowed to regain the privilege.

If we, the children of this land, do not show more honour, respect, caring and sharing for the special privilege of living on this—The Mother Earth—then she and Grandfather Sun, through the power of the Great Spirit, may take away this great privilege which we have selfishly taken for granted. This great reward is called "Life." It is experienced by showing Love and Respect for all natural elements—earth, air, fire, water, wind, and for wildlife and all living things on which Human Beings are dependent, remember. Let us remember that the way to live in peace and harmony with each other and our surroundings is to be at peace with ourselves. Many of the things which have tempted Red and White men alike have made him seemingly very unloving and unpeaceful. May we overcome all those qualities we do not need (such as greed), by showing the Good Qualities of our True Nature—like "Giving." Most importantly, may we know and remember that we have, deep within our beings—a Peaceful and Loving Spirit. It is time to let it out!

May we remember these truths as life, here—in this valley, in other valleys, and on this Planet depends on us knowing and living them.

We can choose to learn from our Traditional and Spiritual Elders to live in harmony and balance with all things. Or, we can choose to learn from those who seek to profit, no matter what the cost to Mother Earth. If it is to survive—the natural world, the world we all know and love—needs protection and understanding. IF IT DOES NOT SURVIVE, OF COURSE, NEITHER WILL WE!!!

Witness Testimony (excerpt)

The 1st of January of 1994, like a cry of despair, the struggle of the liberation, the National Liberation Army of the Zapatista emerged. The Zapatista National Liberation Army emerged.

I know the reality of the Chiapas. That's where the petroleum lies in the Indigenous regions. That's where wood is. That's where the fish in the rivers are. That's where electrical energy is produced. And in the Indigenous communities they only see that the cable go by that transport electrical energy.

So it is a constant theft in Indigenous regions.

And then there's no possibility of arrangement with ourselves who are now claiming our own autonomy which is an internal sovereignty of our communities and regions. It is not possible and this is in contradiction because we don't only want economic autonomy or cultural autonomy because they only see us as folkloric.

Like the province that we live in, in our regions, extreme poverty is a product of our culture that we have not assimilated from the development of the non-Indigenous culture. But we have analysed that this is not the case. It's not a problem of assimilation, it's a problem of a political nature because our regions, our Indigenous communities, are seeds of votes that give power to those that lead the Mexican State.

So what we want is an economic autonomy, and cultural, territorial and of our educational system as well. We see this as part of a whole and if we do not achieve these things, we cannot have autonomy nor anything, because they're only just cheating us.

So we are living a very serious problem and we do not know right now, we are organizing ourselves to have great trust in our own people because, as I mentioned, we are in danger of being disappeared. Because also the non-Indigenous do not accept us as being different and that we are originating from those lands. And they contribute with their attitudes to try to integrate us or assimilate us through their indigenous policies or *politicus indicanistas.*

They always want to study us and to take things when the things that they bring don't fix our problems. They have not understood that we have the capacity, the maturity, our own institutions, our own internal life, already organized and decided from always, from the oldest of times within our own communities which is the base of where our sovereignty emerges. And that together with our other brothers and sisters of our other communities, we reproduce this way of directing our affairs.

But we always have the interference of the state and this is what has not been understood. And they do not want to abandon us. But we say that we do not want any more paternalism and that from the 1st of January of 1994 in which the Zapatista struggle created a resurgence of the strength of the Indigenous Peoples of Mexico, we stated with a greater strength of process, of recovery of the dignity that had been stolen from us by the invaders.

Now, we are living through a very important process. And very dangerous because all our regions, all our Indigenous regions, are full of army, of armed forces. Because they know that we want everything. And they recognize that we are in the right but they don't want to accept it and they're scared. But we also want to contribute, with these values that we own, of our life in our communities, we want to share it with others. This is an alternative of life for everybody, whether they like it or not. It is a whole alternative because there are many political and economic models that have collapsed, and now there are no alternatives.

We want to reconstruct a new relationship, even with the Mexican State, of coordination. That has not been the case up until now because there we are in cohabitation. It is also a reality that they are there, that they are an historical product, those that are not Indigenous, but they do not understand this and we are not there to be submitted. But we are different peoples and we have to enter into harmony through cooperation. This is what we are proposing:

that even the Mestizo people be recognized but that we have historical reparations for all the historical damages that are being done to us.

So that is the proposal for the reality of our nation state. We do not know what will happen, we do not know if they will accept it or not. We have decided to recover our sovereignty, our autonomy.

Margarita Gutierrez, Chiapas, Mexico
Transcript of testimony given April, 4, 1996
First Nations International Court of Justice
(Simultaneous translation into English from Spanish)

'Indian History Through Indian Eyes'
Excerpts From Keynote Address
National Aboriginal Youth Conference
February 11, 1989
Ottawa

You know, we, all of us, belong to something I would like to call "imagined communities." Imagined communities in the sense that we imagine ourselves to have some thing to connect with really broad numbers of people. I think of that in terms of myself once in the streets of Paris, going along where no one else was speaking any language I spoke and I bumped into a fellow there who was from rural Georgia. Now I am a Seneca fellow. I was born and raised on the Cattaraugus Indian Reservation, a very rural area and I grew up in a house that was built in the 1780s. It was an old house; it didn't have any running water, it had electricity. We had gardens and that kind of business and heated with wood. I grew up in a Longhouse community, a very traditional community and the people all around me were of that persuasion. And that was sort of my background.

So I had bumped into this fellow in Paris and he says: "Well, you're an American" and on some level there is some truth to that. He says: well, he was from Georgia. He started telling what he was about and all this stuff. We were walking down the streets of Paris and here we were "fellows" somehow, you know. I have thought about that experience a lot because the guy from Georgia, he was a brother in the John Birch Society. You know, I am sure he had strong social feelings for the Klu Klux Klan which were positive. In America the guy probably would not talk to me, but in France all of a sudden we "fellows," we were Americans. We shared a kind of imagined community. It takes a lot of imagination for a Seneca fellow and a Georgia cracker to be together. I can tell you that it is not easy to do this. It is an imagined thing.

Go back some hundreds of years and I think a good place to start to tell the story of the Americas is to go all the way back to the eleventh century in Europe and begin to get an angle on who the peoples are. Because my talk today is about who we are. It is about who are the Indians and also who are the non-Indians. I want to locate that in the peoples' minds.

In the eleventh century, the Pope—his name was Gregory the Seventh—announced to the Emperors, Kings and what ever nobility of Europe that the vicar of Christ on earth actually should have more recognized power than the Emperors and he began to claim the right to excommunicate, to throw people out of the Church. And that is what was called the Papal Revolution; it was about 1057 this happened. This revolution started a big stir and people were called upon to have opinions about this idea; the community of Europe was actually formed around this idea. Europe didn't have an identity until this time. The people of Europe were called upon to see themselves as the Christian world. Christ was believed to be coming back; they thought there would be second appearance of Christ. So the mandate of the Christian world, as it was proposed at that time, was that upon Christ's "re-arrival," he was to find his Kingdom in good order. But the Pope was pointing out that the Kingdom was not in good order and that, in fact, the homeland where Christ was born was in the hands of non-believers.

So the Pope started at that time to organize a series of foreign wars, in which the nobility of Europe was called upon to provide the military service to this effort. To go across the Mediterranean to seize the lands of peoples there in the name of a sort of now pan-European nationalism. It was kind of an imagined community for them at the time. I mean, Polish Princesses were called upon to unite with Italian city states in a way that they had never done before. These people had all been at war, or at least had some mutual hostility, and they all spoke different languages and had different histories. At any rate, they were called upon to unite themselves and they did do this.

Imagined communities are extremely powerful. They caused people who lived in western Europe to gather themselves together to march to lands they knew nothing about, to find ways to cross the Mediterranean and to engage in wars with people they knew little about. This went on for generations, and you have to understand the crusades went on and on. Children went on crusades; warriors went on crusades; people went on crusades. It was a powerful movement of ideology of people being imposed upon to think of themselves as having obligations to do things which I think clear reflection would have denied. But it was a powerful movement that went on at that time. I always found it to be a most extraordinary movement because of the way it would later affect my own peoples.

European peoples had come to an adoption of spiritual ancestors who were not their own ancestors. In the Christian experience, western European peoples, Germans, Czechoslovakians, Scandinavians, who had absolutely no lineage whatsoever, connected with the Middle East; were called upon to recognize as their spiritual ancestors'nomadic tribesmen who were a specific nationality of ancient Israelites. Their ancestors became Adam and Eve; became Abraham; became David. The western Europeans, who have absolutely no ancestors with any of this relation adopted them as their ancestors. As this nationalism would spread we find that this community, which is expanding, which has attacked the Middle East, is now an imperialist power that intends to extend over the world and over the minds and identities of the peoples of the world.

In the mid-14th century, Portuguese sailors discovered islands in the Atlantic. The first one that was discovered was Lanzarote Island in the Canaries and then shortly after that, Madeira Islands in the Atlantic, which were actually part of the same group of islands. The Canary Islands were inhabited by a race of people call the Gounches, who were said to be a brown bronze skinned people. The Spanish basically launched a war against them that went from 1404 to 1496, a war of conquest. The purpose of the war was to basically take over the Islands. Now, during this period of time one island was unoccupied, and that was Madeira Island. No people had ever lived there, and the Spanish tried to occupy that place.

By the 1450s, Madeira was the most successful colony in the world. It had become the world's largest exporter of sugar and sugar cane products. At any rate, the Gounches were finally overcome in 1496. If you will notice, this is four years after Christopher Columbus sailed to the Americas. Today there are no Gounches; they are completely exterminated; they are wiped off the face of the earth as peoples. We know very little about their languages.

There is a little bit left of their patterns of their clothing and stuff, but basically, fundamentally, they don't exist anymore.

Christopher Columbus went to the Canary Islands and he prayed to his God when he was getting ready for this trip to the Americas. And he had a pretty good plan. He was planning to sail west across the Atlantic. His purpose for sailing west actually is in his log in which he states that the reason for his trip was to find gold. The purpose for finding gold was so that the Crowns of Castille and Saville would be able to raise more armies to continue the crusades in the Middle East. So the crusades were still alive in Christopher Columbus' mind when he came. People who get a chance should read about this moment in history because it is a very telling moment. He tells that, on October 12th, 1492, they had seen land the night before. On that morning the first thing that they saw were naked people.

Christopher Columbus was the first one to begin the invasion and the so called development of the modern world, the invasions of Europeans around the world. He is the initial viewer, from the deck of the ships of the Pinta and Santa Maria.

You know, these two worlds existed apart. They did not know of each other's existence. There was the western hemisphere—and in some ways you have to include Australia, New Zealand and those other places where Indigenous people live—and then there was Europe. Europe, with its own form of history, its ideologies, and just an incredible imagination in Europe. And here they arrived in the Americas and they saw what they described as naked peoples. And what they really came into was paradise. Listen to Christopher Columbus' description of the peoples he finds. When they arrive at Hispanola, the Spanish say there are probably eight million people living on Hispanola. They described this incredible rainforest and mangrove forest area covered with peoples and gardens, and fruit trees, peoples who paddle out in their canoes and bring fish. They talked about peoples who were dancing, happy and friendly.

The first Indians invite the Spanish ashore and the Spanish are experiencing a moment like no other in history: friendliness, happiness and everybody is getting along fine. There are large populations of well fed people and there is nothing here except what we would have described as paradise. The temperature varied from 68 degrees to 79 degrees. There was always food, there was always whatever people needed. You would want to read these accounts that Christopher Columbus has of his moments of entering this place, his description of the trees, of the birds, of the people. It is an incredible world and one of the greatest adventures. In fact, no one will ever have an adventure like it again. And then you would want to read the other part in the book called, "The History of the Caribbean" in which it describes that between 1492 and 1496 two-thirds to three quarters of the population of Hispanola disappears. Two-thirds to three quarters of the population! Four to five million people disappeared in four years! How could that have happened? Well, it happened!

And Columbus' arrival is a story that is celebrated in the West. The West celebrates this as a powerful achievement, as a positive thing. But, within four years of the Spanish seeking for gold, we saw the enslavement of the Indians, the incredible cruelty visited upon the Indians by the Conquistadors, the diseases, the warfare—the population of Hispanola was diminished by five million. Cruelty did that. Cruelty that was built around this ideology which the Spanish brought with them. You will remember the Spanish were looking for Asia. They were thinking that they were going to find India. And so they looked at the first peoples who they saw on the shores and said, these must be Indians.

There were hundreds of different kinds of Indians just on the east coast of the Americas, from South America along the Mesoamerican shore, all the way around the Gulf and into Florida and up the coast. Hundreds of different types of Indians, speaking different languages, with different personalities, with different cultures. And all of these Indians standing on the shore were lumped into one group. They were described by the Europeans as "the Indians." And the reason for that was because the Europeans did not know who the Indians were. They had only just invented the idea of Europeans a couple of hundred years before. But at that moment in time the Indians were understood by the Spanish to be "the others." They were the people who were not Europeans. The Europeans did not know who the Indians were; they knew who they were not. And from that time to this the Indians are still a mystery to the Europeans. The Europeans and their descendants in the Americas still don't know who the Indians are. But they know who they are not. They are not Europeans.

Europeans, when they described the Indians as "the others," really interpreted "the others" to be some others less than human, less than they were. So the designation of the Indians, I want to say, has two connotations. The first is a connotation of what it is not, and it is not Christian, and therefore, not human, not equal. And the other connotation is that it is used as a designation to disarm people about what they really are. It is phony designation. We are not Indians. Come on, give me a break. I am not an Indian. I am a Seneca. I have a very specific identity, a language, a land base, a right in my land base. But the term Indian recognizes no rights in the land, and it recognizes no rights in self-determination. It recognizes only a difference and the difference is, when you're an Indian you're "an other."

The Spanish conquest was the greatest crime in human history. It made the holocaust that the Germans did on the Jews in the forties seem "Mickey Mouse" compared to the holocaust that visited the Americas between the years 1492 and 1989. Consider this for a moment: when the Spanish arrived in Mexico, in 1520, the estimated population of Mexico was destroyed in the space of a generation. There has never been anything like it, except that it did not stop in Mexico. It went down into what is now Guatemala, Nicaragua, El Salvador, Yucatan. It went into Bolivia. It went to Peru. It went to Columbia. It went to Brazil. And where it went it brought the most horrifying death and destruction ever seen on the face of the earth: the most terrifying enslavements, the most miserable lives, to peoples who up to that point were living really very sustained lives.

Before we leave the Spanish, I want to paint a picture of what life was like in the Caribbean and Middle America. Who were the Indians really? They are now doing excavations of the Indian cities and civilizations of Yucatan that demonstrate that the Indians lived in the rainforests, with populations in the millions, where we today cannot seem to support populations in the tens of thousands. The Indians lived there in a way which did not destroy the rainforest. They had a system of building canals and they used to weave mats to put on top of the canals to raise hydroponic gardens to raise food. They raised food where we cannot raise food with the modern technologies. They had an ideology and a way of living with the environment that regenerated it, that made it possible for peoples to live there over millennia instead of destroying some place in two centuries.

The Indians are the peoples who worked out how to sustain human life, tree life, bird life, plant life, and make humans prosper in the middle of that process. They developed technologies to do it. And now we see that modern agronomists are studying Indian agriculture. They are studying Indian ways of making an irrigation system. Well, who was it who made the foods of the world, the food products of the world? I would like to just point out that we have not even scratched the surface of Indian agriculture yet. The Inca produced more kinds of food than all the other peoples in the world put together ever produced. They were the world's greatest evaluators of environments. Today Indians in Bolivia are raising foods at higher elevations than anyone else on the globe. Indians produced enormous types of foods; from chilies, to potatoes, to peppers, to cucumbers, to tomatoes. It is just remarkable. Whole bunches of stuff that we haven't seen yet up here; grain products that haven't made it out of South America yet. But Indian agriculture moves to the desert. Indian agriculture is in the rainforest. Indians are the saviours of the human race, if you can look at it from a point of view of need of food products!

The process of making this diversity of food products, while maintaining the integrity of the environment, shows the Indian was using the land in a rational way to sustain human and other life. There is no question that they did it better than anybody else in the whole world. If you had left Indians alone there would still be prosperity; eight million people would still be living and eating on Hispanola and there would still be a rainforest there on that terribly devastated and destroyed island. But the Spanish did not know who the Indians were. The Spanish only knew that the Indians were not Christians. And, as time goes by, the definitions of these things will change because the Indians will be given a choice: you will become Christian or you will become dead. And the Indians are forced to learn how to speak Spanish, English, or what ever is the language of the conquest.

In the beginning Indians were nationally Indian. Then, Indians were biologically Indian. As time goes by, most of the Indians are not quite "biologically pure" and after awhile it is hard to tell anyone where the nationality and biology are connected. And so we have this transformation of the identity of the Indian. People have lost track of who the Indians are. Sometimes I think that the ones who have lost track the most are the Indians.

In the 17th century, we saw transformations take place in the English speaking world. The English, by the way, before they were here, were going to colonize Ireland. They sent colonists, to Ireland, just like they would send to North America. And the idea was to get rid of the Indigenous Irish, and take their land, and cut down their woods, and sell all their assets. So they did that. They invaded Ulster in about 1565 and started a war there, which I believe we can all agree is still probably going on. You'll notice that the Irish are physically similar to the English. And the Irish had been Catholic in 1565 for about eight hundred years. But, when they arrived, the English colonists decided that the Irish were not Catholic, and that they probably were not even Christians. They even started to think they were some kind of pagans and then they started accusing them of being cannibals. They did all of this in order to rationalize attacking them and stealing their land. In fact, they were going full blast when the Spanish sent in Armadas in 1588. And, of course, the English beat the Spanish and that meant that the Atlantic would no longer be patrolled by Spanish boats and that English boats could now cross it. And that is why we started having the English colonization in the early 17th century in the Americas.

When the English arrived in the Americas, what they were doing in Ireland is what they started to do here. They took up the same fight. Except here, of course, the Indians were different, they really weren't Christians. This is the main excuse the English speaking people had about why they can take Indian lands and abuse Indian people.

In the 17th century, about the same time, John Locke proposes his theory of "possessive individualism," which goes roughly like this; he says, that with the appearance of money in the exchange system, rational human behaviour will be the organized behaviour which will lead to humans accumulating the greatest amount of money. And possessing—that is what the theory of "possessive individualism" is all about. And he says this rational behaviour is going to be what will dominate and control human activity in the world. He goes on to state, as an explanation of why there are governments, that there is a social contract that is made. But I think the important thing that we want to understand is that John Locke is the founder of modern European ideas about representative government because of his ideas of "possessive individualism." This theory says that greed is the source of human government.

I was once reading a piece by Vine Deloria which says that the purpose of a corporation is to own a planet. That's about as succinct a description that I can get to the realities of Western legal thinking. Western legal thinking is that rational behaviour leads to money and, therefore, the theory becomes prevalent throughout the West—especially in the English speaking countries that the proper use of land will be that use of land which generates the most money. Subsequently, if a trustee believes that the proper use of land is the use of land that generates the most money, then that trustee will always act to see that the people who have the most money to put into the development of land, will get the land.

The second part of this thinking, it seems to me, is that "rational use of land" means that there is a land use which has priority over human beings living on the land. The enclosure system in England was based on the idea that there are some ways to make more money using the land than having people live on it. Now tell me, doesn't that mean that, ultimately, the whole planet is going to be transformed for the purpose of making money and humans will have to live in the sea. It means that the priority use of the land is always for money. There is no priority for use of the land for life. No priority for the use of the land for the future. There is no future! There is just this mad and crazed idea that money is rational thinking—that people who are insanely greedy are the only sane people. That is what that means! Well, I say that the Indians do not agree. The Indians would not agree to transform the planet into a shopping mall!

I think one of the things that the reservation system has done is that it has infused the Indians with the mean-hearted spirit of the Europeans when it comes to being able to reach out to people, to care about people. We don't have that like we had.

I am one of the writers of a book on the subject of origins of a democratic tradition and on the influences of the Indians on the United States Constitution. I said earlier that the white people have this imagined community. The United States is an imagined community. When the United States Constitution was written, the Americans said something along these lines: they said, "We are the people who represent the principles of democracy."

When the United States wrote its constitution, it said; "All men are created equal." But we all know that there was slavery in the United States, and that some people were not created equal. It said that all men are endowed with certain inalienable rights; but where were the Indian's inalienable rights? Those rights were not real. It went on and on. Women were not given the right to own property or even have the rights to enjoy the fruits of their labour, their wages belonged to their husbands or their fathers. It was not a country of equality and it was not a country of liberty. It was a country of cruel slavery and of factory systems and all kinds of horrible thoughts and horrible times that were happening—a country of peoples in distress. But the Americans believe that they represent democracy. They have represented democracy in upholding some of the most horrible dictatorships on earth. They have represented democracy, and they represent it now, in countries of the world where there is no democracy. The United States arms and protects some of the most horrible processes in the world. If you don't believe me, please pay attention to what is going on in El Salvador, in Guatemala, in Indonesia, in many of the nation states of the world which are allies of the United States. So this ideology isn't real, is it? I mean, it's just an imaginary thing. It is imaginary that the United States is in favour of democracy. They don't care about democracy. But almost every American will embrace that idea.

I mention it because I say that there are in the world such things as imagined communities; that we are all subject to them. So I raise to you some questions that I want people to put some attention to. What is your imagined community? What is your Indian Nation? What does it stand for? What is it about? What are you about? What is real in your life? And how do you connect to reality? You have been presented, since the time you were born, with a whole list of things to believe that aren't real, a whole list of things to tell you who you are which are all lies. Things that are intended to enable the Canadian Government to more easily integrate you into their process, their process of finding the way to use the land with the highest degree of return on investment.

Who are you? What does it mean to be an Indian? What is this imagined community that we share in the Americas, from the Arctic to the rainforest and to the tip of Tierre Del Fuego. Who are we? What do we stand for? What are we when we are being the best that we can be? And, as much as anything else, what have we lost? What has been brainwashed away from us? What has been taken away from that leaves us now in this condition that I would describe as a condition of extreme distress. What are the issues that we really need to look into? What is the identity that we need to reconstruct for ourselves? How can we use our imaginations to make our world a better place for us and for the future generations of our people?

The Nazis were the culmination of a thing that I like to describe as the Aryan model of history. There was a century in which the Aryans, the white people, the indo-Europeans, Caucasians, whatever, imagined themselves to be the superior race of the world. They imagined their biology to be superior to everyone else's, their brain capacity bigger than everyone else's. They were smarter, they were stronger, better off whatever it was needed to be, and they called themselves Aryans. And in their quest for domination they rewrote history. The way they rewrote history was that they discounted all of the contributions and all of the accomplishments of every other people on the face of the earth. They said that the Aryan culture came from ancient Greece and Rome.

So during the time of the crusades one was imposed upon to imagine that one's ancestors were ancient Semitics. And, in the time of the Aryans, one was imposed upon to imagine that one's ancestors were pure blooded Aryans living in Greece who had no interaction with anybody else. And when it got to the Americas, the anthropology in the Americas was built around the idea of the Aryan ascension also. Their argument was that the Indians were one of a stage of social evolution that was going to one day evolve into civilized human beings. Except that we would probably die off first, so they had better study us to see what we were doing during this stage of development. So anthropology was originally designed to be an argument to sustain the superiority ideology of the West, the Aryan ascension.

When they did this, they wiped out from history all of the Indian stuff. Everything that Indians ever did was wiped out. The Indians were whited out, and are still being whited out. Their history has been distorted. Their philosophies have been demeaned. Their reality has been denied. We are as much the victims of pernicious history as we are the victims of colonialism.

No wonder so many of our young people arrive at this time thinking that to be Indian is to be nothing. Because if you read the history books, it is to be nothing. If you read the anthropology text books, it is to be nothing. So it is being proposed to you; you have been given this ideology. You are to imagine that Indians just sort of sat around here half naked and waited for the sun to go down and woke up the next morning and walked around in the woods. They never had a thought; they never produced a culture. There was never anything here of any substance whatsoever. It is a piece of the ideology, a piece of the propaganda that has been proposed to you. You are supposed to imagine that, and way too many of us do it. Way too many of us imagine that.

You have a right to self-government that you define, that is not defined by the Canada Indian Act. That means you have a right to land separate from Canada's right. Because Canada thinks the only right that you have to land is there is until somebody else comes along with a better way to make more money off of it. Why not argue sovereignty? The right of sovereignty means Canada has no trusteeship; you have that right. I know that it is hard when you have been told forever and ever that Indians aren't capable of being responsible for themselves. The trustee thing says that Indians aren't responsible people; therefore, Canada has to think for them. But really it is an insult. It is Canada saying that Indians can't think. That is what they have been saying ever since they got here.

They say Indians cannot think because they are not Christian and they have the wrong ancestors.

When Indians relate to Canada, they relate to Canada in one of two ways. There are only two choices. They relate to Canada as distinct peoples who are going to assert political rights, or they relate to Canada as part of the Canadian general population who have only civil rights. There is no middle ground here. You have a right to a continued existence or you are going to disappear. It is that simple. If you have a right to a continued existence, then you must insist on rights of sovereignty. Because the right to sovereignty is the right to continue to exist. That's all. That is how it works in international law.

I want people to ask themselves some hard questions, and I want to help direct that discussion a bit. The identity that the Americans laid out for the Indians was of the "vanishing American." And they were not passive about them vanishing. They took active steps to see to it: shot them, chased them away, starved them and did everything they could to them. Finally, they tried to put them on reservations. And the Indians, stubborn souls that they were, refused to vanish in their minds. Schools were brought in. And that is what they were for, people. The schools were to provide two things. One, was to provide you with the ability to do the work that they wanted to hire you to do, to become wage labourers. You had to learn how to speak English. You had to learn how to file horses hooves, and all that kind of stuff. You had to learn how to become servants, so they put schools there.

But the other reason for having schools was to teach you that there is an order of priorities, that there is a ranking of worth in people. This ranking of worth was what the schools led you to believe. To believe that some people were smarter than others and therefore, should have more say in things than others. And that you elect people to speak for you and after you have elected them you have nothing to say about it. That some countries are smarter and better than other countries are. It takes years to teach you that. So they keep bringing you back and they test you; time after time you rank in these tests. Then after awhile you are a "B" student. You're a "B" student, because a "B" student means there is an "A" student above you and it means a "B" student should be subservient to an

"A" student. It means that your rights have been diminished. This is what the purpose of an education is in Canada. It's a socialization process to brainwash you into their way of thinking.

I propose that we need a new imagination. You guys have to imagine that you are going to be around for three or four generations, or fifty or sixty more generations. People have to start imagining that we are going to continue to exist. Our great Grandparents were told that Indians were going to disappear and they were getting shot, they were dying from small pox and all kinds of stuff was happening to them, but they didn't believe Indians would disappear. How come the people of this generation think they are going to disappear? How come you guys are lying down and giving up?

Our peoples in the past really put up a struggle. They put up a hard, tough struggle. In the United States Indians put up a military struggle. They put on a military struggle for over a hundred years. They fought until they fell down dead, most of them. And we lost most of our population. Now our people have begun to come back a little bit. But they have come back a little bit brainwashed. And I am sympathetic about that brainwashing process, because I went to school as long as any of you did.

I think it is time to start questioning. We need to ask ourselves some hard questions. For me, the first hard question is; who are your ancestors? Are your ancestors nomads in the Arabian desert of two thousand years ago? If those people are not your ancestors then where's your culture? Where is your belief about who you are and what you do? And how do you put that together? And what are our Nations? Are our Nations not real? Are they negotiable? Do we take our Nationhood, and our peoplehood, and our culture and all that is dear to us, and do we put that on the auction block! How many dollars is it worth? How many program dollars? What is it worth?

A people must have a vision of themselves. We must develop a vision, a vision of who we are and of who we are going to be and what we are going to like. Not something handed to us by somebody who hates us. We must have a vision of what is positive and powerful among us. We have to learn to start respecting that which is real about us, in the past, in the present and for the future. We have to do that.

Then there is the very question that nobody wants to answer, that has to do with our relationships with Canada and United States. Because, ultimately, I say this: the real measure of our relationship with Canada and the United States asks the question, what is going on on the land? Not what is going on in Ottawa. And what is going on on the land is not pretty, is it? How is what we are doing creating, promoting, and helping that which is going on on the land? And how do we devise a way to see something that we want to see go on on the land?

In my mind, our ancestors lived a very interesting life. No money, no computers, no television sets, none of this stuff. But our ancestors, across the Americas, from the Arctic Circle to Tierre Del Fuego, carried one thing that the whiteman never had; they had communities of people who cared for one another. The whiteman has been here to tell us that that is not important, that what is important is rational thought and making money on the land. But on the land in North America people cared about one another. All the ceremonies, brother making ceremonies, sister making ceremonies, ceremonies of family, ceremonies of Clan, ceremonies of Nation. All that stuff made people belong and they cared about each other. They fought for each other. They made a life for each other. And we are losing that, people. We are losing it.

When we look at what is happening, what is important is not what is happening at the board rooms or the council meetings; it is not what's happening in Ottawa. It is what is happening in your homes, what happens with your families. It's what happens in your neighbourhood. It's what happens when somebody floods land that you grew up on and that your grandfather's bones are buried in. It is what happens on the land. Some of our representatives are going around representing our rights and they don't seem to notice what is going on in the land. Too many of us have lost track of what is going on on the land. But it is on the land that your children will live. It is on the land that your grandchildren will live. It is on the land that life is made.

Reality has been presented to you in all kinds of forms. Reality has been presented to you in the form of phony ancestors; in the form of ideologies that made no sense; in the form of biological superiorities that have been proven to be ridiculous. All kinds of things have been presented to you. What is your version of reality? What is your version of what goes on on the land? What is your version of the future? Could we be a loving, caring and sharing peoples again? Could we continue to ask our peoples to sustain themselves as a distinct peoples? Can we transform the land into a thing that supports human life? Can we envision what we are doing here on this continent? Can we take some pride in what we have done in the past?

They are not easy questions and I don't expect people to come up with answers to them in minutes. But I think they are the questions that we need to have. And we need to urge our leadership in the States and Canada to show us more backbone. They are not showing enough backbone. And they are only talking tough to us. If you go talk to them and say: "Hey, you're goofing," then they will turn around and slap you. But when they are talking to a white-man with a suit on, all of a sudden, they are on their knees and they are just little old Indians again. So I say we need to show more backbone. We need to give our leadership more backbone. And we know how to do that. So anyway, those are my thoughts that I wanted to share with. Thank you.

WIND

In The Sky

He looked down
As though looking down from the very clouds themselves
The down below
where he first walked
Toward the edge of the wood, fog rolled and lifted
Dew glistened in the meadow
The sun was rising
onto the shoulders of the eastern sky
He peered down from the clouds
saw many women dancing
They offered him food
He honoured them with songs
They danced the dance of women
circular, with a side step
toward the rising sun
In a vision of old and new
they celebrated
There in the meadow, at the edge
of a green and beautiful wood

A staff of many coloured ribbons
she offered; red, green, yellow, and blue
The ribbons were wrapped around the wooden stem
a small hoop at one end
long leather fringes hanging from the other
a staff of many coloured ribbons she offered
He took what she offered
The wise woman with long grey braids smiled gently
then left
The coloured ribbons danced
and he lived

He heard the drum songs in his dreams
sacred voices sounding
He was afraid
He sat at old man's drum

in the light of early evening, singing
He stretched the hide of the deer over a new drum
with a younger brother
stretched the hide of wet skin over the sacred hoop
and celebrated
In a circle they sat, singing
Each pole, each leg, supporting the drum
represented with four colours
feathers of eagle staff
drum pulsing to earth
gift from a distant star

Rising to the cacophony of the brotherhood of crow
he hears that a brother has fallen
from the branches of earth
Crow laughter spreads
through the arthritic fingers of bone bare trees
His story is one that spreads
from the roots of trees
that tells of earth
that spreads up into the heart of layered truths
that spreads out onto the branches
that spreads out onto the arthritic fingers of bone-bare trees
cacophonic laughter rising
He listens until he is hungry
He rises
A lone deer in the meadow, at dawn, moves slowly
muzzling green shoots of grass
She is hungry too

He does not know if his dreams are ghosts
of prophecy
He does not ask

Fallen brother
The one who threw caution to horses
The needle in his arm
leaving bloody track of equine poison

He was no equestrian
He was dirt under the hooves
His only bloodline
from the needle in his arm
He was not proud of his bloodline
This was not part of his Horse Nation
That which was his real legacy
The horse ran south

He saw a young man last night
with a gaping hungry mouth
A mouth that could only mouth the words
to sacred sounds
with no sound to emit from his inside
He studied the hunger in his face
in his eyes, the rough face
that peered over the singers
the drum, the women, and wondered
He studied the young man
tough leather jacket
street black boots
touched him
reached to him
with his mind

The young sister at the circle
Telling of her abuse at the hands of the older men
He saw her sigh
letting out huge breaths of air
What was she saying?
He did not know. He did not ask
With watchful grace
she peered from safe vantage point
He once saw a wolf do the same thing
He recognized that look
her pure coat ruffling
silently in the wind
elusive from pursuers and companions alike

she is detached from the pack
moving silently
leaving the surge of her energy
briefly with tall standing birch
No scrolls would tell of her passing
The birch would yield no clues
Her footprints disappearing in time
becoming one with tracks of snowshoe hare, squirrel, and fox
Would she ever know the healing
energy of tall standing birch
peering with watchful grace?
He did not know. He did not ask

Sometimes the search was desperate
Other times, he couldn't give a damn
Sometimes, the blues were as deep as the darkest blue could be
Other times, they were indigo
or the colour of the sky
Still, other times, they were a fierce swirl of all hues
All hues of the colour blue
Sometimes, lonely felt like a bone scraped clean
chewed, and spit out like powder
This reminds him of a story about an Aborigine in Australia
who filled his mouth
with powder that came from the earth
and made colours; white and red
After filling his mouth
placing his hands on the rocks
or the hidden walls of caves
spits the colours all over his hands
leaving an outline on the rocks
or on the hidden walls inside caves, forever
If he could do it
he would fill his mouth with the powdered bone
and spit the outline of his soul
Someone would come along
see a splash of blue alongside white and red
they would wonder who left

imprints of powerful hands and blue soul
A blue whirlwind soul
spit from the mouth of hollowed bone
The mouth
a sacred tool of earth paint
blue bone mixed with spit and sky

This Red Moon
For Steven with love

Tonight
the moon is a hard red disk.

Passpassces predicted it would be so.

Your Grandpa told me the old man
fasted for twelve days
with my Great-Grandfather, Missatimos
at Manito Lake
in the time of the
hungry pup when the people
were starving and fearful
of what lay ahead.

Passpassces dreamed far and saw many things.

"The people shall suffer a long war," he said.

Passpassces saw and knew
in this red moon
flowed the blood of memories;

groping hands in the night,
innocent children crying silent
keeping secrets too fearful
to tell. Too shamed to know

it was not their fault.

black whirlwinds raging anger
turned back inside our souls
men beating women, the
mirrored images of their own self-hate

children watching
        thinking terror is life
        and love too bloody to risk.

Passpassces saw the black water
invading our sacred spaces,
drowning our knowing that
life is to be lived and
love is what heals

Our relations cried out for us
in their love in their love
for our red clay blood
cradled in our land covered in sky.

In that dark night they called
creation to guide us.
and
they smoked together and prayed.

Passpassces held the pipe
and wept and shivered for
the ache of our starving
and the confusion of memory
hardened to shame.

        "The red moon tells us
        the way back to life will be
        by doing battle inside ourselves.

        This will not be war as we have known it:
        Many will die in the fight
        Many will run from the blood letting
        Many will hide in the black water
        Many will try to escape with the colour of their skin

But

More will claim their warrior blood
More will pray their road to peace
More will dance under the thunderers' nest
More will sing their way to freedom
More will make their marks on paper
in the spirit telling of all this
that we pray for those not yet born."

Passpassces fell silent
and the people murmured amongst themselves
fearful for our future
not knowing if we would find the courage
nor even recognize the war

"How will we survive?" they cried
(meaning all of us for seven generations to come)

How will we survive?

There's no way forward
but through
this red moon blood of memory
and the telling of it son.

And the victory.

And the victory.

Heart Butte dance

a fall wind arrived whirling and drying out
summer dreams and travelling clothes.
scented with promises of wood smoke, and edged with ice
it swept us together.
        idle chatter surrounded our hearts,
        fluid and warm words passed over our
        tongues and minds.
the sounding of brass dance bells
stalled the evening's end.
        a breeze passed beneath my heavy dress,
        brushing my uncovered thighs.
duties and diversions pressed against our bodies.
parting with no touches,
        true desires silenced by the past.
whispers of winter time dreams blew against my back.

Walking Both Sides of an Invisible Border

It is never easy
Walking with an invisible border
Separating my left and right foot

I feel like an illegitimate child
Forsaken by my parents
At least I can claim innocence
Since I did not ask to come
Into this world

Walking on both sides of this
Invisible border
Each and every day
And for the rest of my life
Is like having been
Sentenced to a torture chamber
Without having committed a crime

Understanding the history of humanity
I am not the least surprised
This is happening to me
A non-entity
During this population explosion
In a minuscule world

I did not ask to be born an Inuk
Nor did I ask to be forced
To learn an alien culture
With an alien language
But I lucked out on fate
Which I am unable to undo

I have resorted to fancy dancing
In order to survive each day
No wonder I have earned
The dubious reputation of being

The world's premiere choreographer
Of distinctive dance steps
That allow me to avoid
Potential personal paranoia
On both sides of the invisible border

Sometimes this border becomes so wide
That I am unable to take another step
My feet being too far apart
When my crotch begins to tear apart
I am forced to invent
A brand new dance step
The premiere choreographer
Saving the day once more

Destiny acted itself out
Deciding for me where I would come from
And what I would become

So I am left to fend for myself
Walking in two different worlds
Trying my best to make sense
Of two opposing cultures
Which are unable to integrate
Lest they swallow one another whole

Each and every day
Is a fighting day
A war of raw nerves
And to show for my efforts
I have a fair share of wins and losses

When will all this end
This senseless battle
Between my left and right foot

When will the invisible border
Cease to be

Put On My Mask For A Change

See the stripe that divides my face in two.
A vermilion dot marks the tip of my nose.
Take this ancient advice and face up to me.
This is not some recent ritual I picked up.
My beloved cave sister let us dab mud together.
Let us meet at the creek to apply the clay.
Make our healing salves original cosmetics.
Anoint bites, scratches, bumps and lumps.
We then wouldn't mistake each other for ugly.
Let us take back ceremonies to paint our skins.
You be my Zingu mother designing my face.
I the Zingu daughter lift my face from the water.
Then you, then me, take turns smiling Jaguar.
The corners above your lips curl in laughter.
Under healing masques we are twinning spirits.
We are masks within each other holding out.
Whatever we must face is in the winking eye.

The Story of Harry Loon

His story
shoots between my ears
quicker than
a legacy

In ten minutes
he's seen more
done some
heard it all

An unconscious uprising
full of spirit
taking care of business
on parliament hill

He swims in strength's
ocean beauty
of work hours
and shapes reality

He's Iktomi to some
Nanabush to others
the trickster to many
a Harry Loon to me

In a class at school
he came into my hands
through a divine mistake
in a coined disguise

At a convenience store
i gave the cashier twenty
he gave me twenty-seven
back
plus a looney

i was happy i met Harry
he wanted me to know
that nature is great
just don't fool around

a lesson in respect
he acknowledged me
and now rewarded me
with a gold replica

Routine Check

Late winter snow
feathers the sky
as a voice on the line
from some place
I have never been
asks me if I remember
who called my number
from Des Moines, Iowa
on the 17th of September

I don't know anyone
in Des Moines,
but then, disembodied
that business-like voice
suggests the caller
may have been
an Indian
from Rosebud, South Dakota

Leonard Crow Dog,
I think,
but before I can speak,
I am asked this question:
By any chance,
do I belong
to their religion?
What religion is that?
You know,
The Sun Dance.

May I ask, I ask
What this is for?

Just a routine check,
just a routine check,
just a routine check

on a credit card number.

Late winter snow
falls on the Paha Sapa
the sacred Black Hills
which know no religion
which cannot be owned
like credit card numbers

There, routine checks
at Pine Ridge and Rosebud
turn up Indians,
snow in open mouths
government bullets
in their backs

There, at roadblocks
manned by BIA ghosts
voices ask
in that efficient tone
neutral as white paper
Do you belong?

They receive no answer,
only the wind
the spirit of Crazy Horse
thrusting his pony
against the snow,
believing in spring

Studies in Migration

Pulled into Joe Olson's landing. Patterns of the past leaping before us like the frogs caught here for fishing. With the force of long history they return. Welling up in the iron scent of spring water. Pooling amid last falls leaves. Slowly seeping into tennies worn through at the big toe.

Each year someone comes home. Pat moved in next to her dad. Von settled on Grandma's old land. Laurie Brown, gone since after the war, came back that same year as the trumpeter swans. Pelicans have been filtering in for seven summers. Today they fill the north quarter of South Twin. The evening lake black with birds.

Each space held for years in stories. Waiting. Now reclaimed. *Your name was never empty*. We could have told them. *We kept it full of memories*. Our land the colour of age.

Clouded titles fill courthouse files. But spring sap spills out just the same. Boiled in family kettles. Cast iron blackened over decades of fires. Some walk these woods seeking surveyors' marks. Some fingers trace old spout scars.

And flight the birds could tell us is a pattern. Going. And coming back.

Reflections in a Bus Depot

One of the most treasured memories as a young mother was the time when her girl was six. A little four-year-old boy lived next door and he was forbidden to go into the basement in his house. His dad had a lot of fine tools, some of them dangerous, so that boy was told to stay out of the basement.

Well, another older little boy lived in the same neighbourhood. This boy was pampered and spoiled... did almost anything he wanted to do without having to account for his actions. He seemed to be obsessed with the desire to go into that basement. One day he hounded that little four-year-old until finally they both went to the basement. The mother caught them, and oh, that poor little four-year-old got a terrible scolding. Not only that, his mother said as soon as his dad got home she was going to tell on him and he would get punished, for sure.

Notokwesiw's girl saw and heard all this and went running home in a panic. Almost in tears she told her mom what happened. "And Jamie's going to get a good licking and it's not even his fault," she said.

"So what do you think we should do then?" Notokwesiw asked her girl.

"I have to tell his dad what happened because I tried to tell his mom and she wouldn't listen to me. It wasn't Jamie's fault, that other boy made him go into the basement."

Notokwesiw looked at her girl. "What time does this dad come home my girl?"

"I don't know, but I have to wait for him and I have to tell him the truth for Jamie, Jamie's mom won't listen to us."

"Go on then, but if you need anything you call me."

Whimpering and half running. Notokwesiw's girl went next door and sat on the door step. All afternoon that girl sat there, waiting for the little boy's dad to come home. Once she had to call her mom because she had to go to the bathroom. Notokwesiw had to stand outside in case that dad came home to explain to him that her girl had to tell him something before he went into the house. But it was all right; he didn't come home just then. Her girl went back and sat on the doorstep until that man got home.

Finally he was home. Notokwesiw's girl told him everything and saved that little boy from a punishment that he didn't deserve. Notokwesiw was so proud of her girl. She must have told that little story hundreds of times. Now her grandchildren knew the story. She was going to keep on telling that story too. Imagine that, she thought to herself; my girl only six and already she was fair and honest. That girl was now in her thirties and had a daughter of her own. She was still fair and honest.

Things seem to have settled down in the bus depot. The little girl was sleeping now, slumped down in one of those hard plastic chairs. Must be close to suppertime, Old Woman thought. She was hungry by now. Good thing she had packed those fry bread and moosemeat sandwiches. Let's see now, she thought, where did I pack them? Oh yes, in that white plastic grocery bag. Now, where in the world did she put the white plastic grocery bag? Oh yes, in the little brown suitcase.

Old Woman remembered the two Roman Catholic brothers. Trying to set up a new order, those two called themselves Brothers of the Precious Blood or some damn thing like that. They ran a foster home for boys, but the boys they had were all disabled somehow. One of them had a bad heart and two of them were very, very slow learners. One of their boys later came to live at Old Woman's home. He was an orphan and had no place to live.

Well, those two Roman Catholic brothers were evil. They would get those boys drunk; then the one called brother Gerald would rape them. Her boy never really came right out and said it, but Notokwesiw believed those boys were put out for prostitution too. And then they were threatened that if they ever told, the brothers would have to tell on them too. Those poor boys got to believe that it was their fault what was happening and they were scared to say anything.

It took a long, long time, but through Notokwesiw's boy, and Notokwesiw's support, the case went to court. Three times the crown lawyer was changed and so many times Notokwesiw's poor boy almost gave up.

That brother Gerald used to watch him and Notokwesiw from his car. He'd follow them. He'd park his car in front of their house and just sit there. He threatened Notokwesiw's boy.

Notokwesiw and her boy sometimes lived in terror. Months and months it was like that. They were scared to go out. The were scared to come home. But if they gave up, those church people would be free to brutalize other boys. They had to see it through. No matter how hard it was, they couldn't give up. And it was hard. How many times had Old Woman talked her boy into seeing it through when he was ready to quit. They would talk and discuss it for hours. Always they came to the same conclusion. They didn't want any more boys to have to suffer those indignities, that shame, that fear.

Somehow, they got through those long hard months. The time in court seemed so long. Notokwesiw phoned as many friends as she could think of, and invited them to sit in the courtroom while the trial went on. One of those brothers went to prison for that, but he only got three years. She didn't know how much time he spent in prison, but last Notokwesiw heard, he was trucking all over the north, preaching around again. Was that the way God's workers were supposed to conduct themselves?

Sad memories. Sad, sad memories.

But there were good memories too. Some of her boys came from reserves. One of them was a big strong young man. He wore glasses and everybody like him. His name was James and he found lots of things to laugh about. The others used to try and make him laugh because he sounded so funny, like he had the hiccups or something. He was such a happy guy, that James. Seemed like he sparkled.

Oh yeah, then there was Cecil. Stubborn Cecil. Old One had taught all her boys how to cook and look after themselves, but Cecil was kind of lazy. Always watching TV with his finger buried in his mouth. Used to be scared of some TV shows, that boy. Wrapped himself in a blanket and covered his head when scary parts came on.

One time it was Cecil's turn to cook supper. All they ate that night was boiled potatoes and macaroni. Cecil didn't want Notokwesiw to tell him what to do, so he made supper the way he wanted it.

Another time Cecil got stubborn and refused to cook. All evening the boys sat around and went hungry. Then Cecil got hungry enough and he went in the kitchen to make himself a sandwich but the other boys wouldn't let him. "We want a decent supper," they said. And they kept trying to get Cecil to cook. He just sat and watched TV and tried to ignore them. But when the big Mac came on and he heard their stomachs grumbling Cecil had had enough. "Okay, okay, okay," he said. "I'll make your fuckin' supper."

It was a hungry bunch of boys that ate a late supper that night, but it was the last time Cecil got stubborn about cooking. Most of the time he was kind and gentle, and he felt guilty when he remembered how pitifully hungry they looked just because he was too lazy to cook. Even worse, their stomachs growled at him.

Ah, there were lots of memories of those years. Most of her foster sons came from away up north, all Cree speakers and they talked to one another in Cree most of the time. Old Woman only knew a little bit. They used to go car riding a lot and one time Notokwesiw told them a story that she thought was funny. When she finished her story there was no reaction but one of the boys was bright and intelligent and in Cree he scolded his brother and cousin, "It's a joke," he said in Cree, and he told them to laugh. So they all laughed hard, never mind that they didn't know what they were supposed to be laughing at. They had to be respectful and co-operative, they thought, even if that meant laughing at bad jokes they didn't understand.

Although there was nothing wrong with their intelligence or capabilities, they weren't all that good at English and sometimes used the language inappropriately. One of them brought a sock to Old Woman one time and asked her if she could fix it. "It's broken," he said.

They were quite thoughtful and protective of Old Woman too. They knew she didn't like fighting so they wouldn't tell her about the fights they had or had witnessed. Years later, she learned that one time two of her boys had a hell of a fight, but they hid their bruises. Stole her make-up and every day they carefully put on the make-up. What was their fight about? One of them told her, "We fighted over a nickel."

Kind of funny how those boys used to get back at her, too. One of them was mad at her for a long time. He was in art classes at school and one day be brought a gift home for Old Woman; it was a piece of clay work he did in pottery class, very well done piece of work, too. It was a closed hand with the middle finger sticking straight up in the air. She always knew when one of them was not happy with her; when it was his turn for cooking, he cooked all the things she didn't like. Another one didn't do or say anything, just gave her dirty looks at every opportunity.

Old Woman wanted her foster sons to be strong and independent, so she made sure they all made decisions together. They had to do as much around the house as Notokwesiw did, so they all learned how to cook and keep house. One of them even learned how to knit and another one could sew and crochet. When the Indian Affairs counsellor need a home for a new boy, everybody got together and decided whether the new boy would move in or not.

Notokwesiw had loved her foster boys. Even when they were rotten little turds she loved them. She remembered those two boys who were always sleeping in. She couldn't get them up in the mornings. As last she talked with their school counsellor, and didn't he come right to the house...went right up to their room and got them out of bed for school. It was kind of amusing to see those two sleepy-headed boys coming down the stairs with bewildered looks on their faces. They kept looking at each other; didn't quite know what to think.

They didn't sleep in too often after that.

Notokwesiw snuck a look at the little girl. Poor little girl. Maybe...maybe some day something good would happen for her. Old Woman would pray hard for all the little kids who were scared.

Well, soon time for the bus. It was good to sit and remember sometimes. Now that she was getting old, Notokwesiw had time for herself and she often sat alone with her memories. Good memories, sad memories, funny memories, inspiring memories and painful, hurting memories, too. She'd often thought that if she could write, she would write stories about her special memories. There were so many of them.

Notokwesiw had to go to Thompson. Her girl was going away to school for a week, and Notokwesiw was going to look after her grandchildren. That was her job now. Look after grandchildren. It was a good job.

When she thought of little ones, she always remembered something a white doctor told her. Somebody wrote it she thought, something about... 'children are our most valuable natural resource. They're non-renewable and they deserve the very best we can give them.'

It was a good way to think about the little ones.

The young mother and her little girl boarded their bus. That young mother still looked as though she was scared of something. It wasn't until their bus began to move that the mother relaxed. It looked as though she breathed a sigh of relief. She closed her eyes briefly, and then she looked at her little girl and smiled. Her girl smiled back and crawled onto her mother's lap. The last Notokwesiw saw of them they had their arms around one another. Their eyes were closed and they were both smiling. Notokwesiw smiled, too, as that bus took them to safety. Strange thing she thought, that bus is a safe place for those two.

Oh... there was her bus. Good places sometimes, these bus depots. Mind you, they could at least provide chairs that were comfortable.

Letter Excerpt

Bojoh

Here's The Minotaur.

It's context may interest you: this is a dream I had sometime before the issue of "cultural appropriation" made headlines. While the dream was exhilarating and I gained a real sense of my own personal power and awoke feeling triumphant, I was nevertheless cheesed-off that this non-Native monster had invaded my dreams. I would rather have faced a windigo! After relating this dream to Daniel Moses, he commented, "so, you're a warrior woman." Then during the whole "cultural appropriation" thing, especially during those times when I felt so alone and helpless, I armed myself with Daniel's comment, and drew great strength from this dream (now poem) and did what I could with what little I perceived I had—no one was going to bully me or my people (haha)!

I give thanks to this dream and that nasty ole Minotaur for giving me power and testing my strength. Now, I give this dream to you.

Resonance In Motion

In the time when they brought forth
symbols those syllable markings
indicating patterned speech The Old
Ones utilized in every spoken word
those characters translating oral tongue
without need to touch lips in our
language. In that time when Sequoia made
these available to The People enabling
those who chose to communicate
by touching ink to page, paint to
bark, by tracing design with
bent fingertip to record events.
In the time if they signed away the
mother they were put to death
by The People in accordance
with unwritten traditional law. In that
time when people of importance
showed themselves to be of
unique character. They gave their
lives to spare a friend, or relative.
When a warrior always respected
women, children, old people.
They laid down their bodies to save
The People. In the time
when all believed visions
and dreams even from the tiniest child. In
the time when honesty gave birth
to mental and spiritual freedom.
In that time we were humble,
simple as the dew on
petal tip budding fresh from
pastel pink and white dogwoods, as simple
as phases of the moon,
as simple as pass of day.
In that time we were humble,
as humble as furry

snowshoe rabbit, as young
doe with fawn internal,
as humble as The Old Ones, those turbaned
philosophers, the ones who
truly know all we can ever hope
to question. Those who are comfortable
with the flower of knowledge.
In that specific day and time,
lunar cycle, cyclic calendar.
In that ever certain movement in
time event, era span of the living and of
the dead. In that splitting fractional
second spanning up until those
foreign to this world appeared
that second in centuries of
millennium. In that time, then,
we enhanced our resonance
and place, that specific centre
of existence, we fasted,
retreated our projections
to visualize clear beyond
clarity of sight to observe
to hear the sounds resound
above, below here in this place
to understand our relation
to the skies, to those heavens
spreading every night before
and above us. Those multitudes
of lights, heavenly bodies,
seven pointed stars,
Grandmother Night Sun, the
path of the spirits
those that leave here and go
onward, those that teach
us in the singing, that vast
sky of beings united so intricately
to our own being, to the
Earth's beings, to the place

from which we come where
we find sustenance. Those
skies we follow like charts,
those suns, Mother and
Daughter, the two that
will return one day and
the one that remains for our warmth
and for the tasseled green corn to
emerge again. Sky that
holds both day and
night, light and dark,
window to the eyes of
Creator and those
spirits dwelling with him.
Even though Creator has both sides
we say Him out of respect
to our Grandfather Creator,
that giver of life, the very
point of light matching the great
peaks of earth surrounding
valleys, that giver of life Grandmother Earth
mammoth mountains her breasts, backbones,
jagged buttes, rolling hills we climbed to
pray. From these we observed to centre our-
selves. In that time we believed
that which is important which
now in this time still continues
to exist under the surface of
this world, the facade of this
time which gives us sustenance
even though we often neglect
its place of honour and importance
so significant. It allows growth
of all living beings, continuity.
Now the resonance appealing
to those with eyes of the swallow,
the openness of the innocent,
aged, infants, and little ones,

never yet jaded in humility.
This importance now in need
of blessing, of spiritual tribute
as newborn and elder
need nurturing to gift the
people with their wisdom and
renewal. Now in this time
resonance beckons nightly
in stars, in moon, in
cloudy, milky, passageway, daily in
sky, in sun,
in the masses, common man,
save the most jaded individual who
returned to a violent time in
heated latitudes. Now in this time,
we search for what we
knew thousands of eras
ago, we bleed in quest
for those flowers. Then we
lived to a hundred and seventy-five
years and were not allowed to share
knowledge as teachers until we matured
at around fifty-two. Now
we die before we begin
approach to this span,
diseases and evils from
foreigners, our downfall. Now
pupils spring rivers check waterfalls
without looking to the sky
to find what appears to
be out of reach and is actually
only out of hand. Now,
in this time, we begin
again. Listen as crickets mark
these occurrences and changes
watch as sun patterns
a new depth of sky. Feel
twist in surroundings

be again. Come again to the
place from which you came to
where we do finally go, to where I beckon
you as I have been called.
It is turning. The dawn of
the next world approaching.
The generation coming.
It is turning. Do you remember
they told us. Do you remember
they brought this to us. They
directed us to live so. Do you
remember we are to always live
so as they instructed us? These
voices belong to skies, to
mountains. They belong to
past and present, they sing
future. It is in motion.

My Voice

When I was young
too young to speak out
my mamma spoke the words for me
She'd ask me
Are you hungry?
She'd answer for me
Sure you are
She'd ask
Would you like breast milk?
She'd say
Sure you would
I couldn't speak
I'd cry
I'd cry out
No one listened
I didn't have a voice

When I learned my first words
my mamma put them in front of me
She put them in my mouth
She spoke the words for me
She'd say
Can you say mamma?
Can you say dadda?
I'd listen to her
She'd listen to me
say what she wanted to hear
I'd cry mamma
I'd cry out dadda
I didn't have a voice

When I was four
they took me away
They took my mamma from me
They took my dadda from me
They put new words in my mouth

They spoke the words for me
They'd say
Can you say new mother?
Can you say new father?
I'd listen to them
say what they wanted to hear
I'd cry mamma
I'd cry out dadda
I didn't have a voice

When I was sent to school
teachers taught me
what they wanted me to learn
They spoke the words for me
They'd say
Do you like French Science and Math?
They'd answer
Sure you do
They'd listen for me to
sound like them
At home I wanted to cry mamma
I wanted to cry out dadda
No one would have listened
I never had a voice

When I was sent to church
they washed my forehead
They washed my brain
they taught me what to pray
They spoke the words for me
They'd say
Do you believe in God?
They'd answer
Sure you do
They'd say
pray to our god
pray without a voice
They'd listen to the prayers

they wanted to hear
I wanted to cry mamma
I wanted to cry out dadda
No one wanted to listen
I never had a voice

When I got older
old enough to speak my mind
they still spoke the words for me
They'd say to me
You're useless aren't you?
Sure you are
You don't know French Science and Math
Can't you do anything right?
They taught me to hold my head low
I prayed
but not to their God
They'd say to me
Can't you even pray right?
I prayed again
but not to their God
I yelled Mamma
I yelled Dadda
I spoke the words for me
I had a voice

Valley Of The Believers

I'll say it this way:

you know they're going to
walk deep
into the forest & dissect it,
they're going to bring
microscopes & dirt samples &
there'll be seekers
of wine & the bread I broke
with you
or anyone. they'll peer
between the leaves
& note the smudges, yes, &
they'll find the bodies
strewn everywhere, & there'll
be a collusion
of confusion & blood &
screams,
(some of them mine) & they'll
gut the place
of gold & emeralds &
desecrate my sacred ground
& they'll water down every
element
of purity & quality they find,
except for one thing:

by that time, you'll be able to
smell me
in their pores, & I'll have
touched upon
the essence in them
of every thing, & in that valley
of tears
we shall already have
become One.

A Fast Growing Mold Bitter As Shame (excerpt)

SCENE 1

(Bedroom area; two figures silhouetted as a dark form. They are supported against each other and are upright, but each is asleep and does not hear the other's voice. Their voices come from the crack between the dreamworld and the waking world.)

WOMAN: The fine hairs, the cilia, seductive tendrils as permeable as smoke, soft as mist, insidious as fog that obscures the path, mutes the footfall.

MAN: Invading all boundaries, searching, probing, creeping like a fast-growing mold. It lays its sucking tentacles across my mouth and nose gulping, swallowing my breath, devouring all light.

WOMAN: I don't know how it got in here! My door was locked and bolted, my windows sealed, and still it seeps through the floorboards with its familiar stink, and here it is, in the bedroom, between the sheets. Between my skin and yours...

MAN: A taste, sometimes only a half-remembered taste between our lips of something vaguely familiar-metallic like blood and bitter as shame.

WOMAN: Vigilance that doesn't allow for rest...

MAN: ...against a constant intruder...

WOMAN: ...a spreading haemorrhage, an oil slick. Violation!

MAN: Violation! Trespasses in this territory...

WOMAN: —desecration.

BOTH: From this thief there is no luxury of sanctuary... (pause; pacing changes; words tumbling out and overlapping, sometimes simultaneous.)

MAN: Something about the vacant blue eyes, the lipstick mocking from the glossy pages of the girlie magazines we used to sneak a look at in the drugstore. Mmmmmmmm.... No questions asked, no talking back, no reminders of the brown face, slanted eyes, large lips in the mirror. The door was locked and bolted; it isn't my fault!

WOMAN: ...dark, mysterious, devastating... succulent, exotic morsel of dark meat. "Would you care for a bit of thigh?" Pale and immaculate, he offered to share his micro-waved luxury. Served me up a generous helping of nuclear power. Eat your heart out Snow White.

MAN: The Ice Goddess...

(Lights snap to full, stark morning light, the woman and the man are on their bed, centre stage, awake now they look at each other.)

MAN: Good morning. (turns away abruptly)

WOMAN: Good morning. (also turning) What time is it?

MAN: 10:15.

WOMAN: Shit. I meant to get up earlier.

MAN: Sure.

WOMAN: I did! (gets up huffily and goes to kitchen area to begin her dance of washing. She wears a light nightgown or a slip)

MAN: (reaches for her, then withdraws his hand and falls back onto the bed; slowly begins to dress, socks first. His movements are ordinary but carry the precision of personal ritual.)

SCENE 2

(In kitchen area; Woman is washing herself, the gesture evolves into washing clothes, washing dishes, or other mundane daily activity. Her movements transform from one into the other. She speaks through the movement.)

WOMAN: Crossing the frontier from sleep into wakefulness you first touch the borders, then enter the tourist trap of my colonized body; this body that I can barely remember belongs to me. Gaudy, numb and bloodless, a carcass from a wax museum in Niagara Falls. Am I the woman who fell from the Sky World? Changing Woman molding bloody clay from the soft underside of her breasts? Can you still hear the warnings of White Buffalo Calf Woman? The wails of the earth?

MAN: (from the bed) What day is it? No, never mind. Let me be lost.

WOMAN: Thursday.

MAN: (groans; beat) ...and where is the testimony heard of the territory stolen from between our bodies? (on his feet engaged in ordinary daily tasks; work. He is engaged in the same kind of transformational gestures and we see their dual dance.)

WOMAN: Evidence.

MAN: Somewhere a woman screams. Who is she? Someone tell her to be quiet! (as if scolding a child) What's the matter with you?

WOMAN: Just who do you think you are?

MAN: (on his feet) You'll stand with your nose to the wall until I say you can move. Get those hands back up over your head!

WOMAN: Stolen: a way of knowing passed from nipple to mouth; replaced by sterile latex.

MAN: (agitated) A ripping sound of splitting skin, deep moaning comes from all directions. No... (he locates the sound coming from deep within the earth)

WOMAN: It's garbage day. (pauses for response) Do you hear me?

MAN: (with increasing hysteria) She's in such awful pain. Some body shut her up!

WOMAN: I don't want to miss another garbage day. There are ants marching all over the kitchen. They obviously never heard of immigration laws. Roach prisons, ant traps, lemons on the back floor sill; and still they swarm.

(During Woman's last speech, Man rushes between kitchen and living room areas, with great anxiety, he puts some food on a plate, smudges it ceremonially and holds it out in front of him)

MAN: I offer this... (pleading) Stop screaming! (begins to sing softly; a prayer; a mourning song)

WOMAN: You see, first they send out a scout. Once the scout discovers where the food is, he transmits back to the rest of the ants, and that information forever becomes part of their ant memory. (sings) "The ants go marching one by one... Hurrah, hurrah..."

(Woman's last syllables blend into Man's song and they sing a bit together, weaving in and out of near laughter and near tears. Woman dresses while she sings.)

SCENE 3

(Living room area. In transition from previous scene, Woman breaks into robust round dance beat.)

WOMAN: (sings) "Travelling down this lonesome highway thumbing for a ride, Sure wish that pow-wows never end, way ya ha, way ya ha yo!" (raucous laughter) C'mon! C'mon, let's go to the pow-wow.

MAN: Where's the party? You know what I heard?

WOMAN: WHAT?

MAN: I heard that pow-wow's fixed. They got their favourites, and they got their family and they win every time—even the ones that dance like turkeys making a milkshake.

WOMAN: I knew it! I coulda won last year, 'cept for that head judge was crooked. They're all crooked.

MAN: That's what I heard.

WOMAN: That pow-wow princess, Minniehaha, all the time snapping eyes at me—cross-eyed thing—And trying to steal my moves!

MAN: Who?

WOMAN: You know the one! Don't try and tell me you didn't notice! The one with the neon fringes.

MAN: I got better things to do than to watch you women scratch each other's eyes out. Had to watch my own back real good. Yeah. You see that one drum come in? Swaggering like their shit don't stink—

WOMAN: —or like the nails are coming through their boots.

MAN: Jeans so tight you'd swear they took a Brillo pad to the crotch just to wear 'em down. Don't tell me you didn't notice.

WOMAN: (shrugs)

MAN: A singer from one of the other drums lost his voice. Couldn't make a sound. Medicine wars.

WOMAN: That's what I heard.

MAN: (explodes) I should've kicked all their asses! Ground their teeth into the dirt—the whole damn family! Nobody messes with me! (screams) I'M A WARRIOR!

WOMAN: A thief stalks the perimeter of the sacred hoop where the centre is not honoured.

MAN: (calm) Y'know, they don't have McDonald's in Newfoundland.

WOMAN: No?

MAN: Unh-unh, they're afraid of Micmac attacks.

WOMAN: Oh, you...

MAN: Wanna braid my hair?

(Their laughter folds into a very intense embrace on the edge of desperation. This first real connection between them resonates a common memory and they see themselves as who they might have been. The transition into the next scene starts from the embrace and all the strength, fear and duality within it. The transformation spans time.)

SCENE 4

(The next section is gestural; strong, clear, rhythmic movements describe the work of daily life in a pre-contact world: planting, fishing, gathering, hunting, caring for children, grinding corn, prayer, and ceremony. The man and woman work sometimes separately, sometimes together, but always in balance. Suddenly the Woman stops working and peers out as if trying to hear a faint sound. Her breathing becomes audible and rhythmically erratic.)

MAN: What is it? What do you see?

WOMAN: A floating house with huge wings coming out the sunrise.

MAN: There's a ship on the horizon. (very slowly they draw closer to each other)

WOMAN: (very quietly) ...soft as mist...

MAN: ...a fast-growing mold...

WOMAN: ...between my body and yours...

MAN: ...bitter as shame.

(FADE)

she is reading her blanket with her hands

my son tells me that he writes depressing songs sometimes. people say to him that he must be depressed a lot. he says, no, that he's not. that he can't write when he feels down anyway. he says he just writes what he sees, man.

I like the way my son looks at things. for instance I very recently unrepressed my metisness. I'm metis. I used to say, "my mother was metis." I thought I wasn't because I'm white-skinned. I thought it would be rude to say I'm metis because I don't experience racism like my mother did. I'm not oppressed in the unrelenting way that aboriginal people are and I don't want to be accused of jumping on the minority bandwagon in order to appropriate other people's perspectives as a way of getting published. I think that would be cheesy and unethical.

my son looks at me and gives me his best knowing smile. he says, "mom, listen to what you're saying. metis means mixed blood, mom. you shouldn't have to be ashamed of who you are."

"you're right," I say. when my mom was a kid, the word was "assimilate!" my mom and all her brothers and sisters were fostered out into my dad's family. I didn't learn about my mom's family because nobody talked about them. they were all ashamed of that family. my grandfather (my mother's father?), they say he was a falling-down drunk who did because he froze himself up to his waist when he fell asleep in some gutter in the middle of winter. I've never even seen a picture of him, they say he was white, though. but then they said my grandmother was white too. she didn't look too white to me. I met my grandmother but not very often because after all she was a bad mother and she had her kids taken away from her by the children's aide. shameless, unnatural hussy, is what my father said.

my father was an evangelical white supremacist. I wondered why white skin was such an issue in my family.

a woman I know is metis. white skin was an issue in her family too. I knew her when she identified herself as "white." now she's a strong metis woman who's politically active in the aboriginal community. so I called her up and asked her if she'd share her story with me. she said my responsibility will be to the first people of this land first. that I'm a writer and an artist and so my job will be an important one. she said to find out who my metis grandmothers are. they'll help me to know what to do.

now, I took what she said very seriously. before I called her up I had this dream. in this dream I'm sitting on the right-hand side of a couch waiting for an appointment with someone. there's a briefcase lying flat on the floor near me and on top of it, also lying flat, is a small leather bag. it's in the shape of a briefcase too but it's small, about eight inches around. it's a golden tan colour with intricate weaving or beads or painting around the edges. I lean over to get a closer look at the bag and I feel a kind of physical feeling of its beauty, of the love in the hands that crafted it.

then I begin to see pictures forming on top of the bag and in the air above it. the pictures are three-dimensional, each one forming very slowly into focus and showing itself before changing its shape into the next. four pictures it showed, each in golden brown diaphanous light, like particles of sand.

then an elder comes out from an appointment and picks up both bags, one in each hand, the smaller bag starts to dance around in the air and pulls him about with it. he makes a "woahhh!" sound and I say that the bag's been doing some pretty amazing things that it's been showing pictures. the bag pulls him to the floor and opens. its contents spill out onto the carpet. I realize it's a medicine bag and I feel I must hurry to help the man; is he okay?

yes he is. he wants me to help him put the contents back into the bag. I start to collect his things into my hands and I get slivers of wood stuck into my finger tips. the slivers hurt a lot and they also feel to heal.

the elder's gone when I'm finished. he's left without his bag. I'm concerned about that and I close the bag and start to carry it away and to look for him.

a young man—husky, rough—blocks my way with the whole front of his body. I say in a strong voice to leave me alone I am a metis woman. he says he's a white man from some european country and he puts a knife to my stomach and says he'll slice me in half if I move. I don't move.

he keeps pushing at me with his body and his black clothes and I ask him what he wants but he just grunts and pushes at me. grunts and pushes at me.

across the way are three native women with a child and the women are weeping with despair. the child has left them and gone down a hill to die. the women call to me they want me to help them. I break away from the man and run past the women and down the hill. they're afraid to go down there because it's death down there and they're not ready for death. I'm able to reach the child and carry her back up the hill. she's limp in my arms but she is moulded, moulds into me. and when I reach the top of the hill and the women, we all know that I've saved the child and that the child is in me. is me.

I hear some of my metis grandmothers when they talk to me now. one granny in particular. she says it's about time I started to hear her. her voice comes up from below smooth and warm. honey-soft. she's trying to tell me something. when I turn to look, she's gone. she starts to wear a little red knitted hat so I can see her. she's really very unromantic-looking. she's short and plump and she has no teeth. she laughs a lot and she's funny. I wanted to tell a funny story. some people tell me I have a good sense of humour. I think it's true too because lots of times when I say something people break out laughing.

a woman recently told me a funny story. she's metis, on welfare, and a single mom with four pre-school-aged kids. she asked me if

I'd repeat this story whenever I had the chance because it's funny and it isn't just her story.

she said she didn't wear a bra. after she got married, it bothered her husband that she didn't wear a bra. suddenly her breasts were his concern. he worked with crass men, he objected. they made rude comments. could she please just wear a bra when she went out of the house? he even cried real tears. heartbroken. she'd almost forgotten why she didn't wear a bra. for sure her mom made her wear one when she was a teenager (whenever she could catch her). she'd decided sometime during puberty that no woman would've invented a bra. she looked it up in the library for sure. sure enough, some man had decided that women's breasts needed hiding and hiking.

so, to please and appease this once passionate lover and now moody husband of hers, she began to wear a bra. most of the time. pretty soon he began to use her bra as an object of debasement. often, when he happened by, he would slip his finger under the elastic and snap it onto her skin, laughing loudly. then he began to deftly open the snaps here and there. when her breasts fell from their little lace prison, he'd grab at them from behind and squeeze them until the pain was unbearable. she told him this was painful and degrading to her. he would just laugh louder. "she used to love it when he coddled her breasts," he said. then he'd squeeze them even harder. "say daddy loves me, and then I'll stop. say daddy loves me and then I'll stop," he'd say. having her back turned to this guy became a dangerous position to find herself in.

so eventually, she bought a bra with a frontal snap. when he began to open this bra (sometimes even in public), she realized (but was by this time five years, three-and-a-half kids into an abusive marriage) she realized she was trapped, just like her own sweet breasts. her husband's abuse was so subtle and so socially acceptable. he kindly pointed this out to her himself.

her husband became overtly abusive after her fourth baby was born. mentally, and sexually, verbally and bodily. no bruises. no broken bones. very little outside contact.

she began to think of herself as lucky. lucky that he didn't beat her too badly when he raped. lucky to have food to eat. lucky to get a new pair of shoes. lucky to have an old beaten down second car. lucky to go to the library. to be allowed to read. yes, even lucky to wear a bra.

I was very moved by this woman's story and I didn't think it was too funny.

"don't you get it?" she asks. "you don't, do you? ah well, that's okay," she says. "other women'll get it. do you at least know why I want you to repeat my story celebrating my beautiful braless breasts?"

my face is blank. she pats me on the back like I'm a child. "because I can," she laughs. "because I darn well can."

women don't tell too many funny stories. it isn't that funny things don't happen to women but women are pretty serious these days. we have to be anyway because who knows when we'll be cut off again. it starts slowly and at the level of poverty. lots of women there. one woman was cut off social assistance because they told her she had to get a job because her three kids were all in school now. they didn't ask too many questions and she killed herself anyway.

I don't see this world as a safe place for my kids to grow up in. and what about if they should decide to have kids? what'll be left for them? so often I find myself asking rhetorical questions or watching someone's disinterested middle-class gaze looking over my shoulder at some shiny thing or another.

a woman I know says she can't imagine what she'd do if she didn't have her parents to go to for money. me?, I can imagine having parents to go to for money, but I can't imagine what that would be like. she says her greatest fear is a fear of poverty. me? mine's a fear of wealth. so how are we so different? I wouldn't advocate radical riches to rags, I tell her, but then there's so many things about people that I don't understand.

there's things about me that I don't understand too and trying to sift through how I became who I am is exhausting (though I never seem to tire from trying). maybe I'm an incurable narcissist and pretty soon I'll wake up one morning and I'll be a flower right there in my bed. my daughter will come into my room, see me the flower, and think, "oh, how thoughtful. mom must be gone out already and she's left this beautiful flower here for me to find. I think it's a tube-rose because its scent fills the room and now it makes my nostrils flare. here, I'll just put it into some water. it's a desert flower so it'll last a while, maybe three weeks if it's fresh. I love the hollow stems. I think I'll pin it down later and start my own collection of dried petals, like mom has."

but then when she gets home from school, she may be a bit confused because the flower will have put herself back onto the pillow of my bed. she'll have covered herself up to her blossom and she'll be wondering how it is that she came to be who she is. she'll be wondering why she's still okay after having experienced the childhood she experienced. she wonders about that one a lot. she thinks that maybe repressing the most tender parts of her scent is what made her who she is.

she's still puzzled about having the ability to literally slow time down so that she can see and hear things in a slow and lazy way and then remember body language, words, details, that she knows very few people see or hear because they're busy being self-conscious or ambitious or some other self centred thing. but her, she's mostly fluid when she goes from here to there she mostly listens and looks, listens and looks, but rarely does she shell her thoughts around her own. rarely does she censor past her skin her limbs her senses colours breezes that other people share.

this one gets to her the most. there's so much in the air that's missed. why can't they see? why can't they hear?

oh dear.

she wants to pull the blankets over herself and hide in there in the warm sweet darkness of her bed but then she remembers that no one will see her and no one will smell her and she has a job to do anyway. so she turns herself around and her petals are her silver hair and her hollow limbs they fill themselves with laughter.

Lonely Metaphors Are Story-less Figures

What's it worth
to play charades
and look for
the wishing
rock?
At an Indian assembly,
a relative is talkin' Indian,
and feelin' good about bein' mad,
mad at those who don't understand.
He did have to shift
so all would know and
remember how babies talk.

Mat swit i xn numt
Do you know what
I am saying?

Wanna hear about mountains?
"Noble-majestic-great-epic."
Beautiful words? original? mine?
You see, I learned 'em from books.
We've so many people with wonder
in their voices—and yet

there are so few
gifted translators.

and that's why I look
for the wishing rock
and play charades.

user-not-so-friendly

We're squareheads
Archie Bunker's
Humptee Dumptee
meathead mechanic
monkeys near far
En'owkin wall in
the Romper Room

on fullmoon days
we like to steal
assigned scrolls
chew them up at
no man's land
no woman's land
excuse says "moi"

don't like smokes
but coffee breaks
our lines become
crooks & warriors
even Mohawk hair
Crees & Micmacs
& Oka army tanks

we are programmed
to raise flags
for Ira Hayes
run through Inuit
syllabics rarest
Japanese writing
& h-bomb scribes

I Will Go And Pray

Truly, I will walk
alone into the forest
Truly, I will talk
to the winged in his nest

With the four-legged that run
I will speak to the wind
raise my head to the sun
and never look behind

I will fear, only fear
not that which I make
I will hear, only hear
true words, I want to take

WATER

Untitled

The water is falling, surrendering over the wet rocks. It is teal blue in the moonlight. The brightness of summer touches the midnight blue sky. I remember my cousin speaking. One wall is windows in the room we are in. He sounds the same talking to this room packed with people as he does when we stand alone. He is wearing a faded denim shirt and jeans. His hair is braided, silver runs through it now. He has large hands, with long fingers and he traces the air as he speaks. His hand flows downward as he talks about water, how it symbolizes humility and how humble we have to be to do this work. He says that water is flowing underneath this building we are sitting in now. We are on ground level facing the lush green sunlight filled woods. I feel grateful when it is my turn to speak as I have followed my Elder, Kayendres and three chiefs, beginning with the eldest. I am the youngest—the water is flowing in the right direction.

Lines Upon The Flow

Our paddles are deep in conversation with the river. Hear
how they enter it, each stroke questioning the current? And hear
how the stream replies with an eddy or splash, syllables so

obscure, who can be sure they're adding at all to what's been thought
about night? Neither you or I can tell by a push, a pull
in the thick of dark, in the dark of the flow, its quickness or

direction. Will putting up paddles, letting silences come,
move us out beyond discussion, beyond what carries us
along? Will we come to some conclusion in the current? But

some other tongue slips through on an old and liquid idea
and off into song. And we would join in, sing along if we
could, if only we knew the tune or some words in the language.

How the river mocks our desire, breaks up in bubbles of
laughter in our wake, won't ever take us seriously, as long
as we mistake talk for speaking in tongues. Tongues of light, it says,

tongues both dumb and bright. The ones, it whispers, that push upriver
through the sounding dark into a night so clear, you're afloat light
years out in space right here along the shore, the moon in your throats.

Stars, Tadpoles And Water

as a youth I often wondered
why everything needed a specific name
why a star swimming in the dark night sky
was not a tadpole swimming in water on the earth?

to understand that Crow is the keeper of knowledge is to say
a great many people would gasp and prefer the square hole
although they are by all outward appearance round peg legs
in the cycle of life-long yearning/learning to adjust
to the noise of falling rocket ships and dreams overhead
at the stock exchange at the bus stop shuffling their feet
in the unemployment line waiting for the highly esteemed
over priced politician to amputate what remains of hope
submerged beneath the junk pile of things to do places to be

actions reactions
and all these things

running together as they often do held prisoner by
chain smoking alcohol aspirin dope the next morning cancer and
aids
to prove how much we are dis-connected on from the other
from the tribe from the earth from water from touching
feeling the familiar roots of a familiar place familiar faces
in the clouds roll along day upon day in the sky of your dreams
reflecting the birth and movement of Stars and Tadpoles

itself a reflection of other worlds too quick for the eyes

other times

in other words
the bone laden fossil stones collected with a living pinch of
tobacco at the creek bed left by moving mountains of water
in the long ago teach tell us that our lives are not permanent
indentations on the sacred water sacred circle sacred red path

water decides wind decides earth decides sun decides how
each symmetrical duplication of the pattern of the body of each
living thing frozen in time has returned to the hard stone
reality that life escapes is gathered back by forever moving
rivers of changing energy each in their own time wordless timeless
each by their own ice age moved
a whirling fire storm unexpected
to understand that plants and trees share secrets among themselves
communicate their eating habits feel pain rejoice at the onset
of the new spring rains is to know that life is fragile just ask
the dinosaurs who thought nothing of chasing the others around
tearing apart the vegetation plotting the conquest of the world
by sheer numbers and force of arms legs and sharp jaws unaware
of the immense power of our Mother to straighten Herself out
when the asteroid weight of the fiery monsters became too great

just ask the Full Moon
        ask the Old Ones waiting
        as the Water you drink everyday
        ask the child with Starshine in her eyes

Swimming in the Cannon River

sleepy

eyes heavy

forgot to keep
my balance

fell into
the unforgiving
river

panic

followed by
release

slept
till they
pulled me
out

visions
of ghosts
and demons
never came

found
myself
swimming
with the
fish
i was to
catch

the terms of a sister

begins in the womb
we swim
towards a nation

umbilical reach
blue infinity

severed by lightning
striking the core
of this hemisphere

we emerge
brown as earth
red as sun

children of chiefs
medicine women

this is me
this is you

power preserved
to ignite
the darkness

I'm age

i'm age
image of woman
female of species
enchanting
light of the moon
passion, encounter
vital fluid of life
cosmic clockwork
eternity.

illusive dream
image of woman
short tight skirts
fast cars
twenty foot round
rotating bed
mirrors of prove
mirrors say
that is me
you
us.

image woman
skeletal
full with child
she stumbles
through a desert
a desperate search
for hope
a bowl of sustenance
plague free water
i hear a voice
from the back
comment on her bare breasts

Crystal Globe

We live in a crystal globe
glittering, revolving, adapting, even though
it is not meant to lack truth
someone in the beginning instructed not to forget
in our lifetime
but somewhere, sometime parts of it were forgotten
then passed on to those willing to listen
fractions remained unmoved by the motion of time;
unbounding power which tested those willing to speak
in this universe which never lies
The fragmented parts passing
like an eclipse
where there is no turning back
where there is no reversing
and in that minute moment
the power of the sun is shielded
blinded by a creeping transparent moon:
It only takes a second to block light from entering the crystal
and it is inevitable to stop.

We live in a crystal globe
and go on forever multiplying with repetition;
somehow there is a mystical beauty hidden behind this
somehow none of it makes sense until we remember the truth
in its simplest form;
this is caused in the accuracy of memory
and it is then
it becomes all too clear, awesome, yet fearful,
something like feeling the penetrating warmth of the sun
just before the eclipse, also
coming to know its coldness before the point
of fading into cold shadows:
The eclipse is repeated and the void is multiplied
with different logic each time,
but, those things are distinct with colours, textures, and feelings

manifested over and over and over
Portions of truth remain
even, pure, and without limitations
like the process of water turning to ice
and ice reverting back to water.

We live in a crystal globe
gentle, warm and with the ability to melt those things which freeze
All of us are born and die soon
with questions unable to be answered;
this does not stop
and there are no words to describe this;
not in colour to be seen
not in sound to be heard
not in any aroma
none in these earthly textures.

It is a beauty deeply hidden
within this crystal globe

The Ogopogo

To Lynn, who believes.

Ogopogo:
a large marine animal of unknown origin said to inhabit the Okanagan Lake in the Canadian province of British Columbia. The Ogopogo has many parallels to the Loch Ness creature in Scotland.

Fencing is slow, methodical work, and I was glad for the excuse of my sister's visit. I took off my hat to wipe the sweat from my face and waited as Lillian hurried towards me, a storm of kids swarming around her. Behind her the lake cast a perfect mirror reflection of the low hills. On the other side, a mile away, a single blue motor boat plowed along the shoreline, a distant drone of annoyance in an otherwise peaceful world.

The kids reached me first, most of them trailing towels and assorted clothing with them from the beach. Lillian was yelling, "You've got to see... bigger than... my Uncle said that... pogos don't look you..." Lillian's excitement was contagious, which explained why the kids were so noisy. I couldn't make out what they were trying to say. My sister's black eyes were round and her shoulders were shaking.

"I'm sorry. I can't hear you," I yelled at her, and I gave up as the small hurricane of activity swept around me. Lil suddenly sat down, hard, onto the ground. The kids swarmed around me and then, in a trail of dust and sound, were gone, dashing up the dirt road towards the distant houses.

"Sis, you okay?" I asked. Lil looked up from the ground and swallowed.

Lil shook her head and again swallowed, trying to speak.

"If it's Ralph acting up again, I'll speak to his mom. That boy has to learn some manners. Always going and coming like he does, it's enough to..."

"Shut up! Will you shut up! You're as bad as the kids."

I moved half a step back from the force of her voice. Lil reached up, grabbing my left arm for support as she pulled herself to a standing position with a grunt of effort. Her long braided hair was made blacker by the sun's brightness, so black that I could see the bluish tinge that glinted when her hair caught the light in a certain way. Lil stood there staring at me.

"Well, what is it?" she demanded.

"What is what?"

"How come you're staring at me like that?"

"I wasn't staring. I was just looking at your hair."

Lil reached up and smoothed down the top of her hair. She half-turned her head to look at one of her braids. The next thing I knew she was staring up the road at the receding whirlwind of dust. Her right hand shielded her eyes from the sun but even so she squinted.

"Where are those damn kids going?"

"Probably up to the house. You were saying something before you fell."

"I didn't fall." Again, Lil glared at me with those dark eyes, daring me to say anything to the contrary. I knew better, and remained silent, twisting the rim of my hat in both hands.

"Hmph! If you were listening, you'd have heard what I was trying to tell you. There's something down by the lake. Something big. I think it's the Ogopogo.

I must have been staring blankly at Lil because she went and kicked me in the shins.

"Hey! What'd you do that for?"

"Ah, you asked for it. Don't you believe me?"

I thought better of reminding my dear sister about the time six months ago when she'd seen a flying saucer near the garbage dump by the reserve. She still had a hard time living that one down. Humour her, I thought.

"Okay, so what's the gag?"

"It ain't no gag. I tell you, I saw something down by the lake. It darned near scared the shit out of the kids who were swimming."

I played along. "Okay, sis, how big was it?"

Lil's eyes became round again. "Big! It was really big."

She must have seen my eyes glaze over because the next thing I knew she'd tied into me and I was staring up at her.

"Get up! Get up and I'll show you. I'll bet you don't dare come down and see."

I was getting up when I saw the distant dust storm of kids once more heading our way. Only this time it'd grown. There was no use fighting the inevitable. I nodded and Lil led the way back down to the lake's edge. A single frail pier jutted some hundred feet onto the lake. There was no wind and the waters were still as a mirror. I could see several small white clouds reflected in the lake's stillness. The power boat had moored somewhere unseen, leaving the entire lake empty of movement. I stared the length and breadth of the lake for as far as I could see but there was nothing but water.

Lil stood by my side, a look of triumph on her face.

"There. You see. I told you so."

I was missing something here.

"What am I supposed to be looking for?"

Lil gave a snort of sheer disgust just as the whirlwind of kids stormed up to us. Several adults had joined them and for the next five minutes people were yelling at each other and pointing to the lake. I continued to stare at the water but there wasn't a sign of movement. The voices of the kids dominated everything.

"... a giant beaver that got lost in..."

"... Dad said....this big, maybe bigger, and..."

"... sturgeons at least a hundred years old were..."

"... ain't nothin' but your imag..."

"... close to it I could almost touch it..."

I finally turned to Lil, trying to ignore the kids yelling at each other and at the adults.

"So what did you see?" I yelled.

Lil pointed at the waters. "It was over there, about a hundred feet out. And it was big. As big as a whale, maybe bigger."

Having no idea how big whales were, I stared at the spot where she was pointing. Nothing. No matter how hard I stared there was nothing.

Lil saw my baffled look and pointed again. "I swear, it was there. Geoff," and here Lil pointed at one of the yelling boys. "Geoff was the closest. It almost hit him and he panicked."

"Sis, where were you?"

"I was laying on my blanket. I heard the yelling and turned to see the kids running for shore. I could see at least two humps behind them. The thing was so dark so I couldn't make out what it really looked like. And it was moving fast."

I stare at the water, my eyes hurting from the want. And then a shadow moved under the water a hundred feet from shore. A long dark shadow which twisted towards the surface as Lil screamed and turned to run.

"Wait," I yelled, but it was too late. A torrent of people poured up the dry road towards the safety of their homes. I took a last look at the shadow and saw a second shadow, longer and thinner, below that of the first. The first shadow broke the surface of the water and I saw the single broken branch rise in the air from the lower part of the trunk. Disgusted, I turned to follow the clouds of dust.

That night I heard the stories around the campfire. Excitement filled the voices of each speaker, some of them elders. It seemed half the reserve was down on the beach, but nothing was found. Of course, not many boats travelled too far from the beach and the lights. I told my story, but I was careful not to fuel the imaginations of the kids. They'd be up half the night as it was. Nor did I mention the branch I'd seen on the trunk of the old tree.

A week later I'd almost forgotten the whole thing when I happened to pick up the daily newspaper and read the bold headlines. Here we go again, I thought. The story mentioned the sighting. My sister's story was featured as were the scattered quotes from some of the children who'd been there that day.

I was about to skip to the sports section when a single paragraph near the end of the article caught my eye. A man who owned a small blue boat said he'd seen the group of Indians on the other side of the lake. He'd crossed over, saw the shadow and followed it until he'd caught up with it. He claimed that it was just a tree trunk caught in a riptide. Nothing more would have come of it except that the man swore that as he pulled the tree to shore he saw another shadow, deeper in the water, follow his boat's trail for a good quarter mile before it sank out of sight. That shadow had been longer and narrower.

Is there an Ogopogo? I don't know, but I no longer turn off my sister when she starts speaking about it. Now I'll never really know.

The feast was going well. Some two hundred people were

seated in the hall, filling it with a low hum. Very formal, very boring. I bolted down my food, trying to finish as fast as I could so I could make a quick run for the door and freedom. Tomorrow I was going deer hunting and I needed my rest.

"Hey, Martha, there's Joe. You know, the one who saw the Ogopogo."

I looked up in a panic. Several people nearby turned to stare at me and I looked down at my plate. The emcee swept by and I hunched down in my seat, trying not to draw any notice. The single slice of fried bread and the almost empty cup of coffee were the last things in front of me. A minute and I'd be out of here. I was doing this only for sister, Lillian. I hated crowds.

The emcee reached the stage where he fumbled with the mike, tapping it gently. The dull thumps echoed through the hall and conversations dropped as people, including those near me, turned their attention to the stage.

The fried bread tasted so good that I chewed a couple of extra times rather than simply swallowing.

"Thank you, ladies and gentlemen, for coming to our annual feast and fund raiser. I hope you all enjoyed the meal? Well, did you?"

A wave of applause broke out, and I joined in rather than finishing off my coffee.

The emcee smiled, clearly enjoying his job. The applause died down and I reached for my coffee.

"Tonight we're going to have entertainment for you all. We scheduled a dance to begin the ceremonies, but on the way up here I noticed Joe."

It wasn't fair. Give me five more seconds, please.

"You all know Joe, don't you?" The emcee smiled and pointed at me. Everyone turned and I sucked in my breath feeling the whole world stop. I knew people could see the blood rushing to my face.

"Stand up, Joe. Joe and his sister Lillian saw the Ogopogo last month. You all remember that, don't you? It was in the papers. Come on up here, Joe, and tell us about it."

As everyone clapped I felt something pull me to my feet. The something turned out to be my sister, who was in her glory as she waved to the audience. “Get up there and don’t make idiots of us,” she whispered to me.

Before I could protest, she pushed me towards the front of the stage. It was worse than “Aliens.” The walk to the stage seemed to last forever, and by the time I got to the mike I was soaked with sweat. In ceremonies no one can hear you scream.

I stared at the audience, who stared back. There wasn’t a sound in the hall, and I felt like Sigourney Weaver. Any moment the audience would turn into creatures ready to suck my face off. I was defenceless. Remember the crewman they always beamed down with Captain Kirk and Spock on *Star Trek*? You always knew the poor sap was going to bite the bullet. Dog meat. Chopped liver. I kept staring at the audience and they kept staring back. The seconds turned into minutes which turned into hours, and they just stared at me, not making a sound. I was losing pounds of sweat every second and they just stared at me, waiting for me to crack, which I did, of course.

I smiled, my eyes big as dinner plates, and I slowly took the mike in my hands. Still watching the audience, I pulled the mike closer to my face and then I bit into it.

The next thing I knew I was staring at the ceiling. Everything hurt, even my hair, which stood straight up, what there was of it. My sister’s face was among those who looked down at me. I must have looked like a demented Chihuahua on steroids. As they carried me out amid the ensuing bedlam, the last words I heard were from the emcee.

“Give Joe a hand, folks. What an act! What a card! I told you he’d be great.”

The End.

Those Things That Come to You at Night

"Old Woman, Grandmother," she said. "They come to me at night."
"What is it they want?"
"Can't tell. Ain't like I really hear them clear."

Like voices I've known
sounding off
over the hill
behind the milk shed
under the belly of a car
coming through the woods
familiar tones and rhythms
like surface conversation
heard while underwater
the sliding pitch of sound
but no clear word borders.

"You must try to hear and remember. Sounds, pictures, the stories they bring you, the songs."

Swimming among the fluid notions
of dream space
where voices land
in the hollow behind the house
and echo back to sleeping souls
where ideas ricochet
off of each documented waking moment
but strike home
in the slumbering core.

"They tell me things I'm sure. I want to get up to follow. But I can't pull my body along. When I wake up I am homesick for those voices. And then sometimes, maybe when I am hauling water or frying bacon, I remember something, just a feeling really."

The old woman, bent over her basket, nods her head slowly. "Yes," she says. The younger one waits. Nothing more.

Night speaking
touching spirit
without distinguishable words or voice
calling by name
calling your ancient being
arousing that felt destiny
walking all past
folding the torn moments together
and shaking them out whole.

"Grandmother?"
"It's that way, child. The night things. Like how you learned to walk. Nobody can teach you."

Now a rumbling comes
heard over a heartbeat
beating more rapidly
with a fear of
greatness
felt in the bladder
breathed with flared nostrils
approaching like a flood
it rushes upon you
cleanses you with night desire
leaves you floating peacefully
into daylight.

"They get louder, I'm told."
"The voices?"
"Ayah. Louder if you don't seem to hear. Louder still until you hear or go deaf. Everybody has a choice you know. Some go night deaf. Others learn to listen."

Singing the songs
of midnight
going quiet, smiling shyly
when someone hears
listening inside

voices rounding each corner
of yourself
forming you
from daylight
remembering
those things
that come to you at night.

The Indian Researcher as an Interpreter of History

Listen this research game is everything it is cracked up to be.

No really. I'm wondering how to do this kind of thing the rest of my life! I have no worries and am paid to research and write, and there are lots of non Indians here to help me. What could be better?

I have found out some truly amazing things to report and write about. Some of it quite newsworthy and with all the trashy television networks doing their thing on George Armstrong Custer, I too, have been looking into his seedy past and am hopeful someone will print my thesis.

Not too many people realize that General George Armstrong Custer, known by his friends as GGAC, had a drug dependency problem. He was addicted to Red Man Chewing Tobacco. It was his second reason for going to Montana. The first reason was this Crow woman... but, that's another chapter.

Anyway, while Custer cheerfully wrote one press release after another, claiming he and the military were preserving Mom's Apple Pie, and curtailing the expansion of hostile Indian aggression, he was actually setting himself up as, big horn drug lord of the west. (One source, who refused to be named said Custer even whistled while he typed.)

Custer's insidious scheme was really simple. He would create an incentive for Native tobacco sellers in the West to network with only him. This would effectively cut off tobacco supplies across the country to other military, black marketeers. If the Native tobacco suppliers in the West refused to go along... well, you can guess what happened to those guys.

But, as with a lot of these military, genius-types—he was just too clever for his own set of pistols. His obsession for power and drugs was to be his undoing. His Waterloo. His er-r-r-r, Little Big Horn, so to speak.

When local gossipmonger, Sitting Bull began spreading it around the Big Horn Billiards and Beach Club that Custer's drug of choice was tobacco, a leftist group calling themselves "Cheyenne Dawn's Right-To-Life Coalition" devised a devilishly ingenious plot. They decided to cut Custer's tobacco stash with fresh garlic, making the General's breath totally intolerable. Sitting Bull had told everyone that Custer was out-of-head so much of the time, he'd never realize he was chewing garlic-laced tobacco. The odor coming from Custer was so offensive that even the Crow wouldn't sleep with him. Evidence recently uncovered by non-Indian research-types now suggests that if Custer had not been killed in the Battle of Little Big Horn, his own officers would have put him out of his misery.

Never ones to be left out of the history books, a small terrorist organization made up of Disgruntled 7th Calvary Sergeants (D7CS) had also planned to assassinate poor George Custer. Not because of his bad breath, but because their retirement benefits had been cut in Washington D.C. by PAC-happy Congressmen. They voted to kill GGAC and split his burgeoning tobacco profits because in their words, "drug money is technically not taxable under federal law."

The D7CS cleverly found a way to make Custer's death look like an accidental drug overdose from—you guessed it—Red Man Chewing Tobacco. They planned to leak the story to the international media blaming the overdose on the meddling Indians. But, ah ha, mainstream, Cheyenne, Arapaho, Yanktanaei, Lakota, and Dakota Sioux Indians struck first, and stole the thunder from Custer's officers, D7CS and the Pac-happy Congressman... and, the rest is history.

The End.

(This case in known in Indian circles as The Triple Tobacco Cross, or, THE FIRST DRUG WAR... A little-known trivia fact.)

Ice Screams

It's been three days and I am still here, sitting in this back corner away from everyone. Three days.

People look at me funny. Most of them had been there the first night I'd come in and were surprised to still see me sitting in the corner when they came back but I didn't care. I would just order another drink, but that's why they look at me funny. I wasn't known as a particularly hard drinker, in fact only a handful of people in this bar could claim to have ever seen me drunk once, let alone for three straight days.

I knew they are all dying to ask me what happened out there on the ice but that would defeat the purpose of drinking. I'd have to remember.

So instead I sat here, listening to the same country songs played on the jukebox over and over again. If it had been a weekend, there would have been a band, but not in the middle of the week. The waitress kept eyeing me warily. I guess years of training taught her to watch people who power drink. But I was no problem. I just wanted to be left alone, drink some more rye and try to burn some memory cells.

Stan and David came in earlier and tried to join me but I made it obvious I was not fit for company. I kinda got the feeling my mother probably sent them to talk sense into me or at least keep an eye on me. But Mom knew what happened, and she knew I had to work this out myself. Though I doubt she agreed with my methods; as everyone knows, fear and alcohol often hold hands.

The "Drinking Don't Kill Me, Her Memory Will" song started to play. What little feeling I had left was tempted to smile at the irony. Except in this case, it would be this memory and it sure as hell wasn't a love story.

It had been three days since Ryan's incident but the thought of what happened still scared the hell out of me, a good four bottles of rye later. The sharp reports from the pool table make me think of my buddy William. Normally he'd be at that table exercising one of the few talents he has in life. I wondered what he's doing now, probably hiding at home, since he doesn't drink any more. Stan and David get up to leave. They've been there a good three hours, keeping an eye on me. They've done their good deed but they have families and work tomorrow. They look at me, then open the door to leave. A cold blast poured in and in the distance I can see the multi-coloured light of this small town stretching down the street. Stan and David see the numbed look on my face, shudder and then leave.

They will probably take the 507 to the cut-off, then drive across the lake to the village. People have short memories when they are in a hurry. The lake usually freezes over by this time of year, taking a good sixteen minutes off the trip into town. People from the village always travelled across the lake, even before most people had cars. Years ago people drove sleighs or even walked across the two mile lake. It was usually safe from mid-December to early March supposedly.

Having grown up there all their lives, most of the local people can handle the frozen lake. That's what makes what happened to Ryan's parents so puzzling. What happened shouldn't have happened. It was late February, a safe enough month. All the winter sales were beginning and his parents, always frugal shoppers, decided to go all the way to Toronto to spend four days shopping. It was all planned. Being only nine at the time, Ryan got to go with them while his older sister stayed behind with relatives.

I was told that Ryan was always particularly close to his parents, closer than his older sister. My mother claimed it was because he was a difficult birth. Story had it his mother almost died giving birth to him and then he almost died of some respiratory problem a week later. His mother blamed the nursing staff, saying they didn't watch over him enough. Then his father accused this one nurse of being racist and prejudiced against Indians. You had to know Ryan's parents.

Needless to say, they both survived. Maureen, his mother, liked to say she refused to even consider dying until she knew if her little one would be okay. That sort of set the pattern for the rest of their lives.

By pattern I meant he was the baby of the family and was treated like that. It was a little obvious that he was favoured by the parents but that happened in some families. Of course that was not to say the parents neglected or didn't love Aricka, his sister. He just got the benefit of the doubt, or the bigger slice of the pie. Pretty soon Aricka learned to accept that, though it was through gritted teeth. It's amazing Ryan didn't grow up more spoiled then he really was.

I remembered how excited Ryan was about going to Toronto. He'd never been there before. Aricka, four years older, shrugged off his enthusiasm, a little hurt she wasn't going. All she had to look forward to was a week of exams and staying with her aunt.

Standing at the school bus stop that fateful morning, all she talked about was her brother and the trip. Minus ten degrees and she could still whine.

"He always gets what he wants. Mom treats him better than me. She always does. 'He's the baby,' she says. If you baby someone all the time then they'll be a baby all the time."

I stamped my poor frozen thirteen-year-old feet in response. The school bus was late, probably due to the heavy falling snow. A possible day off from school was rolling around in all our minds so we didn't care much about Ryan or Aricka's problem.

All except for William. William Williams was my best friend then and now, and don't ask me why. He just was. He could be an idiot sometimes, most times, but I accepted that. It was one of those friendships that defied explanation. Now William had little affection for Ryan either. Ryan had never done anything against William or vice versa so there was no real ground for his dislike. You had to keep in mind William's reasoning was that of a thirteen-year-old. He hate the attention Ryan got from his parents because William was somewhere in the middle in a family of nine. You had to fight hard for any recognition at his house. But I supposed the real reason came from a secret crush he had on Aricka. He would agree with anything she said just to get on her good side.

"It must be terrible having a brother like that," he said sympathetically. He could always be counted on to be sympathetic to a pretty girl when it was necessary, even at that age and temperature.

Aricka watched the family truck approach through the growing snowfall. You got used to it. Someday though, he wouldn't always be the favourite. He wouldn't be so hot then. The little scum.

Then the family Ford came rolling down the street, on its way to Toronto. The family was ready to buy out the town and fit as much of it as they could into their beat-up old vehicle. It was a yearly thing with that family and a few others on the Reserve: the income tax refund came in early and already it was mentally spent.

The last anybody saw of them was the beat-up end of their truck roaring down towards the lake, a trail of snow and exhaust billowing up through the snow flakes.

I remember Ryan sticking his tongue out at Aricka as they disappeared into the whiteness of the lake.

Aricka blew into her hands. "I hope they get a flat," she said. William responded with a hearty "Yeah" and smiled like someone who's just scored some victory points.

After that it got kind of strange. Three days passed before Mags Magneen noticed a light on at Ryan's house as she was driving by. According to what she knew, they were still supposed to be in Toronto. No car was in the driveway and nobody answered the phone. Always the curious (and some would say nosey) type, she decided to investigate.

The way she told it the house looked as cold as a Christian's heart as she surveyed it. A blanket of virgin snow seemed to surround the house. She had to break a trail as she walked up to the front door. The light was still on but the house felt empty, as she put it.

A couple of knocks on the door went unanswered, as did the harder pounding that followed. Feeling somewhat uneasy, Mags was going to give up and leave but decided to give it one last try and rattled the door knob. She discovered the door was unlocked. Puzzled, she swung it open.

"Martin? Audrey? Are you here? Hello." No answer again. She shivered, not sure if it was from the cold or the eerie silence. The house was cold, colder than outside it seemed. Some of the lights were on but the place still looked dark. Mags called out a few times but other than the unnerving echo of an empty house, there was no response. The kitchen was clean as always and Mags was confused. It wasn't like Ryan's family to leave the lights on when they went away, let alone leaving the door unlocked. Yet, they weren't there and weren't due back for a few days.

She wandered into the living room and looked around. Again nothing looked like it had been touched in a few days, except of the comforter on their big couch. Mags had given it to Ryan's mother four years before. Now it was lying all in a bundle alone on a corner of the couch.

Mags was beginning to feel the February cold by this time and was tempted to leave, maybe make a few phone calls later to some relatives inquiring about the location of the family. Still puzzled over the strange situation of the house, she absentmindedly picked up the comforter from the couch and started to fold it.

Ryan looked back at her from under the comforter. Mags screamed and jumped a good six feet back, across the worn out Lazyboy and then up against the window, knocking over a plant. Ryan, his expression never changing, followed her with his brown eyes.

"My God, Ryan, you scared the hell out of me! What are you doing underneath that blanket?"

Ryan merely looked at her, still not saying anything.

"Ryan, are you okay? Where are your parents?"

Ryan shivered, picked up the rapidly discarded comforter, and pulled it back over him. He disappeared back into the couch as quickly as he had appeared.

"Ryan?" Mags tried again. Again no answer. She approached the couch again, more timidly this time, still calling out Ryan's name, with the same lack of response as before. Her gloved hand reached out slowly and tugged at the comforter until Ryan's face and upper body were visible.

"Ryan, what happened to you?" Ryan merely blinked his eyes at her and shivered again.

According to Mags, poor Ryan looked like hell. He was still in the same clothes he had worn when he and the family had driven off the Reserve three days ago. His face held no expression, just a steady blankness, and it was thinner. The doctor later estimated that nine year old Ryan had lost six pounds in three days.

A nervous Mags covered Ryan in the comforter and another blanket from the overturned Lazyboy. Ryan didn't flinch, didn't move. You could barely see the little trickle of vapour escaping from his mouth into the cold air. Mags then searched every room but couldn't find anything that would explain Ryan's mysterious presence.

The kitchen was untouched, some of the plants were dead from the cold. It was in the kitchen where Mags found the reason for the intense cold. A large window overlooking the back yard had been forced open and left that way. Footprints outside the window led away into the bushes, towards the lake. They were the same size as Ryan's feet. Mags was beginning to get real scared.

"Ryan, listen to me. Where are your parents? Did they leave you here?" Ryan didn't respond; instead, he tried to duck under the comforter again. Mags quickly grabbed his arm and immediately let go again. "Your arms are so cold."

Ryan stopped moving for a moment, looked at Mags, his brown eyes both looking and not looking into hers.

"Cold," was all he said.

That was enough for Mags. The police were there in fifteen minutes. Aricka was driven in from school; uncles, aunts, and cousins all converged on that little house. But still Ryan refused to talk. The more they asked questions, the more blank he got. Aricka was getting panicky; at one point she screamed at Ryan to ask where their parents were. She had to be dragged out of the room and looked after by the doctor. The doctor then quickly examined Ryan, but it was obvious what was wrong. Hungry, dehydrated, suffering from hypothermia, and, of course, shock.

One of the cops followed the footprints as far as he could. He got as far as the lake but by then the wind had obliterated any trace of a trail. The later theorized that Ryan had been in the house for the last three days, not eating or doing anything, just sitting there under the comforter and occasionally going to the bathroom. That became fruitless after the pipes froze and burst the first night.

"Where are his parents?" became the question for the cops. Everybody had a good idea as to the answer but they were afraid to voice it.

It was Mags who took the first step. After some prodding, her husband finally agreed to take two of the Constables out on the lake to follow the winter road across the lake.

They were out a little over a mile, travelling slowly and studying the surface intently, when they came across a break in the shallow snow wall that lines the winter road. It was almost invisible, hidden by the three day old fallen snow. After that it wasn't long before they found the remains of a trail. A trail that ended abruptly at some freshly frozen ice.

The police later theorized that Ryan's parents got lost in the thick snowstorm that was falling that morning and veered off the main road towards the channel. A half mile later, they went through the ice. Somehow, Ryan must have gotten out of the car and crawled onto the safe ice. He liked riding with the back window open because sometimes he got car sick. He must have walked home, soaking wet, through the snowstorm and sub-zero weather, and then broke into his own home.

And three days later he was found. They never found the car though because the lake was over two hundred feet deep.

Even to this day, a good quarter of the village won't drive across the lake because of what happened. People said it was just an accident but you could still see the shudder sweep across the people when they talked about it, usually around freeze-up or melt-down.

Oh sure, every winter some fool people went through the ice like clockwork. It was usually some white cottagers who decided to go out to try their new snowmobiles on the lake too early or too late in the season. Or sometimes they raced across the lake, forgot where they were going, and drifted a little too close to the channel where the ice was thinner because of the current.

Most of the Native people didn't go ice-fishing near the channel after Kid Johnson caught what he thought was a hell of a big fish there one spring. The Kid, as we called him, still won't eat fish to this day.

Eventually they took Ryan to the hospital. They considered taking Aricka too but one of the aunts convinced the doctor she could take care of her better. The cops wandered around aimlessly, ill at ease and confused. There were no bad guys to chase, no bodies to identify or take away, no tickets to write.

All they had were two kids, one pretty well catatonic, and a big hole in the lake. Pretty soon they packed up and left the house to the relatives.

I remembered playing in the snow as the cop cars drove by

our house. Us kids hadn't heard the news yet but my parents had. They looked somberly out the window at the retreating cars. We knew something was up, but when you had two feet of good snow to play in, who cared?

But that night, everybody knew, regardless of age. Contrary to popular belief, not a lot of exciting things happened on reserves. The news was to keep the phone lines tied up for at least a good month.

Once the news got around, a bunch of us kids would gather by the shore of the channel and look out towards the section of lake where the car went in, looking vainly for anything out of the ordinary. Like we were expecting the car to come driving out through the ice, or at the very least Audrey and Martin's ghost suddenly appearing to a half-dozen partially-frozen children.

Aricka was back in school within three days. Some of her closest friends surrounded her and offered companionship and support kid-style. But the majority of us wouldn't go near her if we could help it. If we bumped into her in the hall we'd say hello and all that, but that was the extent of it. For some reason she seemed tainted with something dark and we didn't want to have anything to do with it. And William swore off his crush on her, preferring fresh game. I even felt guilty about avoiding her.

But one place I couldn't avoid her was in class. I sat beside her in history. Usually a talkative girl, all day she'd just stare at her books, occasionally looking up when the teacher spoke. The teachers knew enough not to call on her for any questions, which surprised most of us who always doubted the common sense of most teachers.

At one point her pencil broke, and she fumbled around in her pencil case for another. She always liked writing in pencil, saying it gave her a chance to rethink things. I offered her mine—I'm a pen-type guy. She looked at me. I think I even caught a bit of a smile from her.

"Thanks." She took it and went back to work. That was our conversation for the day.

Ryan on the other hand was a different story. He was in the hospital for two weeks, in bad shape. His body temperature was really low and other problems were happening. He wouldn't eat, wouldn't do nothing. They even brought in one of them psychiatrists but with little results. It was like talking to a disconnected telephone.

One day, about a week after my conversation with Aricka, me and William paid him a visit. Actually that wasn't quite correct. Rather my mother, in exchange for a trip into town to see a movie, told William and me we'd be making a pit stop at the hospital, whether we wanted to or not. It was sort of Mom's Reserve version of home psychiatric treatment. Only dogs could talk to dogs and only kids can talk to kids.

William was not amused. The last thing he wanted was to spend Saturday afternoon in a hospital talking to some orphan kid gone crazy that he never liked in the first place. William was like that.

And to tell the truth, I didn't want to be there much myself, but neither of us could or would say "no" to my mother.

"I hate your mother," was all William could say as we walked down the antiseptic-smelling snow-white hallway.

That's how we found ourselves going into room 413, an ominous number if ever we'd heard one.

The door was open and we entered. We could see him from where we stood. Ryan was almost lost in the sheets. We were surprised at how different he looked, how much weight he'd lost. He almost disappeared into the pillow and sheets; only his dark skin told us where he was.

We shuffled nervously, neither of us wanting to break the silence in the room. There were two other beds in the room, one was empty and the other had some white kid reading a stack of comic books. Ryan seemed oblivious to everything.

Finally I broke the silence. "Hey Ryan, how you doing?" The silence returned. William and I looked at each other.

"He doesn't talk. He's kinda spooky." It was the comic book kid, some redhead with a leg in a cast.

"He hasn't said anything at all?"

"Nope. The nurses, the doctors, everybody talks to him but he doesn't say anything. Why's he in here anyways?"

A little more reassured that Ryan wouldn't jump up and grab him, William edged a little closer to Ryan, his curiosity getting the best of him.

"His parents went through the ice in a car," I said.

The comic book kid looked surprised. "They put you in the hospital for that?"

"He was in the back seat. Barely got out. I think that's why he's like this," I found myself edging closer. By now we were both at the bedside, looking at Ryan. Seeing all the tubes and medical stuff running everywhere almost made the trip worthwhile.

"Ryan?" No response. "It's Andrew and William."

William managed a feeble "Hi." Ryan couldn't manage even that.

"I told you." The comic book kid was getting annoying. William looked at me.

"Well, we tried. Let's go. The movie starts in half an hour." William was already edging his body towards the door but for some weird, no doubt morbid reason, I was fascinated by Ryan. I didn't want to leave just yet.

"Look at his face. I wonder what he's thinking about? What do you think, William?"

"I don't know. The Flintstones. Let's go."

"He looks cold."

"Not any more." This time the voice came from Ryan. If it were possible for two thirteen-year-olds to have heart attacks, that was the time. Even the comic book kid looked up in surprise.

"Ryan?" My voice quivered. Slowly he turned to look at me. The glazed lack of expression had left his face. He now looked like he was either concentrating or constipated.

"I'm in a hospital?" William and I could only nod. "My parents are dead, aren't they?"

Again we nodded.

"I'm hungry."

William, still a bit nervous, reached in his pocket and brought out a package of gum. He removed one stick and held out his hand towards Ryan. "It's all I got."

Ryan looked at it for a moment, then reached over and grabbed it. The moment his hand touched the gum William jerked his hand away.

"Thanks." Ryan then mechanically removed the wrapper

and put it in his mouth. The chewing looked like it took some effort. The only noise that could be heard in the room was the sound of gum chewing and comic book pages being turned.

After some moments of silence, Ryan pulled himself up in bed and looked out the window. "So, what's new?" he asked.

"Ryan, are you okay?" I always seemed to find myself in the role of the perpetual big brother. Ryan still was not looking at us; he stared into the glaring sunlight.

"Yeah, I guess."

"How come you haven't talked in a week?"

"I don't know. I just kept seeing Mom and Dad in the car, going through the ice. And pretty soon, I didn't want to see that any more, so I went to sleep."

"But you were awake."

"Didn't feel like it. Then I heard your voices, like in school, and I remembered I have a test in Math. Mom always liked me doing good in Math."

How about that, my mom was right. Only dogs can talk to dogs.

"Um. That was four days ago."

"Guess I failed, huh?" Then his whole body started to shake. His face contorted and it was obvious what was coming next. The sobs rolled out of him, gradually becoming louder and louder till they filled the room. They were gut-wrenching and it looked almost painful. Everybody had seen crying before but this wasn't ordinary. We bolted for the door, grabbed the first nurse we saw and pointed her in Ryan's direction. Then we got the hell out of there. We'd seen enough scary things for the day. Needless to say, we didn't enjoy the movie much.

The next day at school Aricka made a beeline for me on my way in. "I heard you visited my brother yesterday."

After what had happened, crying and all, I wasn't sure if this was necessarily a good thing or not. So I tried to play it cool. "Yeah. We dropped by."

"Thanks. He's talking now."

I shuffled my feet. "And crying."

"Yeah but doctors say that's good. What did you say to him?"

"Nothing really. Just said hello and talked how cold he

looked. That's all."

Aricka smiled at me. "Well, what ever you did, thank you." Then she leaned over and did the most amazing thing. She kissed me on the cheek. I'd never been kissed on the cheek before, I'd never been kissed anywhere. It was the strangest feeling I'd ever had; my insides were melting and I would have died for this thirteen-year-old girl but I was terrified that someone would have seen us. I figured I was too young to die of embarrassment. I just stood there, stunned. And she was still standing there too. "Could you do me another favour?"

Barely trusting myself to talk, I managed to sputter out "What?"

"Help me do something. Come with me out on the lake."

I came to instantly. "Are you crazy? Your parents just... well you know."

"I want to put some flowers on the spot where they were. I was so mad at them when they left, I'll feel better if I say goodbye. Please come with me."

There was no way I was going out on that ice ever in my lifetime, let alone within ten days of what happened. Not for any girl.

"Sure. When?"

She smiled the most incredible smile. "Tomorrow, after school." She kissed me again and went in the school. That set the future pattern for the many stupid things I would find myself doing for women over the next dozen years.

The next thirty hours were less than enjoyable. The thought of going out onto that ice terrified me. The weather was getting warmer yet my feet were getting colder. All through school the next day she would smile and give me the thumbs up. Finally three o'clock rolled around, as did my stomach.

She was to meet me at the doors of the school. I was half tempted to make a run for it but I had made a promise. I was scared but proud.

The last few students made their way through the doors; then she showed up.

She solemnly buttoned up her coat. "Let's go. We have to stop at my house first," she said.

It was there where she picked up her flowers. She had moved back into the house about a week ago and one of her unmarried aunts had moved in with her. Somehow she had scammed her aunt into getting some flowers for her, saying they were going to the grave site.

"I'll deal with my aunt later," she said as she gathered the flowers up. This was the first time I'd been in that house since it happened. It was unnerving. Nothing looked changed, except an 8 x 10 picture of the family that had once been a 5 x7. The smiling eyes of Audrey and Martin seem to stare out at me. So did Ryan's.

We retraced the same steps Ryan had used from the lake to the house. There was already a path broken in the snow: Aricka was talking on about the state of her family but I couldn't listen. I kept thinking about Ryan walking the entire distance, wet, and a zombie. I shivered from more than the cold. Aricka led the way, her arms full of roses. I followed.

"Ryan's doing good. Doctors say he can come home in a few days. I saw him last night. He misses me, and the family, but he won't talk about Mom and Pop. The doctors say not to force him."

I almost tripped over a buried log and stumbled off the path. In the freshly overturned snow, I say a flash of red. I picked it up and it was a red mitten of some sort.

"Aricka? What colour were Ryan's mitts?"

Aricka trudged on, without even looking back. "Red. Why?"

I threw it away like it was covered in ants. "No reason."

We finally made the wind-swept lake. I tried to see the other side but the glare from the snow made me squint. Walking on the ice was a lot easier. The constant wind had packed the snow quite well, giving it a little padding, almost like walking on long grass.

The wind howled by us as I stupidly put one foot in front of the other, wishing I was anywhere but here. Aricka led the way, a good two feet in front of me. I couldn't help but think that if my family knew I was out here, I might as well go through the ice. I tried to look through the blinding glare to make sure nobody could see us, or even just identify me.

Suddenly Aricka stopped, then I stopped. We had been walking for about twenty minutes until we came to a place where it was obvious a lot of people had been standing around. Cigarette butts littered the area, as well as the odd pee stain. The police had been here. And there, in the centre of everything, was a refrozen jagged blot in the lake. I couldn't take my eyes off it, knowing that somewhere beneath it, a couple of hundred feet or so, was a 1970 Ford with two overweight Indians in it. And they would probably be there forever.

Aricka stood there for a moment. Then took a deep breath and walked forward. Her foot gingerly tested the new ice but by then it had frozen solid enough to support the weight of a thirteen-year-old girl. She walked to the centre of the blot, and kneeled. She put the roses down gently and seemed to pet them for a moment. Freezing, but not wanting to say anything, I shuffled from one foot to another.

"Good bye, Mom, Pop. I'll remember you." I think she was crying but I couldn't see because of her coat hood. In the coldness of the lake, I was worried the tears might freeze.

We remained like that for a few minutes before she stood up and started walking back to the shore. Thanking God with every step, I followed.

Without looking at me, she had to shout above the blowing of the wind. "It's over now. Thanks, Andrew."

Even out on that frigid lake, I felt a little warmer.

Then she stopped and turned around. She had been crying. "I know you didn't want to come but you did. I knew nobody else would come with me. Or they'd try and talk me out of it. Thanks so much."

Then surprise number two happened. She grabbed me and hugged me. A little embarrassed but instinctively my hands went around her. She wasn't crying or anything, it just felt like she wanted to hold on to something. Out on that barren lake, I guess I was the only thing.

After that, we quietly went home.

Ryan came home a few days later, looking more sombre than ever. They had managed to put some weight on him but he still looked small. Hoping for another hug and kiss I went over to visit them. Ryan almost looked normal, but there was still something about him, something that hovered about him crying out that this kid has seen some seriously scary stuff.

He still wouldn't talk about his parents, or what really happened that day. All the doctors were worried about that but Ryan didn't care. Neither did Aricka. She was just happy to have him back. And to think just two weeks ago, she had called him a little scum.

By the summer Ryan had pretty well become his old self. He was playing with his old friends again, doing things, even laughing. There was a big party on his tenth birthday. I was there, and I even managed to bring William. It was held down at his aunt's place near the tip of the lake. After all the festivities had happened, everybody decided to go swimming. The lake was alive with the sound of splashing and laughing kids.

All except for Ryan. He refused to go in the water. He just sat on the dock watching, occasionally waving. But he never went in the water that day. He blamed it on a cold he had but there was something more. The fact that he never went swimming, canoeing, fishing, anything water-related ever again in his life, let me believe I was on to something. Aricka just shrugged it off.

"He'll get over it. Don't worry."

Aricka and I were spending a lot of time together. By the first anniversary of the accident, we were officially an item. Again she talked me into accompanying her out onto the ice, and again we put the roses down, though we had trouble finding the exact spot. We hung out together until we were seventeen, and then the time came for me to go off to college. It was an amiable separation, we just grew apart.

She got a new boyfriend and every time that anniversary rolled around, she'd drag that poor sucker out onto the ice with her. Same with the one after him. But eventually she married a guy from the reserve a couple of years ago and moved to Peterborough, about a half hour from home.

Ryan did well at school, even became a decent baseball player, but he never left the reserve for any length of time. He never had the inclination to go anywhere or do anything. He still lives in his parents house and I'd see them occasionally when I came home. I even went out drinking with Ryan a few times. And whenever I wasn't around, William would keep me informed as to what was happening around the village. William was quite happy. He ran the local marina and was living with a beautiful girl named Angela. He had everything he wanted, except a charge account at the beer store.

Me? I kicked around the city a bit, doing a little of this, and little of that. I came home every couple of months, though, to recharge my batteries. I finally came home two years ago at the ripe old age of twenty-four. Now I had a steady girlfriend, and an occasional job at the band office, whenever they threw me a contract like somebody throws a dog a bone.

But in my two years back home, I realized more than ever how true that old saying was. "The more things change, the more they stay the same." The village had a few more houses, a little less forest. In some of the local bars, I ran into cousins I used to babysit. These little things didn't add up to much when you considered that the tone of the village was the same. To this day, most people didn't know what was going on up at the band office, and didn't really care. Old people still sat by their window looking out at the cars driving by, dogs running everywhere fertilizing the world. Home was home, what could you say?

It was winter again and I was back staying at my mother's when Aricka called. It was the first time I'd spoken to her in almost a year or so. Teenage romances are hardly binding ten years later. Especially when you live in two different towns.

"Andrew? I hate calling you like this out of the blue but I need your help."

She still had that breathless quality about the way she talked. When we were young I think it came from girlish enthusiasm, her brain working faster than her mouth, but now I feared it was from too many cigarettes.

"You sound serious, what's up?"

"It's anniversary time."

I knew it was this week. You didn't forget a thing like that but I had long ago stopped being a part of her ritual.

"Yeah, I remember. I hear you still go out on the ice with them flowers of yours."

"Not this year. I'm pregnant, Andrew. The doctor says I could deliver anytime. He and Richard won't allow me to go out on the ice this year."

I almost dropped the phone in surprise. "Don't tell me you want me to go out there!"

She was quick to respond. "Now calm down, Andrew. Richard offered to but Ryan told him no. He wants to do it."

"But he never goes out on the lake, summer or winter."

"Well, he is this year. I don't feel right about it. It scares me. You know he's never been right about water since the accident. Something could happen out there."

I knew where this was leading. "Yeah, so?"

There was a deep breath on the other end. "Go with him, Andrew. Make sure everything's all right."

"Why me? You've go more cousins and relatives than you know what to do with. I don't want to sound rude but why me?"

"I was thinking about that too," her voice got softer. "You brought Ryan out of what ever he was in, remember, in the hospital? And you went out with me that first time. I knew you didn't want to go but you did. It has to be you, Andrew. Promise me you will?"

I was silent for a moment. Those feeling from thirteen years ago came back to the pit of my stomach. I was cornered. "You win. I'll go."

Aricka was ecstatic. She thanked me profusely but I barely heard her. I was thinking about how to handle this. I'd found that as you get older, your sense of courage tended to evaporate, disappear like the wind that blows across frozen lake. I had promised I would go, but I wouldn't go alone. I immediately phoned up my buddy, my pal William.

He was not pleased, even less than me. "I don't even like the guy. It's your promise, you deal with it."

Luckily the gods had allowed me to go to a hockey tournament a few months back with William. There we met these two girls from another reserve and, well, so on. Also as the gods would allow, I had Angela's phone number, his long-suffering girlfriend. I casually mentioned this to William. You have to do these things with William, just to keep him in line. That's what friends are for.

He was flustered for a moment. "I'll tell Barb," he said. "Then you'll be in trouble." I could hear the smile growing in his voice.

I wasn't going out with Barb at the time. "See you tomorrow at five. Bye." Before he could protest, I hung up.

I picked him up in my car the following day. He was glum, cranky and generally not impressed with me. "I hope you're happy," he said. I was, sort of, as happy as I could be, under the conditions. "Let's just get this over with." Good old William, the milk of humanity overflowed in him.

We arrive at Ryan's house, and it had changed little since that winter thirteen years before. Maybe a little more run down (bachelors are like that), but not much. Ryan was already sitting on the porch, his hair blowing in the stiff wind. A bouquet of half-frozen flowers on the porch beside him. You could tell he didn't want to do this, even from this distance but he had to.

Something inside was going to make him do it. It was necessary. Like going to the dentist.

"I really don't want to do this, Andrew," said William.

"Neither do I but we gotta."

"My, aren't we plural these days?'

Once our car stopped in his driveway, he got up and walked over, breath pouring out of his mouth like a little steam engine. I opened my window to talk to him.

"Hey Ryan, ready to go?"

Instead, he opened my door and motioned for me and William to get out.

"Let's cut through the woods. It will be quicker than driving around to the lake, then walking. It's about half the distance."

William looked at me with worry. We would be following the same path Ryan took coming back from the accident, and we were going to the lake to remember the accident. This was becoming too much for William, almost too much for me. Ryan motioned for us to get out of the vehicle again and we did. I could hear William muttering under his breath, "You owe me big, Andrew."

"Well, let's go."

Ryan closed the door behind me and started walking across his yard towards the woods a hundred feet in the distance. He grabbed the flowers and nestled them in his arms. William and I followed along like ducklings behind their mother, every once in a while William giving me a shove to remind me he was here at my insistence, or actually, threat. Nobody said anything until we reached the lake.

I'd never been one for ice fishing. I always found it too cold, and the fish never tasty enough to warrant the cold. Still, I always found myself out on the lake for one reason or another at least once a year, the same with William. But this was the first time for Ryan in all these years, winter or summer. He stopped walking just short of the ice. He looked out across the frozen expanse. I couldn't tell if he was working up nerve or lost in thought.

"It's been so long, I wasn't sure where it was." His voice was almost lost in the rushing wind. "Aricka sort of gave me directions. A little off to the right of the spit, she said." We all mentally found the spit, then the direction. "That way, I guess."

Nobody moved. Again William was muttering to himself, "Oh Angela, where are you? Your arms are so warm. February on our reserve can make you very romantic." Then suddenly Ryan was out on the ice, walking at a brisk pace. We were a good ten feet behind him before we started moving to catch up.

Other than the wind, the only thing we could hear was the dry crunching of lake snow under our three sets of boots. Again we walked in a row, barely able to keep up with Ryan. There were old skidoo tracks all around us. It would have made walking a lot easier by following them but Ryan had his own course set.

Approximately half way to our destination William finally said something aloud. "For God's sakes, Ryan, slow down. My sweat is freezing."

Ryan stopped and looked around. "Oh sorry, I wasn't thinking. Actually, I was thinking too much."

"What's the hurry?" William looked miserable, his hands shoved way down deep in his pockets.

Ryan started to walk again. "No hurry, just lost in thought. It's all so familiar. Except it's not snowing."

Again William muttered to himself, "Give it time."

We were walking again but not so fast. The shoreline was slowly drifting off behind us, and we were squinting now from the glare.

William tightened his hood to keep the wind out. "Been a while, huh, Ryan?"

Ryan looked like he wasn't listening but he was.

"Yeah, a while." He kept walking. "You two didn't have to come with me, you know. I could have handled it myself."

"I know but your sister asked me as a favour. You know I could never say no to Aricka." This was true even now, pregnant and all.

"I almost wish you hadn't come Andrew. You make it more real. I remember the two of you at the hospital, then the crying It's like I'm nine years old again."

The wind started to pick up and we soon found ourselves shouting three feet from each other. In another few minutes we'd be there.

"You know, I always told people I really couldn't remember what went on that day, when they died. Actually I do but I never wanted to talk about it. At the time I thought it was nobody's business, not even Aricka's. She wasn't there, she didn't see anything. Now I don't know."

We were approaching the channel; a couple hundred feet to the left was the other shore. The ice would still be quite safe but it was like looking over the edge of a tall building, you knew you were safe but...

"I was sitting in the back, the window was open. You remember how I used to get car sick? Dad was cursing about the snow, worried that he might be lost. Mom had just told me to roll up. It was too cold to have it open. That's when it happened."

"The car just lurched, dropped and I was thrown to the floor. Mom was screaming and I heard Dad call my name. Then I felt wet, and very cold. I climbed on the back seat, and saw water coming in my open window so fast its all a blur."

William and I felt like we were being told a ghost story, in a very ghostly place, with a very ghostly person. It wasn't a very warm feeling. I was beginning to wish Angela was here too.

"I was only little then," Ryan continued speaking. "So the ice could hold me up. I crawled across the broken ice to the solid stuff. It was cold, so damn cold, but it soon went away. I actually felt numb, then warm after a while. All the time I could hear Mom and Dad behind me. They were trying to open their doors, but because of the water pressure, the doors wouldn't open."

"You don't have to tell us this." William said what I was thinking. I don't think Ryan heard, either because of the wind, or the memory.

"I remember sitting on the ice, crying. The water was up to the windows, and there were bubbles everywhere. It looked like it was boiling. Mom rolled down her window and tried to crawl through but she was kinda big. She wouldn't fit, I've never seen her try so hard at anything. She actually looked wedged in the window, then she reached for me, like she wanted me to pull her out, or maybe pull me in with her. I don't know. But the look on her face... It was then the car went under the water, with a large plopping sound. It wasn't there anymore. There were more bubbles then her purse floated to the surface."

Ryan stopped both talking and walking. Evidently we had reached the spot, or as close to it as we were going to find, both in his memory and our reality. He was looking down at the ice about six feet ahead of him.

"I just sat there for the longest time. I was nine years old, I didn't really know what was going on. I was scared, cold, in shock. After that it gets kind of blurry. I guess I found my way home."

Way over on the other side of the lake, I could see a car driving across the ice, heading to the reserve. I wished I was in it.

"Is this why you've never been out on the lake since?"

"I guess. I just remember my Mom reaching for me. They're still out here, you know. Somewhere below us. They never found the bodies."

William stamped his feet from both impatience and cold. "Can we get on with this please?"

"You're right. Let's get this over with." Ryan walked ahead a bit, then kneeled down and placed the flowers quietly on the ice. Then he started to stroke the flowers, like he was afraid to leave them. "Since the accident, I've always been afraid of this place. But Jesus, I'm twenty-two years old! You've got to stop being afraid at some point. In all this time I've never been able to say goodbye to them. After all, it's only water, right?" "Goodbye Dad.

Goodbye Mom." He stood up and turned to face us, a slight smile on his face. "I was always Mom's favourite."

It was then he went through the ice. It all happened so quickly. There was a sharp cracking noise, Ryan looked down, and then, like bread in a toaster, he slid straight down into the water, the ice buckling around the edge of the hole. A plume of water rushed up to take his place for a scant few seconds before falling onto the ice.

Then there was silence, even the sound of our breathing had stopped. We stood there for a moment, not believing what we've just seen. I remember instinctively racing for the hole and William grabbing me and wrestling me to the ground. I tried to crawl to the hole but he held me.

"Forget it man, he's gone. He's under the ice somewhere. We'll never find him."

William was right, there was no sign of Ryan in the three-foot hole, just the occasional bubble.

"Come on, man. Let's just get the hell out of here. Tell the police."

We stood up. I looked at the hole again, not knowing what to do.

"Don't, Andrew, let's go." William grabbed my arm and turned me towards home. We slowly headed back to the shore.

William took one last look backwards. "Like he said, he always was his mother's favourite."

On the way back, it started to snow.

That was three days ago. Three long days ago. We told the police; they went out with divers but never found anything. I never thought they would. The community went into mourning, and the funeral was today. Even drunk I found it mildly amusing—them burying a body they never found.

Poor William. Fortunately or unfortunately, depending on how you look at it, he doesn't drink. From what I've heard he hasn't come out of his house in the last few days, won't take calls either. The police had to practically threaten to arrest him if he didn't give them a statement.

And here I sit, waiting for the waitress to walk by so I can order another drink. I keep seeing Ryan disappearing into the ice over and over again. I now have a new respect for alcoholics and why they drink. While I don't think this phase will last forever (I'm really a terrible alcoholic), it will hopefully last till I have new thoughts to think, and new memories.

I have just enough time to make last call. I manage to flag down the waitress as she passes. She nods at me.

"Yeah, yeah, I know. Double rye and and coke, no ice."

The End.

Reflections of Your Glory Days

Memories unwind
pausing my stride
as I see you
meander the streets.
Gestures and mumbles
enforce the depths
of your dis-orientation.
Passers-by react differently.
Some recoil with disgust,
others pause compassionate.
Very few remember your past.
The ones who do,
give you something
cash or smokes
sometimes both.
Bulkiness announces bundled clothes
layered for insulation
against cold or heat.
You look seventy
instead of forty.

Our first meeting,
where the Trans-Canada
flows under the bypass bridge
just past Banff's turnoff,
I, seated on a rock,
nibbled at a light snack
slowly swallowed a tepid Coke
Your and your friend,
fresh from Manitoba,
looking for work—
bound for Vancouver.
Like a tennis-player spectator
my head swung
one side to the other,
Due to your argument:

DO or DON'T pick up the Indian
so obviously pregnant.
You won.
We spent fourteen years committed.
Your declaration of
"the need and will to be a family man.
The unborn would be as your own"
created a change of
You and me
The roles slipped on so comfortable.

The abandonment of responsibilities
other than food and a bed
A totally new concept for me.
Hitch-hiking on Indian time
pausing for a day's work;
then moving on
Money in the pocket.
Two as one
against the world.

The tips of your fingers and thumbs
calloused from shingler's work;
fantastic finger strength
used quarters to flip off pop caps.
An intense tea drinker
Talking eyes behind such long lashes.
You sure had mixed feelings
cause your Mom had given you the boot
right after burying your Dad.
Didn't want no grown boys about
While she talon-held a boyfriend
to be a prospective husband.

You always gave the shirt off your back,
a fierce fighter for the underdog.
The inseparable twins
compassion and consideration

were the heart of your daily life.
Never lost in idleness
always doing something.

The most silver warped board
made into creative art-
creations of beauty and usefulness.
The laughter you produced
when you'd test-proof your work.
Does one forget a one hundred and eighty pound man
dancing on a child's table?
Tin-rusted, warped and mangled
straightened and polished
lovingly shaped and moulded
toys, furnishings, knickknacks.
Leatherwork lived and breathed
under your touch
"Jack of all trades,"
You could fix anything
wiring, autos, childish woes.

At the Vedder Crossing Motel,
upon returning to pay rent
we were met by eight determined men
bent on gaining our welfare cheque.
You stood your ground.
Clenched your teeth.
Your eyes had already picked the ringleader.
Ordering me behind you,
(Me—eight months pregnant)
You told me to find you a club.
Sent me to phone the cops.
Then demanded I wait at the café
until your arrival.

Darren at three-months-old
truly deflated
your ego

all because we thought it was too cold
to take our daily walk after supper.
How his eyes were drawn
to sparkling jewels,
flashing traffic lights.
His complete attention captivated
by anything that moved or made a sound.
His angry screams raged throughout the hotel
till we dressed him and donned his woolen cap.
For three days
he turned his head from you and
stilled his gurgling chatter
that penance tortured you indelibly.

Residing at the Sunora Hotel
you picked apples;
You had never ever done it before.
The straps created blisters
two inches high on your shoulders.
I sat you in the sun
poured on Johnson's baby lotion.
Each time the sun's heat
penetrated it into your skin
I'd reapply it.
You tolerated my actions.

Early the next morning
Ol' Frank was amazed
you hale and hearty,
ready for work.
He couldn't believe you were blister free.
He asked you the remedy,
you winked and said
"Old Indian medicine. Ask her."

The Sunora room,
like a cellar pantry
all walls, no windows

only one door to enter.
You had just left,
gone to the Valley
for a couple of drinks.
A late fall storm
blew out the town's power.
Everything was impenetrable black
I grabbed the baby and
backed against the wall.

Eyes locked on the unseen entrance
voices... sounds intensified
swelling fears battled logic
my heart threatened to rupture,
burst through my rib cage.
My mind locked, concentrated
"Breathe normal"
my brain screamed
"Black be my friend;
Black be their enemy."

"She's home alone. He's gone."
"Are you sure?"
"I seen him leave."
"I don't know."
"It's black, nobody will recognize us
Come on! We're safe."
"They'll hear us."
"They won't see us."

The two men's footsteps
cautiously approached the door.
But behind them
heavy steps rustled
with forward determination.
A voice commanded
"Hey! You two! Stop!"
A candle sputtered... quavered for life.

Across the hall to the left
its light flickered towards the door
but fell short
revealed Ol' Frank's shadowy presence.
He grabbed two men,
knocked their heads together,
and tossed them toward the descending stairwell.

As Ol' Frank demanded a chair and candle,
placing his bulky frame dead centre of the doorway,
your protective panic slammed the front door shut.
Haste bounced your body off the walls
in your ascent to me.

At the stairtop you leaped over
the fetal cowards,
and made a mad sprint into our room.
Still feeling desperate,
I clasped you to me
drawing so much energy from you
I almost smothered the babe.
Your intuitive radar
always placed you near
in times of dire need.
Marian Elizabeth named for your sisters
holds a certain spot in your heart
because she's the first-born that you've raised
which was a bonus for family members
to use as a lever to attend family-do's.
I remember if we wanted to go somewhere,
if each one of us asked, you said "no".
But you could never say no to Marian.
How your eyes shone... flamed!
Mingled emotions of frustration, pride, love
the battle of wanting to say no but couldn't
radiated from your body at my underhandedness.

Frederick William named for our fathers

exploded into an early birth
due to a shower suddenly turned cold.
Three pounds four ounces.
If he made it over forty-eight hours he'd live.
Vivid are the agonizing hours of praying,
willing strength into that minuscule life.
Tubes were plugged into his mouth
navel, nostrils and behind his ankles.
Little patches stuck to his head and chest.
All our senses screeched—he's a hair from death.
Your parental instincts were strong.
You'd put your hands into the incubator cubby holes
talk to him, lift him and stroke him with your finger.
I was petrified of holding him in case I broke him.
He was so soft and warm.
Like a piece of sponge covered with velvet,
his little body was half the width of your wrist.
I never held him until he was two and a half months.

Robin Laura, our English Rose,
named for you and my Mother.
The first time I went into labour
they induced me to reverse the contractions.
The second time they wanted to do the same.
I demanded to deliver now
or I'd catch the next bus to Penticton.
Three days after her birth,
the doctors said it was critical to operate.
If her skull wasn't opened
it would grow deformed and her brain wouldn't grow.
It's a miracle she never drowned.
All those tears we shed.
Stricken with horror and terror we debated.
Finally I signed the paper for the go-ahead.
She was such a happy smiling baby.
Her eyes would sparkle alive with her emotions.
She is still a dreamer.

The day at Kingsway and Broadway
we were headed to Safeway
(you and "Sissi" being regular chatterboxes).
Suddenly I saw an elderly lady fall
about three steps off the curb into a crossing;
noon hour traffic just a whistling by.
She lay belly down in the street
raised the length of her arms,
paling with each whizzing vehicle.
Fear-locked words couldn't mobilize my ironed muscles.
My eyes bulged as my mind willed her to rise.
My unguided hand finally clutched your shirt sleeve;
turning, you followed my gaze.
Towards the fallen lady you flew
in the process you grabbed a "four x four x ten"
Stepping in front of the fallen one,
you stood with the raised board
like a titan gladiator, defiant and brazen
Ready to take one and all through death's gate.
Drivers whitened and swerved around you.
A little red sports car came, turned and
blocked traffic securely in the double lane.
The driver, a young man, jumped out to assist you.
The poor woman had elephantiasis,
couldn't bend her knees or ankles.
Together you raised and aided her to the curb.
We, the family, waited at the bus bench.
You slowly walked her home
and carried her things while she talked,
made a pot of tea and waited till her colour returned.

Christopher John, our last babe.
2 A.M. Born New Year's Day.
A howling blizzard raged.
It was a tight situation to get a sitter.
Everyone was off to a New Year's Eve party somewhere.
I told you not to come until you found a sitter.
So between each breath you had to run home.

You'd open the door, gasping for breath,
and stand in the doorway,
leaning the left arm on the door frame,
the right clasping the doorknob;
breathless, you'd quickly babble
as wind and snowflakes danced chaotic
past your perspiring body.
No wonder Chris is the calmest during the wildest storms.
No wonder he's such an action person.
Chris, our own stormwalker.

Society laced and braided your downfall.
Certified and papered carpenters came to you
inquired, received and used you knowledge
learned from your father and grandfather
yet ironically refused you full-time jobs.
Social workers continually agitated.
It pinched your esteem.
Your future dreams shrivelled and died.
There was so much support to drink and forget your troubles.
Finally you admitted defeat and
signed everything over to me,
released me and the children,
you decided to play the game they called alcoholism
and released yourself totally.
Now... you're a wino... on the street.
Will it only be a passing phase?
Please don't let it be until death do you part.
Shared hardships and good times
created a special place in our hearts
that can never be taken away or replaced.
The offsprings asked if I'd ever take you back.
Oftentimes, I replied there's too much water under the bridge,
only God can see and predict the future.

Sally Stands Straight Stands Her Ground Shocks the Salesians

Yes,
I know I am late.
Late to Mass,
Late to Mission,
Late,
so late,
to the Mayflower.

Yes,
I know how late I am.
I may be latest woman you know,
keeping your time and mine.
Two pulses,
two heartbeats.

My circle time surrenders
to hours struck from iron.
Straight lines win,
in the end.
I am late anyway.

This morning I entertained angels.
I was aware.
They wandered up the walk,
wrapped in beads and feathers,
let themselves in,
asked for oatmeal.

I saw glory in the faces,
and served them.

This morning I saved a burning bush.
I stopped to blow on the blaze.
The flame died,
tired as I right now am.
I would be late to Mass, again,

but I paused to whisper *wado*,
thank you,
and bandage its charred limbs.

This morning I greeted the sun.
I opened my eyes at dawn.
I blew kisses at creation,
smudged the saints.
I could have dressed for Mass right then,
made it in,
but I went to the window,
fancy danced.
In my own time,
I saw God.

Sally Stands Straight Scolds the Dominicans

Our words echo in the air
remembered by mountains,
told again by thunder,
as lessons in drumbeats,
and dance steps.

Jingle dresses carry our verbs.
Grass dancers are our poetry.
We have all the rosary we need,
since eagle feathers shelter Scriptures.

Our confessions are in our eye,
watching weavers and warriors
lick their fingers clean of fabric and fire,
tasting God.

Our indulgences are in our ears,
bronze heads tilted toward the worship in the whirlwind,
counting coup,
breathing God.

Our supplications are in our souls,
mothers and mankillers trade wisdom and weapons,
making master's degrees from a night by the fireside,
talking God.

Nga Roimata

Girl of sorrow, tears spell your name
Your cry burst out as the green leaves
Welcomed this mourner, this
time traveller, this
manuhiri arriving in dread
In the fading light
Broken, I came

The breath of the Dark Lady swirled in the uncarved
house
I heard her sighing in the welcoming speeches
I felt her sobbing in the ritual embrace
I came out of respect for her
To stand between her and you—
Pale in your black clothes
Watching beside your small white-boxed treasure
Pink camellia clusters laid out above
Your unlined face too young for this
This is unseasonal
That coffin should be full sized, man sized, the body
in it old

Next day the busload that had travelled all night
One high-pitched *tangi* outside the house pierced the
morning
Black-clad women wailing, green fronds threading
their hair
Even a moko blue on the chin
Advancing in response to the shrill *karanga*
Family photos carried in front, hands green waving
You sat there taking the grieving, you waited
Your face impassive, your crying done for a time
Your breasts were bursting, they had to be bound
Your child could not suck at the food, nor pull at
your pendant to get it

Rain misty between the house and the kitchen
Ringawera worked through the night
The new block dining hall there in front, almost
        completed
The heaped builder's mix an improvised sandpit
In the meantime we slithered in mud so the wait
        could go on
Speeches and singing, argument and prayer
The small fat face colder and greyer

After three days we emerged into clear air
The sea limpid blue currents below
The islands, green and brown, sharp silhouetted in
        their pattern
We walked again down that winding clay road
To where clay deeper dug would clasp
the tiny body to the breast of *Papatuanuku*
assisted by leather-coated spadesmen
Handfuls of earth crumbled between the fingers,
        flowers

In the small church, murmured incantations,
and the host of *kohanga reo* children
sat on the floor up front
They were an observant congregation
They were witnesses
This was children's business

The low lamentation of waves greeting the shore
echoed our weeping, girl
Let your tears of grief cover the sky
Your ancestor, double arched *Uenuku*
will give you his sign to stand
Battle on,
Find the sun again

Janice's Christmas

(The following is a monologue written for the New Play Centre's production of "Voices of Christmas" at the Vancouver East Cultural Centre, December, 1992. It is a retelling of actual events that occurred when I was a little boy, during Christmas, 1972.)

Christmas ended for my family when I was five years old, back home on the rez. Some days before Christmas, Old Mabel's house across from the graveyard had burned down and three of my cousins had died. That same night, my sister Janice—she was eight—asked my father, "What happens when you die?" He was quiet for a moment, then he answered, "You go to heaven." "I know," she said, "you sit in the arms of Jesus."

The next day, my dad was at work and my mom was at her sister's. My eldest sister Rose was looking after us. She was fourteen. All us kids were running around the yard as we usually do on a Sunday morning. Morgan, the boy from next door, came outside. He had a rifle. He said he was going to shoot some birds. All us boys ran along behind him into the smokehouse. He closed the door behind us. Pretty soon, we heard a "knock, knock, knock." Morgan opened the door—all these little girls looking up at him. "Go away," he yelled and slammed the door, right on the tip of his rifle. Bang! Right near my face. A little girl started to scream.

Morgan opened the smokehouse door just in time to see one of the girls fall. She was crying, "My arm, my arm!" By her long hair, I could tell it was my sister Janice. Morgan ran and picked her up and started to run towards our house. We all ran along behind him. He was so fast he left us all behind. Up the stairs he went. But the door was locked. He started to kick the door. I caught up to him and I remember looking up at him as he moved. Janice's long hair swung back and forth as he turned. Finally Rose opened the door. "What did you do to her," she cried. "I shot her!" "What did you do to her?" "I shot her." Over and over again she kept asking, not understanding. Then she began to cry hysterically.

Morgan pushed his way inside and lay Janice on the couch. Rose calmed down enough to phone our mom. "Just come home," she said. We waited. We didn't know how to call the police or how to call an ambulance.

Finally someone said, "Look for a bullet hole!" So we took off her jacket and pulled down her dress. Nothing. We looked on her coat and found a small hole in the shoulder. So we looked at her shoulder. There was a tiny mark, so small it wasn't even bleeding. By this time, Janice was unconscious. Then we heard gurgling noises in her chest. Morgan blew into her mouth, then pressed down hard on her chest. Blood poured out of her mouth like thick paint, across her face, down the side of the couch and onto the floor.

Then my mom came in. [pause] She just stood by the couch... nothing. A woman told me once that mothers live with the thought that something might happen to their children. My mother looked, and I think she knew, she knew that Janice was dead.

A few days later, we had the wake. I'll always remember it because it was my sister Maureen's seventh birthday. The house was full of chrysanthemums and I'll always remember having to steer around this white coffin, sitting in the middle of everything. I started to cry that night—not because I was sad, but because I was scared, scared of Janice's ghost. My father wouldn't even look at me as I cried, he was so disgusted with me. But my mother picked me up, carried me into her bedroom and lay with me until I fell asleep, even though the house was full of people.

The next day, after the mass, the coffin was opened up and everybody lined up to see the body one last time. I remember someone lifting me up so I could look at her. Janice had been an extraordinarily pretty little girl; not the little, tiny beauty of little white girls, but the broad, healthy look of an eight-year old Native girl. But now she looked grey and blank, her long hair pulled so you couldn't see it.

At the graveyard, my mother fell. Suddenly she just went, "Ohhh!" and she fell. I think if her sisters hadn't been there, she might have fallen into the grave.

Just before Christmas, I had to go to court to testify. I was so small, I didn't even fit on the witness stand. So the judge stood me on his desk and held onto my feet. He told everyone, "This is a very smart boy and I want you to tell everyone here what happened that day." So I did, and as I was telling them, I looked down. There, scattered across the judge's desk, were pictures of Janice, naked, lying on a table—photographs from her autopsy that he had left out.

The coroner later explained that the bullet had passed through both her lungs and tipped her heart, she didn't have a chance. He ruled her death accidental.

A few days later, it was Christmas. Everyone was trying to be bright and happy for a change. I was so excited. Even my mom had a nice little smile on. We all sat around the tree, opening our presents. We open our presents in order. I was the last one. I was so excited—my present was big and square and HEAVY. Finally, it was my turn! I tore it open, and inside was a great, big... dictionary. [pause] I started to cry. I didn't want to... My father was so disgusted with me, he wouldn't even look at me. But my mother leaned in close and said, "Evan, you're a smart boy. You can get out of this place."

It's been twenty years since that Christmas, and my family hasn't talked about it one bit. But maybe this year, we will. Maybe we'll have a little memorial ceremony for Janice out in the yard, like we should have done. Maybe we'll get to remember her brief life instead of her horrible death. But I have to ask, what does a child's death at Christmas mean? And I'll finally get to ask my sisters, and my mother and my father, "Do you really think she's sitting in the arms of Jesus?"

[Author's note: the telling of this story was not to make the audience aware of my personal tragedy as a First Nations person. Rather it is told as an affirmation to all those people—especially other First Nations people—who carry loss and tragedy into the celebration of events like Jesus' birth—a man, in whose name, many of us have been persecuted, punished, stolen—even murdered.]

When A Grey Whale Sings to a Swan

When a grey whale sings to a swan,
A shrill cry leads a wisp of thought
Through the mist of an alley sky.
And a wolf screams at the south
Where warmth gleens snow crisp, white,
Blinding his eye.

An Inuit hunter drives a spear through a blowhole in ice
and catches tomorrow's food,
And the sea wolf swims
to the sea's depths of cold and dark,
minus one of her brood.

A whale bleeds at a propeller chop
Beneath the hull of a schooner ride.
Teens ride waves
And tots sculpture sand
As a cow drifts in with the tide.

A gull picks at a carcass
It's feathers ruffle as it swallows meat.
Upon a fire a crab screams
Into an echo chamber pot
Boiling water as cedar burns sweet.

A family drives home through forest and mountain,
Sea breeze trapped in the folds of a tent.
The gas they drive sucked through refinery
In a port from a half empty load
A tanker sent.

Another half remains in the sea, floating, breaking,
washing on rock and sand,
Globbing thick.
The lion turns black and dead birds bob
In sludge as crude turns sea sick.

Through the watch humans' eye,
air and sea die, and bird and whale are gone.
Through the wind and the rain,
The Haida feel the sea's pain,

and listen

as a grey whale sings to a swan.

Fasting

I went up to a barren place
on a high hill
seeking a vision on my mind.
I saw a bearded man
hanging from a tree
and backed away.
They kill their visionaries
in this place
I thought.

I went up again to a quiet place
on a far off hill
seeking a vision still on my mind.
I saw a rich man
sitting guru-like atop a pole
and quietly left.
They sell their visions
in this place
I thought.

I went up elsewhere to a lonely place
on a desolate hill
seeking a vision foremost on my mind.
I saw a black man
suspended from a tree
and sadly turned away.
They fear their vision makers
in this place
I thought.

I went anew to an unknown place
no other tracks approached the hill
finding a vision furthest from my mind.
I saw a small tree
growing from a rock
too small to crucify a saviour

too humble for a rich man's pride
too weak to lynch a slave who dares to dream

I approached him
sat down
and waited for him
to grow.

What More Than Dance

what more than dance could hold the frame
that threatens to fall and break the kiss
of foot and floor in time with your partner
what more than chance could draw out space
between you to its breaking then back to close
what more than dance could make your body answer
questions you had been asking all your still life
what more than dance could make you come to your senses
about where and how hard your foot falls
between starting and stopping.

what more than push and pull
this symbiotic rumba of sorts
what more that this and
all the more reason to dance a jig,
find your own step
between fiddle and bow and floorboard
to live to dance, to dance to live, what more
what more calls your name, makes you trust
another will know the step and won't let go
'round and 'round till the dance is done or complete

what more than dance could make you lean t'ward another
as if you'd been leaning that way all your life
between yours and "other" space
the steps you learned as a girl to follow instead of lead

"Oh, you knew how, you just didn't
for fear of having to answer"

what more than dance could make you climb
out of your darkness into another's
so you could find your own light
what more could make you answer,
set you cold in bright light
and bring you blooming through it all.

Tears From The Earth

ROM
F #
S #
R # #
A # #
E # #
T # #
H # #
u E # #
p # #
u E # #
p A #
u R T H
p
str
eam
a silver
brook trickles
tear-like from the
craggy face of a receding
glacier time has eroded valleys
ravines underground caves and the stream
tumbles forward picking up speed silt poisons
from man fish gather and die great hunters eat
the numbers perish and pass into the earth the brook
moves on dragging effluent and chemicals from shoreline
mills mercury is the silver in the silver brook the
children play in their blood soon to burn in the
choking industrial air marine life lives with
the label toxic waste pinned to their
sightless eyes and stillborn babies
and the horrors of extinction
and they cry... upstream
a silver brook trickles
tear-like from the
craggy face of a
receding
glacier

River In A Tree

Upside-down as it can be
There's a river in a tree!
Rushing ever upward
From root to leaf it flows
Branching ever outward
It's up, up, up it goes
Pulled by the sun
Lifting water by the ton
From ground to tree to air
There's a river rushing there!
Flowing ever upward
Upward does it run
The air will be its ocean
In the clutches of the sun

EARTH

Ko'olauloa

I ride those ridge backs
down each narrow
cliff   red hills
and bird song in my
head   gold dust
on my face   nothing

whispers but the trees
mountains blue beyond
my sight pools of
icy water at my feet

this earth glows the colour
of my skin   sunburnt
natives didn't fly

from far away
but sprouted whole through
velvet   taro   in the sweet mud

and this `aîna
their ancient name
is kept   my piko
safely sleeps

famous rains
flood down
in tears

i know these hills
my lovers   chant them

late at night

owls swoop
to touch me:

`aumâkua

earth walk talks

i heard
you took that long ride
out to clouds and sky and blue
heavens around you now
all finished with
this earth walk
it was a good one Tom
and i'm really glad
we met those times
coming in from around
all ends of this country
talking about the work we did
and sort of keeping
everyone straight on things
i can still see you talking
and smiling and talking
the earth walk talk
even here
at coquihalla
between clouds
and blue and shaman's mist
really needing
to be kept straight
and don't worry Tom
i'll be keeping
an eye on things
til I run into
you again
and remain
your friend
always
wayne

at allison pass

mountains
grow
along
the trail

and
climb

a slow sky
path
to
crow's nest
float and
drift

to eagle and raven

sail
through
clouds

turn and face the wind

and mist
haunt
me
like
some shaman's
dream
rising
along side
these earthly trees
reaching for the peak

your voice and spirit
everywhere
now

if only i could
have you
here

but summits
wash
away

ascend
and
slowly

ascend
slowly
now

and
slowly
ascend
ascend
and rise
away

Wolf Warrior

A white butterfly speckled with pollen joined me in my prayers yesterday morning as I thought of you in Washington. I didn't want the pain of repeated history to break your back. In my blanket of hope I walked with you, wolf warrior and the council of tribes, to what used to be the Department of War to discuss justice. When a people institute a bureaucratic department to serve justice, then be suspicious. False justice is not justified by massive structure, just as the sacred is not confineable to buildings constructed for the purpose of worship.

I pray these words don't obstruct the meaning I am searching to give you, a gift like love, so you can approach that strange mind without going insane. So that we can all walk with you, sober, our children empowered with the clothes of memory in which they are never hungry for love or justice.

An old Cherokee who prizes wisdom above the decisions rendered by departments of justice in this tilted world told me this story. It isn't Cherokee but a gift given to him from the people of the North. I know I carried this story for a reason and now I understand I am to give it to you. A young man, about your age or mine, went camping with his dogs. It was just a few years ago, not long after the eruption of Mount St. Helens, when white ash covered the northern cities, an event predicting a turning of the worlds. I imagine October and bears fat with berries of the golden harvest, before the freezing breath of the north settles and the moon is easier to reach by flight without planes. His journey was a journey towards the unknowable, and that night as he built a fire out of twigs and broken boughs he found on the ground, he remembered the thousand white butterflies climbing toward the sun when he had camped there last summer.

Dogs were his beloved companions in the land that had chosen him through the door of his mother. His mother continued to teach him well and it was she who had reminded him that the sound of pumping oil well might kill him, turn him toward money. So he and his dogs travelled out into the land that remembered everything, including butterflies, and the stories that were told when light flickered from grease.

That night as he boiled water for coffee and peeled potatoes, he saw a wolf walking toward camp on her hind legs. It had been generations since wolves had visited his people. The dogs were awed to see their ancient relatives and moved over to make room for them at the fire. The lead wolf motioned for her companions to come with her and they approached humbly, welcomed by the young man who had heard of such goings on but the people had not been so blessed since the church had fought for their souls. He did not quite know the protocol, but he knew the wolves as relatives and offered them coffee, store meat and fried potatoes which they relished in silence. He stoked the fire and sat quiet with them as the moon in the form of a knife for scaling fish came up and a light wind ruffled the flame.

The soundlessness in which they communed is what I imagined when I prayed with the sun yesterday. It is the current in the river of your spinal cord that carries memory from sacred places, the sound of a thousand butterflies taking flight in windlessness.

He knew this meeting was unusual and she concurred, then told the story of how the world as they knew it had changed and could no longer support the sacred purpose of life. Food was scarce; pups were being born deformed, and their migrations which were in essence a ceremony for renewal were restricted by fences. The world as all life on earth knew it would end and there was still time in the circle of hope to turn back the destruction.

That's why they had waited for him, called him here from the town a day away over the rolling hills, from his job constructing offices for the immigrants. They shared a smoke and he took the story into his blood, his bones, while the stars nodded their heads, while the dogs murmured their agreement. "We can't stay long," the wolf said. "We have others with whom to speak and we haven't much time." He packed the wolf people some food to take with them, some tobacco and they prayed for safety on this journey. As they left the first flakes of winter began falling and covered their tracks. It was as if they had never been there.

But the story burned in the heart of this human from the north and he told it to everyone who would listen, including my friend the Cherokee man who told it to me one day while he ate biscuits and eggs in Arizona. The story now belongs to you too, and as much as pollen on the legs of a butterfly is nourishment carried by the butterfly from one flowering to another. This is an ongoing prayer for strength, for strength for us all.

Joy Harjo, Albuquerque 22 June 91 for Susan Williams

Bear With Me

Part One

Today we stand on new ground
Raspberry bushes spread abundantly
A hot afternoon sun wraps sacred gifts
around this red-speckled field
Just for us from
up above (rock/bluffs/cliffs)
down below (valley)
all around (universe)
There are no clouds in the clear blue sky
unlike my mother's warning eyes
"Don't go too far away
stay close by where I can see you."

Old dead trees and stumps under raspberry bushes
thick green moss grows in cracks
on top hop scotch rocks

Her feet steadily check balance
Small stones fall between two large
opening layers of flat rocks
Must be hollow ground below
She reaches a branch of big red raspberries
Under her feet a crackling sound
One foot almost goes through a big dead tree
laying on the ground
The sound continues to murmur growl
She stands quiet picks berries wonders
Is it some other life?
She remembers stories about bear
from her mishomiss (grandpa)
One is big bears don't hurt nobody
if she sees one or more bear cubs
she's to walk away not play with them
because close by would be mother bear

Bear With Me

Part Two

Somewhere below straight down
sounds like bear
She drops her biggest berries
into the dark cave-like hole
She stands on top crisscrossed log
at the mouth between rocks
somewhere in the distance
pass the many sounds of birds
crickets bees and other insects
"Mary, where are you?
come here right now!"
It's momma's scary voice far away

Binder twine string holds her
little raspberry container
catches a prickly rose bush
She tries to pull it loose
Instead all her raspberries spill
pass the bushes long grass
into opening ground below
She takes another slow step
stands firm and slides into
soft sawdust like tree log

A family of red wood ants scatter
Try to run and hide
Instead of hit her legs
She feels a hairy something
Soft feather like movements
brush her ankle laced high tops (leather shoes)
Hears a burpy grunt
a deep contentment

Bear With Me

Part Three

Momma's loud voice comes closer
Wide eyes look for a way out
She breaks loose runs and climbs
rugged layer rocks
from which she came
Mishomiss sits on top of this rock ground
There's trees everywhere
You'd never know there's underground
Mishomiss puffs his pipe
He knows this place
She was with him when he picked
this spot last fall
To make winter firewood
and this raspberry field

Now, his straw hat keeps his face in the shade
He takes his red cotton handkerchief
from his back pocket overalls
Wipes his sweaty face and neck blows his nose
Puts his handkerchief back
into his back pocket
Beside him on this rock ground
is a birch-bark handmade bowl
or pail shaped container full of raspberries

"Brother (nickname)
you're just in time...
it's time to eat...
"Let's gather dry twigs
and cedar to make fire...
we'll boil water for tea...
"The others will soon be here."

Bear With Me

Part Four

Over the open fire her momma turns over
a golden fried scone (fried bread)
in a cast iron frying pan
Her momma's eyes tell her
not only of flowers in her head
She sees momma trade with a relative
some of these raspberries for
some coal oil for their lamp
She sees a handful of dollar bills
after momma sells maybe half a pailful
of these fresh raspberries
She will then buy white sugar
to make home-made jam
She sees jars of raspberry jam on shelves
underneath their kitchen floor cellar
She will climb down a short steep ladder
Pick one jar when snow is on the ground

Tonight after hot sun goes down
she may get to watch momma cook
fresh clean sugar covered
sweet smelling raspberries
on top of the old kitchen wood stove
(and momma may even bake a raspberry pie
for tomorrow's dessert)
Before her bedtime she'll tell momma
she heard bear and gave bear
an open log of red ants for it's meal
and a five pound lard pail full of the
biggest, ripest, juiciest
raspberries for its dessert

How do you tell momma something like this?
When all you don't want to see is a
long stick make deep razor sharp
red blood streaks on her body
"Momma, no! Momma, no!
please momma, nooooooo."

Star Nations
for Tasina Ska Win

I

we a nation of women
joined together
by seeds we carry
buried deep
even those of us
who have lost
have the memory
of our ancestors
our grandchildren
sewn to our souls

we together
are the stars
lighting
the blue black
we the adobe light
sky bricks
primordial
blue
the mortar
dark

we the seeds
we the stars
flowers
petals pollen full

II

look at me
I am not
a separate
woman
I am the dna
of my great grandmothers
the future
past
the present
both

we are apple
serpent red
we are moon swept
lapis oceans
full of spells

we are first life
star seeds sown
future past present known
from our blood
new ancient flowers grow

Gift of Stone

Once, upon a sandy beach
miniature dunes etched by wind
were a written record of waters
  a half mile distant.

A trickle from a nearby mountain
was mother to a grove of willows
which dry-clattered their branches
  for most of the year.

A terrible stench permeated all
within this shaded stand, the putrid
odours of creatures whose task
  is devouring the dead.

The feared-by-many vultures
brood and belch here, communicating
by scent, flapping heavily away
  when summoned by death.

At the edge of this haven, circling
to avoid its foulness, I saw
lying in the sand like an offering
  a carefully crafted stone.

A weight, designed to absorb water
and sink nets in this desert lake,
perhaps detached and lost here
  when this was an island sea.

I carried it in awe and respect,
this treasure given only once,
to drop into deep blue waters
  returning the gift to the giver.

I raised my eyes to the mountains
and studied ancient beach lines
hundreds of feet above, standing
  there beneath a former sea.

I thanked the vultures for detouring
my steps, I thanked the rains for
nourishing the lake. I thanked the
  hands which fashioned the gift.

I built a small fire and spent
the night star-gazing, in wonder
that the vast universe can be
  mirrored in a silent lake.

Decisions

Emilie stood at the corner. She had to make a decision: to go to school or go to the restaurant and wait. Emilie's mind was on the man who danced in her dreams each night; the man who made her blood tingle with anticipation. School didn't matter. The only thing that mattered was being alone with him.

Ten minutes before he started his shift Sam, the waiter, sipped his coffee. What, he thought, do I do now? What do I do if she comes in? She's only sixteen, yet I really get a charge outta her. I like the way she looks and the way she swings her legs off the stool when she's done her coke. Hmm, I really could make those legs swing. I can't do anything about it though. She's too young, and yet? Maybe later.

Emilie was sixteen and yearned for the tall waiter with dark wavy hair, and electric blue eyes fringed with thick dark lashes. She craved for his arms to hold her. She wanted his hands to mould her flesh and touch her heart. The ache was unbearable. Emilie no more wanted to be in school than she wanted to be at home babysitting her brother.

Brunette hair hung about her thin shoulders. Her ebony eyes held generations of memories; the pain of her grandmothers as they spoke of the residential school and the education system that had changed their lives; her grandmother's songs of grief as they left their natural teachers behind in their villages. She didn't want to be like her grandmothers sitting in their homes or at bingo with a taste of bitterness on their lips. Emilie knew she wanted the taste of sweetness and she knew where she had to go to fill that desire.

Sam wasn't interested in waiting on tables, and he wasn't waiting 'till the end of the week for his pay check. He was free, twenty-one and Cree. With twenty bucks in his pocket, he gazed at the door of the diner. He knew in a moment he would leave. He remembered the old men as they sat with their beers in their hands, their stories on their lips and the dim lights flickering in their eyes. That light would go out soon. The spirits were quietly leaving town.

Emilie set her books in her locker and left. She walked away from the school. School no longer mattered. The halls of polished tile, and the walls of painted wood, were like a prison. Emilie needed light. She needed the spirit and the freedom of youth. And she needed the freedom to fly with her dreams. She strode toward the centre of town. Emilie was no longer a school girl but a woman full of want.

Sam was ready. He hung up his apron, and donned his Blue Jay's cap. He tilted it a little to the side and pushed it to the back of his head. Sam was ready. Throwing his Wrangler jacket over his shoulder and crooking one finger in the neckline, he ambled to the door. Turning, with his free hand he tapped his finger to his forehead in recognition of his boss, as he opened the door. Just as he did, Emilie's outstretched hand turned the handle and entered. Sam took her hand in his and together they sauntered off.

Emilie's mind was a flurry of thoughts. Where are we going? What is happening? Are we going away together? Oh God, he must love me too. Would they live together forever in his little apartment? She noticed the palm of her hand in her left coat pocket was sweaty and nervously twitching. Her heart raced. She had imagined all kinds of things laying in her bed alone at night. She had let her hands caress her body and imagined them to be Sam's. Emilie had never been alone with a man before. Her casual friendships with boys were a disappointment every time she came home from a date. She never let them touch her because to her they were mere babies.

Sam glanced down at Emilie by his side and smiled his sideways grin. This could be a dream he thought. She is so beautiful. Oh man, I could just take her right here on the street. This could also be a nightmare. I know that this could be the best day of my life or it could be... what? Is this my ticket to heaven or is it my ticket to jail?

Emilie followed him, just as naturally as if they were together for the last one hundred years. Oh, this must be where he lives. Is his room here? In the bar? It was at the top of the stairs above the hotel bar. He took her in his arms at the bottom of the stairs and ran his hands in her long hair, twisting it in his fingers and holding her close. Oh God, I'm so happy. Her body trembled as she felt his arms around her.

Her shampoo smelled clean and fresh like lemons as it mingled with the stale smoke and beer that was floating on the breeze outside the bar. She smells so good, he thought, holding her tightly. Taking the stairs two at time, he ran, hand in hand with Emilie. The tingle of their touch electrified the air as he reached under the mat for the key.

The dimness of the room was unnoticeable in the lights that danced around their bodies. He left the lights off and the bit of light that shone in the windows gave them a clear path to the room. They stopped long enough to remove their shoes as they made their way to the couch. Sam tossed the cushions on the floor and pulled out the thin spring filled mattress. He attempted to straighten the sheets and the one thin blanket crumpled from last nights sleep. Dam, he thought, why didn't I make the bed proper. As Emilie made her way to the bathroom, Sam nonchalantly tossed his shirt to the chair across the room.

She turned the water on in the sink and let it run. The thoughts of him knowing that she was sitting on the toilet made her blush. She took her barrettes from her hair and loosely brushed it back over her shoulders. Thoughts of forever drifted and mingled with the fear that inched its way throughout her body.

Emilie returned to the room. She twisted her barrettes in her right hand. Her fingers of her left hand twisted the curls of her hair which draped down the front of her right breast. Sam took the barrettes, set them on the table and took her in his arms. He held her close to him with his right arm and gently rubbed her back. His hand crept up towards the nape of her neck. His fingers slid down over the curve of her buttocks.

A shiver ran through her as Sam caressed her behind. He nuzzled her hair and placed little kisses on her ear lobes and neck. She's so young he thought and just as quickly let that thought drift from his mind. He helped her remove her blouse and slide her skirt over the gentle curves. Her skin tingled with every feathery kiss.

Emilie in turn let her fingers twine in Sam's hair and stood on her tip toes to reach his full lips. Her fervent kisses, wet and biting, left his lips and trailed down his neck to his chest. She was there with him forever. Nipping his flesh she made her way to his nipples and took them between her lips and drew little circles around each. Sam could no longer stand on his wobbly legs. They fell in each others arms to the battered old couch that was now their chariot.

It was now late afternoon. He thought of her and then his mind flew to his job or the fact that he had walked out on it. What now, he thought, as he reached across Emilie to grab a coke and take a gulp. His palms were sweaty, and his hair all a tangle. Emilie lay among the sheets, her hair tumbled over the pillow, like wisps of dandelion fluff on the wind. Sam looked at her and thought of the eiderdown that covered him as a child, how soft and warm that was. He traced little trails over her arms and along her neck to her breasts. He gently kissed each soft globe and cupped them softly in his hands. His kisses ignited the flame that smouldered inside her and she reached for him again.

Long into the evening they held each other. Gentle caresses mingled with fiery branches; her passion unyielding and his stamina spurred on by the drive to consume all of her. The lights of the night danced across the walls as they made love.

As darkness fell, Sam and Emilie untangled themselves from their euphoria. Heading for the shower Emilie asked herself —what now? She was no longer a school girl. Sam sat, running his fingers through his hair. What was next?

Emilie soaped herself and let the water rush over her head. His shampoo smelled of tar, but she had no choice. Her hair clean and her body tired and sore, she stepped from the shower and looked for a clean towel. He had one towel and it lay in a heap on the floor. She hung it over the shower curtain and thought of fixing the place up. She would buy new towels and maybe some curtains for the windows that overlooked the streets. Emilie put her jeans and shirt on over the damp underclothes, and made her way into the living room.

Sam glanced at her and smiled. He wrapped the sheet around him, tucking it in toga style. He nuzzled her neck as he led her to the door. Sam didn't speak, just kissed her and looked into her eyes before opening the door for her. As she left the room, he locked the door behind her and leaned against it. His stomach plopped to the bottom of his feet. Had he made a mistake? It was too late now. He had no job, and she was only sixteen. Sam knew the consequences.

Emilie danced on wings as she made her way down the stairs and up the street to her home. She didn't think of her mom and dad until she rounded the corner. She prepared herself for every answer to every question that they might throw at her. At the door her mother looked at her and hugged her. Emilie felt the twinge, a small spring coiled and unsprung. She stepped over the threshold into the next level and never looked back.

Sam showered and dressed and made his way down the stairs. He turned at the bottom of the steps and entered the bar. The smell of stale smoke, and the sourness of spilled beer attacked his nostrils. Country music droned from the neon lit jukebox shoved against the wall. Sam ordered a draft and took a gulp. The pungent taste couldn't remove the doubt that trickled down his throat.

After hours of smoke, music and beer, Sam stumbled up the stairs. He didn't flop on the bed as he had done in the past. He grabbed his bag and tossed in his one clean change of clothes, tooth brush, razor and comb. Sam knew he could buy whatever else he needed in the next town. His trip down the road in a big rig was his ticket to "hauleeewood," and the life of perpetual freedom that he craved.

It was dawn. Emilie rose from a troubled sleep and padded to the bathroom for a shower. She dressed in her school clothes and made her way down the stairs. Emilie stopped in the kitchen and grabbed an apple. She wrote a note about some early school activity and left the house. Emilie bounced down the sidewalk towards town.

Upon reaching the building she ran up the stairs. She took the key from under the mat as Sam had done the day before. Emilie entered the dim room on tip toes. She made her way towards the bed. She felt for Sam. The bed was empty. Emilie stood, and turned on the light. The bed was just as they had left it. Sam wasn't there. Gone. The word "NO" came to her lips along with thoughts of "fool" and "love." Tears flowed down her cheeks to lips that just yesterday had kissed and nibbled.

She made her way to the stairs. She remembered her mother and the words that she had said over and over again. No one ever takes anything from you. You are always in charge and you have the choice to give something or not. If you give something away, remember to give it with love. Have no regrets. And always be proud of the gifts that you give. Though she was a woman in sorrow her thoughts were now on how to succeed. Her determination showed in the sharp, steady steps that carried her to school. She did not want to end up like the grandmothers, sitting at bingo, with bitterness on her lips.

Emilie strolled into the school and went to her locker. She picked up her books and walked in a deliberate step to her first class. This was no longer a prison to contain her. This was a stepping stone to the future. She knew in her heart that somewhere out there Sam was waiting. He just didn't know it yet.

Standing At The Crossroads

Marina died a lonely death on September 27, 1987, in a quiet room at the Intensive Care Unit in the hospital. The nurses failed to retrieve her after another alcohol seizure. Marina's hand was buckled to the bed railing during her final attempts of clinging for more breaths.

I am deeply moved by her death, not only because she was my cherished friend, but the mysterious events that surrounded her drinking. Marina had nine-and-a-half years of continuous sobriety. She was cheerful, bright and lively, always encouraging me to try her way of life; however, I had not hit enough bottoms yet. Still trying to wipe out the pains of my unhappy past, I drank until the ritual of taking pills and washing down the sadness nearly led me to a lonesome grave. Finally, I was able to put "the plug in the jug" and get sober.

Marina, an attractive, proud Blackfoot Indian, came from the Blood Reserve in Alberta. She was stocky and stood about five feet six inches. She had dark brown eyes and a dazzling smile. She looked much more youthful than her forty-seven years and always stood out in a crowd by wearing fashionable outfits with matching accessories. Her personality was filled with bursts of spontaneous laughter and gaiety. Her warmth attracted many who became close friends.

When Marina started boozing the progression of drinking consumed her for three years. My friend hit a lot of bottoms—spiritually, emotionally and physically. She'd drink and then she would stop. Off and on, her relapses were almost parallel to the number of years she had in sobriety. Ironically, during those three years she had about nine relapses and each one was unbelievable. To this day, I'm still amazed! It's almost like God gave her nine lives and still thirsty, she plunged into destruction.

In the last year of Marina's drinking, on a cold blistery evening in January when I was only a month sober, I was thinking about drinking as I drove around. Instead, I travelled along Highway 33 toward Marina's secluded home. It seemed like I was being guided there and before I knew it I was driving down the street near her house. An ambulance was parked in her driveway.

The flashing red lights caused me to become panic-filled. I rushed inside and found Marina held down by paramedics as they tried to tighten the restraints on the stretcher. There was blood spurting from her mouth, yet she still struggled for release. I assured that everything would be all right and I would be following the ambulance right behind her. In living colour, I relived my own personal experience as I gaped at her. It had always been hard to visualize my recent stay in the hospital. I bled profusely from the nose, mouth and rectally from a ruptured stomach caused by excessive drinking and abuse of prescription drugs. Seeing Marina this way quickly removed thoughts of drinking I had earlier. I thanked God for my new-found sobriety and sped to the hospital, wiping away tears and praying for Marina's life.

During that night, I sat by Marina's bedside, staring with wide open hopeful eyes, comforting her. I helped the nurse to hold her down each time she had another alcohol seizure. Unbelievably, Marina pulled through. Eventually, she got strong enough and left the hospital. She stayed sober for almost three months, living life to it fullest.

Unexpectedly, I dropped in to visit her one afternoon and tears welled up in my eyes as I gaped upon her. This time she lay in her crumpled bed, almost blind. She kept reaching for her bottle of beer but couldn't find it. As I sat by her bedside she begged me to give her a beer. Unwillingly I took the opened bottle of stale beer from the bed stand and placed in her hand. I told her she did not have to drink and there was a better way. I did not want her to have that beer, yet knew she would get it, regardless. I placed a blanket on the carpeted bedroom floor and reached for a pillow. I lay there beside her and during the night got up and called the ambulance a couple of times. Help was denied. The dispatcher said they were unable to send anyone because Marina had refused to cooperate whenever and ambulance was sent. She continued to take sips of stale beer during the night and the next morning I returned home, unable to help her in any way.

Several days later, Marina partially regained her sight. She had called a cab and was heading out to replenish her supply of booze when she fell on her front steps. Because her body was losing its potential to fight off infection, the cuts on her leg from the fall became swollen and infected. Following another trip to the hospital for detoxification, the doctor also warned her it was certain her leg would have to be removed. Despite the doctor's warning, Marina left the hospital and continued to drink at home. One night, a small group of concerned Christian friends came to her house and vigilantly prayed over her. A miracle happened. Gradually Marina's leg healed, although she still needed to use crutches for awhile. Her sight improved too but she continued to drink.

Over the next few months Marina and I slowly grew apart. We didn't talk on the phone as much and I knew I had to associate with people who were alcohol free in order to stay sober myself. The odd time I phoned Marina to see how she was doing. Sometimes she'd pass out still holding the phone.

One Friday night, I joined a small group of sober people for an evening out of dancing and drinking cokes. I still enjoyed the odd night out. In the disco, I spotted Marina, sipping on a cocktail in a dark corner of the crowded night spot. She didn't notice me but I felt saddened to see her wavering on the stool as she sipped from a goblet of booze.

Summer had come and gone. It was nearing the end of September. Around eleven-thirty one night, I received an unexpected telephone call from Marina's daughter, Tracy. She said she had been to the hospital earlier and her mom was in bad shape and asked me to go to the hospital right away. I jumped in my car and rushed into town, speeding on the dark highway. I stopped long enough to pick up my closest friend, Morag, who had been sober quite some time. Shortly, we arrived at the hospital. Marina looked grave. I turned to Morag, looking for some assurance. She responded, "she knows we are here. All we can do is pray for God's will." We stayed at her bedside for quite some time until Morag suggested we go home, wait and pray. I phoned Tracy when I got home and assured her, her mom was going to be okay.

Early the next afternoon, I went to visit Marina again. This time she was sitting up, talking with Tracy, eating a fresh orange, laughing and looking much better. We had a nice visit and upon leaving her I told her I'd be over to visit her at her house in a few days.

Unexpectedly that same evening, I received another phone call from Tracy. Frantically, she asked me to come to the hospital right away. I rushed into town and felt chills go up and down my spine during the quick drive along the deserted highway. Marina was now in the Intensive Care Unit. I met Tracy in the small waiting room on the second floor. She looked so worried. Quickly, Tracy buzzed the intercom and the nurse released the locked double doors. Because Marina had specifically requested my presence, the nurse didn't question if I was a family member before letting me into the Intensive Care Unit. Inside, Tracy's dad was pacing the floor in front of the nurse's station, directly adjacent to Marina's room. In the bed, Marina lay, wrenching in pain. Her face looked all twisted and yellow. It seemed that the fatal malady of alcoholism had launched its teeth into her and was slowly chewing her bit by bit. I stood by her bedside, wiping her face with cool cloths and placing paper trays at her disposal as she filled them endlessly with blood spurting from her nose and mouth. Tracy stood nearby, grief-stricken. When it was unbearable for her she'd leave the room. Marina spoke the odd time. Once she said, "I'm so tired, I just want to go to sleep." She told me she was afraid and I asked her if she still believed in God. She said, "Yes, I do." She then began asking for a minister and close family members. I assured her everything was going to be all right and that she was in God's hands and to hang in there. I was certain she would pull through. Shortly, the chaplain was called to her bedside. The nurse had also called their family doctor to come immediately.

It was well past midnight and Marina had settled down a little. Tracy and I went downstairs to quickly get a coffee, expecting it to be a long night. At the coffee machine we bumped into the family doctor as he was leaving. In passing, he informed us Marina was "on her way out." He didn't comfort Tracy. He seemed to be in a hurry to get home. We dashed toward the elevator and went upstairs to her room. The nurse was standing at her bedside, turning off the machine that had measured her irregular heart beats. Tracy's dad stood nearby, silent and sad. At 1:07 A.M.. Marina's struggle had ended. She transformed into a beautiful ashen colour and her lips became soft, silky and glazed. I stared at her. Tracy was beside me, holding back tears. We stood for a long while.

When the nurse covered her with the sheet we left the room As we stood at the front entrance of the hospital I told Tracy she was a pillar of strength for what she had just been through. I hugged her and left her standing there as she waited for her dad to come down. I drove home, utterly shocked, hurt, mystified and angry that her own doctor could be so cold-hearted.

Five days later we attended Marina's funeral. It was very sad. Her wake was held at her house and many of her family from the Blood Reserve attended. We all reminisced of how she had touched each one of us with friendship, loyalty and love. In the bedroom, her husband Alex neatly folded her clothes and put things in the drawers. Still in shock, he mused how Marina liked to go shopping and would probably like to wear a certain outfit he held up, clutching a matching pair of earrings in the other hand. The few of us who were in the bedroom agreed on what Alex had decided she would wear. It was a long, beautiful peacock-blue dress. We were amused at how he could light-heartedly reflect on her perfectionism for matching clothes and accessories. No one person scorned Marina for having drunk too much; everyone could identify with her disease of alcoholism and sympathized.

Today, I accept the death of my beloved friend and I understand it was God's will to take her out of her suffering because Marina could not find continuous sobriety anymore. I am assured her resting place was pleasant and her final journey was peaceful because she surrendered and put her life in God's hands to take her out of her misery. As I reflect, her memory still lives inside me gracefully. Nearing my seventh year of sobriety I strongly believe Marina's experience is a strong reminder of what could happen if I ever decide to pick up a drink or pop a pill. Her memory will stay vividly etched in my mind forever. I miss her.

Our Blood Remembers

The day the earth wept, a quiet wind covered the
land crying softly like an elderly woman, shawl
over bowed head. We all heard, remember? We were
all there. Our ancestral blood remembers the day
Sitting Bull, the chief of chiefs was murdered. His
white horse quivered as grief shot up through the
crust of hard packed snow. Guardian relatives mourned
in our behalf. They knew our loss, took the pain from
our dreams, left us with our blood. We were asked to
remember the sweeter days, when leaves and animals
reached to touch him as he passed by. You know those
times, to reach for a truth only the pure of heart
reflect. Remember the holy man-peace loving. He was a
sun dancer—prayed for the people, water, land and animals.
Blessed among the blessed, chosen to lead the people.
He showed us the good red road, the one that passes
to our veins from earth through pipestone. Our blood
remembers. He foresaw the demise of our enemy, the
one with yellow hair. Soldiers falling upside down
into their camp, he told us. Champion of the people,
a visionary, he taught us how to dream, this ancestor
of our blood. He asked us to put our minds together
to see what life we will make for our children—those
pure from God. Remember? Pure from God, the absolute
gift, from our blood, and blessed by heaven's stars.
And, we too, pure from god, our spirit, our blood, our
minds and our tongues. The sun dancer knew this,
showed us how to speak the words and walk the paths
our children will follow. Remember?

(On December 15, 1890, Sitting Bull was murdered outside his home in South Dakota shortly after his arrest was ordered. He is remembered by his people as a great man, a holy man and a leader.)

My Mother Told Me A Story

Many years ago my mother told me a story
a story about when she was a child
and it goes like this:
It was a cool and sunny day
and all the coloured kids
were playing around in their way.
But coming in the distance my grandmother saw
white people
coming towards the station.

My mother told me this story
a story about when she was a child
growing up on the station—
my mother told me this story.

Some of the mothers started to run
and hide with their kids
down towards the waterhole in the bush—
but they took every half-caste kid in sight.
But my grandmother hid my mother
in an empty hay-sack bag.

My grandmother waited for the whites to go
but it was sadness that day
for the mothers of that land
'cause their children were taken away
from their dreaming and their culture.
This story makes me sad—what my mother told me.

promises

i promised to lie with you
in tall grass, green, soft
under sunlights' full
spectrum
in colours of warmth
with bird songs sweet
and to gaze upon you
from above
and to involve myself
in nothing
but your naked beauty
but an ugly paper wrapper
blew close by
and the sound of the city
crept into the field
where we lay
and behind the grasses
i saw the great beast
for what it was
i trembled
you pulled me down
wanting me
wanting what i had promised
your fingers playing in my
hair
searching my body to
bring me
into you
but my thoughts were
about the Messiah
and i was calculating time
i stood
and shouted to the heavens
"come on, come on!"
"fulfil the promise!"
and i danced in victory

as my ancestors did
naked in the field
around the one
the one, i loved so dearly,
her beauty ignored
for my love of another
stopping now as times before
without breath, without answer
anger gathered in my heart
and a curse conceived
that i would abort
and looking down in shame
i see my loved one lying, waiting
her hand raised suggesting
to finish what was promised
the ugly wrapper
rests lifeless around a grass
stem
and coming out of empty
distance
a coyote's laughter
that brings me to this life again
with bird songs sweet
and the colours of warmth
and the tall grass, green, soft
i echo his foolish laughter
ignoring the other reality
i focus upon my own promise
and accept my loved one's
hand...

The Ruby Necklace
(The Raven's Tale of the Origin of Corn)

Long ago there lived at the foothills of the mountains a Medicine Man and his wife who had two daughters. The first daughter, Dagu'ne, was frail and helpless and couldn't do much of anything. She spent most of her time looking at her reflection in the water, and brushing her long, black hair. But because she was so pretty, everybody loved her and didn't mind doing things for her.

The younger daughter, Selu'ji, was strong and healthy. She wanted to do everything all at once. She ran like a deer and climbed like a bear cub. She wandered far and wide and tasted all the wild roots and fruits and berries to see if they were good to eat. When her father saw that he was not to have any more sons, he spent more and more of his time with this younger daughter. He taught her to use the bow and arrow, to track animals, and to sing the War Songs, which was perfectly all right, because among the Cherokees a girl could grow up to be a Hunter or Warrior or Medicine Woman or anything else she chose.

What Selu'ji liked the most was helping her father gather the wild plants that he used to cure sick people. She soon learned their names and where to find them. She found that some were to be gathered in the morning and others only when the moon was full. And most important of all, never to take all of them. "Take some and leave some," her father would say, "so that there will always be more for those who come after us."

One day an Indian trader came by with a pack on his back. The people of the village gathered round to see what he had to offer. He opened the pack and laid out his treasures for all to see: shell necklaces from the east, turquoise rings from the west, red stone from the north, and carved jade dolls from the south, black obsidian and white ivory—little, tinkling, silver bells.

When he held up a dainty little strand of seed pearls, Dagu'ne cried out that she must have it. Her mother placed it around her neck. The price was very high, but the mother insisted that it was worth it. Her father counted out many deerskins in trade.

Dagu'ne wore her new necklace to the dance that night. Everyone came to look and told her that she was even more beautiful than the pearls. She smiled and thanked each one. She was very pleased. Her father and mother and younger sister were pleased, too.

The Trader had planned to leave at sunrise the next morning, but during the night he fell ill. The Medicine Man was called in to treat him. Selu'ji helped her father to gather plants and mix them together. She watched while they simmered for hours over the fire. Everyone thought the Trader was going to die. But by the time the moon had waxed and waned, he was well again and ready to travel.

Before the Trader left, he went by to thank the Medicine Man for saving his life and to give him a necklace of bright red beads.

The father gave the beads to Selu'ji. She could hardly believe that they were meant for her. Red was her favourite colour. She could see right through each one. But how they sparkled in the sunlight! People began to notice. When they found that the stones were rubies, and very valuable, they talked of nothing else.

Dagu'ne was very jealous of her sister. Now she hated Selu'ji and all because of those silly red stones! In her anger she wanted to get rid of them. So she stole the ruby necklace and buried it in a hole at the edge of the garden.

Now the pearl necklace was the finest in the village, and Dagu'ne was happy.

Selu'ji looked everywhere for her rubies, but she never found them. She asked around, but nobody could help. It was hard to accept the loss. When she asked her sister about the mound of loose earth at the edge of the garden, Dagu'ne explained that she had planted some cattail fuzz to see if it would grow. Selu'ji kept it watered because she liked cattails.

And sure enough, several green blades pushed their way up from the top of mound. Selu'ji watched and cared for them, but they weren't cattails at all. There was one main stalk with long green blades growing out from it. A tassel appeared at the top. Silken threads peeped out from a pocket halfway up the stalk. Later the pocket bulged and when it turned brown it cracked open. Selu'ji reached in and pulled out a hard ball that looked like a great big berry. She rubbed off some of the seeds in her hand. They were small, almost round ruby-coloured! She remembered her ruby necklace.

Could these be the lost rubies?

She called her family to come and look. Her father said he didn't know what they were. Her sister scoffed at such a fuss over some worthless seeds and threw them into the fire. In the heat of the coals, one popped and bounced back at her. the rest popped and flew in all directions.

Selu'ji picked up the nearest one and looked at it. The red seed had burst into a white bud. She smelled it. It smelled good. She tasted it. It tasted good, too.

It was popcorn. That was the first corn.

She saved half the seeds and planted them in mounds of earth as before. From these plants came corn of other colours. Grains as blue as smoke from the fire appeared along with the red ones. Then came yellow and finally white. The multi-coloured ears of corn were very pretty. They were very small. They kept getting larger, and most of them turned yellow or white all over.

It was called "selu."

Selu'ji, the Corn Mother, gave to The People something far more valuable than rubies.

NOTE:
Dagu'ne is the Cherokee word for "Pearl"
Selu is the Cherokee word for "corn"
Sel'ji is the Cherokee word for "Corn Mother"

Speak *Sm'algyax* Grandma, Speak Haida Grandpa

Dear Gram:

I am writing you too long after you are gone. But never so gone that I do not weep your absence and miss your voice. I was wondering if you were wondering how I was doing? Do you know that I went to university and got a degree? and now I am getting another one—a Master of Arts they call it. They say it's important to have this piece of paper because it will give me the way, the passage, the ticket, the language to tell my story. But, grandma, I wonder if you really want me to tell my story. You see I learned about why and where the night and pain and all of the things that you would not let us speak about came from. I learned about what happens to people, like grandpa, when they're sent to residential school. In university, there's nothing in the textbooks that say anything about who we are. I mean gram, we go to school to learn about them and when they think we can think like them and speak like them, then we get a degree. But even though I know how to speak and act like them, I am like you. I am not sure if I can speak and I don't know if it's okay to speak, to tell the story of our pain, to talk about the abuse of the our people and why grandpa abused me.

Did you know gram? Did you know that the pancakes he cooked us in the morning were part of the nightly ritual of visiting me in bed in secret in the dark? Did you know that the good smells were a lie? Did you know that my morning baths couldn't make me feel clean? The water, rocking the boat, the boat where he abused me, where he led to the galley and into the engine room. Did you know that after I walked down the wharf onto the boat and entered that voyage of self-hatred cloaked in family smells and nurturing sounds that I knew you knew? It makes me feel dead inside oh so so tired. Yes nights, nights, and rocking. Rocking alone downstairs by myself. No hands to cradle me, no soft palms to wipe away my fear, no tears, just me rocking, empty and alone with my fear that I was a pregnant eight year old. So so alone, so alone that I remained there, too alone to name my fear and speak the act. Semen sliding down my leg in the middle of the night, too afraid to move, lying still waiting and waiting, waiting to slide down the wall, waiting to disappear into the darkness. Jesus Christ, how long do I have to be alone? When is it alright to tell my family, my community? I was raped over and over, over and over.

Say fondled. No... abused. No... touched. No. Not raped. Don't say the word, he made you pancakes in the morning. He made you pancakes and he was so quiet when he touched me. Not a word, not a threat, not a sound, just heavy breathing and grunting and touching. And silence. I am so quiet in this world. I will not be silenced. I write now using a huge Webster's dictionary like the one he used to use for cross-word puzzles. Grandpa was so smart, he always used that great big dictionary. He learned a lot at the residential school.

When I wake up in the morning I sometimes think this is the day to die. Death, inevitable when I think I am all alone in this world with my pain and I wish somebody could fix it because I don't know how. Maybe that wish is like when I was a little girl and I used to dream about saving all the poor dirty kids standing outside the bar waiting for their parents. I wanted to take them home and bathe them in the tub that you used to bath us in. I think about being clean and being loved and I wish I could clean up the whole world with that same gesture of love that we experienced in the morning in our tub. Did you think you were washing away the secret and your silence? I don't know grandma but my faith in the need and the ability to truly clean the world up with a bath is an act of love that ignores life's ugly realities. This is not something I want to do. I want to love but not in silence. I want to speak the night and speak your gesture of love. I want to speak, to scream, to wail, and to cry out, yet, I need to dance, to heal myself. I want to expose the night so we can have our day.

When I write, I dance my words on the page. I speak sadness with the joy of self-realization, of agency and self-identity. I am whole even in my fractured life of so many worlds: the village, the city, my colleagues, my children, and my family. Oh god I just want to dance. I just want the world to flow out of me. I just want my joy to be true. But it's so rare so far away. Let my joy be true. Let it last a little longer next time. At times when I think life is pretty good for me as an Indian woman like right now this moment as

I speak to you, I take the words, and dance them on the page. But then my Indian woman /child surfaces and is angry and frightened and tired and sad. I work hard to put the punctuation where it belongs (belongs?). To make her dance to make music for her but the form will not produce the Marcy of childhood, of my young womanhood. I can only dance her with the language that I have now. I hardly remember the joy of childhood. And the times when I experience the satisfaction of being able to write/dance, I must always speak of the abuse of power. When will I dance truly joyfully? I want to write about me dancing for you, scarf whirling around spinning, you laughing, remember? I want to write about the possibility of empowerment, agency, happiness and potential for Native women while she dances. I think that if I keep writing the world that it might happen. But how? Where do I find the strength to continue? It's there in your love grandma. The bath, laugh behind the palm, the gentle proddings.

Go ahead and dance; no one will laugh at you except with delight that you are Marcy, this girl who we nurtured to speak out silence. We cannot speak we cannot tell the secret. Speak for us Marcia. Dance, we will watch and encourage you with our hearts, forgive us for not speaking; we could only teach you. We could only give you partial joy and let you realize the rest your self. We are so sorry we could not say the words to make the night go away. We could only love you in the daylight; it is up to you now to speak the night. We will love you even if other people don't want to hear your words. We will love you because we brought you up to speak, to dance the rest of the story.

Grandma, I want to dance for you again. I want the joy, the self-confidence of dancing for an audience of love. A self with the promise of a future. To become that same child who emerged from time to time despite the pain. I want to tell of the joy I feel when I speak words that come from all the nuances of your love and murmurings, *as shah*, don't cry dear. I want those soft palms that dried my eyes and gentle rocking to mix with this language I've learned in school. I want the caring you had for our family, our community to meld with my text. I want to tell them our story, the one you gave me with songs and stories of the porcupine and the beaver. Remember when you washed us in the tub every morning, grandma, and then gently combed our hair? I can only speak of abuse. I want to tell the story of love.

Oh Marcia, forgive me for not speaking. I could not let my self realize the pain.

I can hardly speak your words because I think you might not forgive me for telling the story you wanted to keep a secret. Yes, some of our leaders, some of our old people and others in our communities want us to be quiet about life on our social and geographical reserves. They want us to be silent and if we are not then we are not family. But your silence deadened me, gram. This is about love and anger. This is about sadness and joy. About strength and the total collapse of the spirit.

It is up to you to speak the night. It is up to you to tell the story of your and our abuse.

It's up to me to speak, to speak the night. I must speak the night of a colonial history that overlaps with the reality of my own night that continues into day. To tell Grimm's fairy tale of colonialism. Will I ever speak it so that people will be compelled to listen to a storyteller? I speak the night with pain and with reluctance but if I don't, I will die.

Why did the porcupine leave the beaver up in the tree? Tit for tat, that's what you get. No big mystery about an old Indian story that sounds more like an Aesop's fairy tale.

I think about what you taught us. How to be white with Indian stories, drinking tea from a cup and saucer and not a mug. Oh gram this is such confusion such pain. I wish you could have said to me you are Tsimshian and our clan is *Gisbutwaada*, Killer Whale and our people came from a strong matriarchal society. I am teaching you the way of all of your grandmothers. I want you to grow up big and strong like all the great matriarchs in our family. But gram you didn't say it. You couldn't say it. Instead you were silent while your husband abused me. You could only pass on the love of nurturing me in a bath tub. Did the missionaries teach our people we could wash away the dirt of being Indian? Where on earth was all of the knowledge of our grandmothers? I want it. I don't want to have to decipher this cryptic code of love and self-loathing in search of some kind of Indian self identity. It would have been so easy if you could have spoken the world in

Sm'algyax. I am crying for us because someone took the language of our grandmothers and replaced it with English, tea in a cup and saucer and such good manners that we could not speak the sickness that happened in our night. Such good English manners that we did not cry rape rape RAPE. STOP.

We are nations of women and men who love our children. We are nations with chiefs because our families eat together at our feasts. What if we gave a feast and nobody came? Help me to tell them gram. Turn your face first towards your children. Speak *Sm'algyax*. Speak Haida. Gently. To us, your families, and then we will speak as nations. Big chiefs. Big names. Big words for white people don't comfort children at home. Oh gram. How could you be silent? To hell with their manners. To hell with their world. Speak *Sm'algyax*, speak *Sm'algyax*.

Speak Haida, grandpa. Speak the language they told you not to speak in residential school. Speak the language of family you could not learn in a school without mothers and fathers and aunties to tell you how to behave. Where they tried to teach you to be like them before you could learn how to love your unborn grandchildren. If you speak Haida, grandpa, will the silence of abuse be over? If you speak our own language will you remember who you are? Speak Haida, grandpa, speak *Sm'algyax*, grandma. So we can be a family, be a community, be strong nations of people. Speak to one another first. Sing our own songs and dance our rights and privileges with honour and love. I want to dance with my own people. It's time to dance with you grandma and grandpa. Time to dance with my daughters, and my son.

So I have to go now. I will miss you as I always do because I love you and I need you to know that. I wish those early morning breakfasts were really so sweet smelling and warm, steaming bathtub beside the kitchen stove. I have to go grandma, to let go of my fear of your rejection and my fear that some of our family and community may reject me, deny my truth. I don't think this is such a great way to say good-bye but I guess it's not really good-bye because it's not over.

Love you,
Marcia

Spirit Deer

The early morning mist hung suspended over the pond below the corral in long willowy wisps, barely visible. The air had a dampness that made it feel somehow alive on my skin.

As I walked home from my early swim, I left a visible trail behind me in the silvery dew covered grass. Meadowlarks were singing in their loudest, seemingly trying to outdo one another. The sun which had almost reached the top of Picnic Hill made it look nice and warm over there, while here it was still shivery.

Even the smoke coming out of the chimney hung in the air above the house in a light blue shroud. It seemed like something was just waiting to happen. Things felt somehow different today, so I stopped, and tried to figure out what it might be.

At that moment the stillness was broken as Mom opened the back door to put some food scraps in a plate for old Prince. He crawled out from under the porch, stretched and wagged his old tail. I could hear Dad whistling as he walked down the hill from the chicken house. He had his hat in his hands and I just knew that he had collected eggs that we would soon be having for breakfast. He saw me and hollered out, "Did you feed the horses yet?" I shouted back, "I did," as I opened the gate to the yard so that Last Chance and Pinda-Ho could get a drink before they were harnessed.

I stopped at the door and waited for Dad to get there so I could hold the door open, because his hands were full. As I opened the door I could smell fresh coffee and deer meat frying. Dad was saying something about the hens laying more eggs lately... I hardly heard him. My mind was still on whatever it was that I sensed.

I looked at the water buckets on the kitchen counter by the sink and silently prayed that they would not be empty just yet. I wouldn't mind carrying those buckets of water up from the spring later, but right now I didn't want to go back down there.

During breakfast my older brother and dad were talking about fixing the dam in the creek and cleaning out the irrigation ditches at the upper ranch. Somewhere during breakfast it was decided that the entire family would be going because there was no school today or tomorrow and that a lot could be accomplished towards getting things ready for planting.

Suddenly my little brother kicked me under the table and pointed at Dad. I looked up and saw Dad's stern eyes on me. He had been talking to me and I had been busy wondering if it was the mist or the smoke that had made things look different. He repeated, "You saddle up Lucky when you're done and ride up to the spring above the pasture and bring the other horses in. Your brothers here will ride to the Upper Ranch... we'll need the extra horses to help with the work up there."

I was still feeling a little nervous, although I was not certain what about, so I asked Dad, "Could I take a rifle with me?" He said, "Go ahead, take the 25-20."

As I rode up the hill I could feel the nice warm sun on my back. It was early spring and the whole hillside was covered with yellow sunflowers. I could hear the call of the blue grouse. In my mind I saw it as it strutted, all fluffed up, it's wing tips dragging on the ground. There were lots of male grouse strutting back and forth on almost all of the little ledges and when one flew up in front of my horse I nearly fell off. It's sudden fluttering made both me and my horse nervous.

I reached the top of the hill and in the distance I could hear the bell that was strapped around Rocket's neck. So I knew that they would be just a little bit further over the hill by the spring. I decided to ride along the edge of the crest of the hill.

The view was something else, and I could hear a diesel engine blowing it's horn at a railway crossing somewhere far below in the valley near the city... suddenly there ahead of me was a deer, it took a few bounds and disappeared over the edge. I'd never shot a deer before but I thought since I had a gun with me, it was a chance to get one all by myself.

I got off my horse, tied her to a *seeya* bush and took my rifle and walked slowly to the edge of the hill. I looked over and there he was. He had stopped almost out of sight. One jump and he would be gone. I raised my rifle without any fast or sudden moves that might spook him. I knew I had only one chance.

He turned and jumped just as I pulled the trigger and disappeared. But from the way that he jumped, I knew that I had hit him.

I ran as fast as I could to where I had last seen him go out of sight. From there I could see both ways along the open hillside, and all the way down to the road, but there was no deer anywhere in sight. I walked down the hill in a zigzag pattern and soon came upon his tracks and a few drops of blood on the grass, but his tracks disappeared... I searched that whole hillside up and down several times.

I was getting tired and feeling scared. I was thinking that a deer couldn't just disappear like that, could it? Then I started remembering the stories my uncle had told me about how a deer will play tricks on you sometimes, especially if it's your first deer and you don't have an Elder with you.

Thinking these things, my heart started beating faster, and I wondered if this deer was doing strange things to me. I shook my head and thought, "What is the matter with me, those were only stories, things like that don't really happen." My imagination was running overtime, so I sat down to calm down and rest a bit.

I decided I would go back up the hill, get on my horse and herd the others down to the corral. I would tell my Dad that I had wounded a deer and couldn't find it. He would bring his old dog Prince, and Prince would find this disappearing deer.

As I was sitting there catching my breath, I was still scanning the open hillside below me. There was only one big tree on this hillside and it was about thirty yards directly below me. My eyes had just looked at that big tree when I saw the deer look out from behind the tree trunk. His head disappeared behind the tree only to reappear out the other side. The strange thing was, that he was facing down the hill. Every time he poked his head out from behind the tree he had to look back at me, like he was sitting under the tree with his back leaned against the tree trunk.

My heart started pounding again, because he hadn't stuck his head back out. I thought, "that's impossible, a deer can't sit under a tree let alone hide from me by putting it's back up against a tree trunk." Just then he stuck his head out again as if he had heard me. When he looked out from his hiding place at me, my heart pounded harder. My heart was pounding so much now I could hear the blood in my arteries rushing past my ears... I was terrified.

I thought, if this is a spirit deer playing tricks on me, should I shoot it if it looks out at me from behind that tree again? Then I thought, maybe the best thing to do is to go around to the side and see if it was really leaning up against the tree... but what if it was... what would I do then?

It took all my will power to get up slow and ease my way to the side. As I got further to the side... sure enough, there he was, sitting with his back to the tree. I was so stunned that I just froze in my tracks and stared at this deer sitting under the tree with his back leaned against the trunk... suddenly he looked at me and stuck his tongue out at me!!! That did it. I was gone.

I ran up that hill to where my horse was tied, like it was flat ground. I jumped on my horse and rode down that hill towards home like I was riding in a suicide race. Dad must have seen me coming down that hill running Lucky as fast as she could go. She ran sure-footed all the way to the tool shop where we usually tied the horses.

Dad was waiting there. I bailed off that horse and before I hit the ground, I was telling my Dad how this deer was sitting under a tree, with it's back to the tree trunk, and how he stuck his tongue out at me.

My Dad grabbed my shoulder and shook me. He told me to calm down and tell him what happened. So I told him everything. He told me to go into the house and have a cup of tea while he saddled the old work horse Pinda-Ho.

I had just finished my tea and telling Mom about what just happened to me when Dad came in. He said, "Come on son, let's go back up there and see." I told him, "I'd rather stay right here." He told me, "Let's go." His tone of voice told me that I'd better go with him.

As we rode back up there, in my mind I could still see that deer looking out at me from behind the tree. I was wishing that he wouldn't be there when we got to the tree. But then if he was gone, no one would believe me.

We tied our horses and walked the short distance to where the deer should be. I was walking behind Dad. I told him, "That's the tree, he's behind there." Just then the deer stuck his head out and looked at us. My heart just about stopped beating.

Dad calmly stepped aside and handed me the rifle. Then he said, "Sit down, take careful aim, and shoot it in the head." My hands were shaking and little beads of sweat suddenly formed on my forehead. Dad told me to take a couple of deep breaths and pull the trigger.

I aimed and pulled the trigger. I kind of expected the deer to suddenly disappear in a little wisp of smoke. But instead it dropped dead. Dad handed me the knife and told me to go "throat it." I was scared but I went anyway. The deer was dead and very real.

Dad touched my shoulder and I just about went straight up. As I dressed the deer out, Dad told my why the deer was sitting under this tree. He said that at the exact moment when I shot it, it jumped as I fired and that I had hit it in the spine. This had paralyzed the deer from the waist down.

Under this tree where I thought he was sitting there just happened to be a deep little hole. It was some sort of a dust bed that he fell into and couldn't pull himself out by his front legs. So he just sort of sat there in this hole propped up by his front legs.

I finished dressing him out. I was looking at this deer and it all sounded very logical, and then the deer winked at me!

I must have turned pale or maybe my hair stood up, because Dad asked me what was wrong. I said, "That dead deer just winked at me." Dad chuckled and said, "That's just a muscle twitch. Dead animals twitch for awhile after they die."

Dad then told me that our people must respect the deer's life. He explained to me what I had to do to show my respect for the spirit of the deer. Then he said, "Don't ever forget this," and he walked away without another word.

While I was doing what he told me, I wondered if he had meant this or my whole experience today.

dark forest

the trees stretch long shadows
moonlight cowls
across the sleeping forest floor
darkness upon darkness
we mistake one for light
but there is not enough light
to call this shape owl
to call this shape fox
only the whispering
feathers stir the still air
furred feet bend dewed grass
our eyes are empty
our cars fill our heads
with visions teeth and talons
the stones are silent prophets
bone-white and waiting

Untitled

grandma pours me a cup of red raspberry tea
with loose yellow leaves
swirling in vibrant midnight blue
sending sparks of fire to radiate around
when i kneel in mud
rubbing red across my crescent body

grandma pours me red raspberry tea
when i want to sleep all day
never leaving my dreams
lay in the stars
lay suckling in my mothers arms
and play peakaboo with my dad

grandma pours me red raspberry tea
when i want to lay cradled in the moon
watch over you
and paint my body with red from my womb
rub my fingers creating pictures
that pulse on the walls of my room

grandma pours me red raspberry tea
when i want to throw porcelain heads that sit on my shelves
shattering windows and mirrors that surround my bed

grandma pours me red raspberry tea
when i want to be a cat
swaying my hips
winning each stare
playing with invisible rainbow spirals
that linger in the air

grandma pours me red raspberry tea
on days when
i want to laugh with the children next door
forgetting the years i experienced before

grandma pours me red raspberry tea
on days when i quiver
tasting salt tears
longing for random words
to send sensual waves
that lull still moments

grandma pours me red raspberry tea
warming unborn babies
that cry
        mama make this world soft
        with soothing sounds of drums
        and clean water swooshing around
causing blows in my stomach
to send me to the floor

grandma pours me red raspberry tea
on my crescent back
cascades across my lips
lingers into my body
spirals in my belly
steeps inside
floats through my veins
sits quietly on my skin

so i can walk strong
with hands sending sweet songs

Mama God

Mama God
the voices cry out
Mama God
out of your womb-mind
the world was pulled
sobbing
its first breath.

Mary Isis
they say is the Mother of God
who then is the Father of God?
and the Catholics pray
with their beads
"Holy Mary, Mother of God..."

Tonatzin
our Holy Mother
virgin of Tepeyac
of Guadalupe
speaker of Nahuatl
Holy Earth Mother
Daughter of Mama God
Daughter of Papa God.

And the Mexicans say
Our Grandparent
the first One
Ometeotl
the Two-in-One Spirit
Male and Female
all in One
who creates
out of the Original Mind

the Mother *Teotl*
the Father *Teotl*

Ometeotl
the two-in-one
everywhere
Invisible Night Wind-Breath
in everything
but no-thing it is
and Lame Deer's teacher said:
the Great Spirit is not a man
like the Christian God
it is a power
it could be in a cup of coffee

Huehueteotl
the Old One
the Fire
in the centre
of all being
the breath
the heat
Mama-Papa
Abuelo-Abuela
El Viejo-La Vieja
Now we know them
the Mother of God
the Father of God.

Kinship is the Basic Principle of Philosophy

The Thunder-beings are alive:
grandfathers!
The Earth is alive:
mother and grandmother!
The trees are alive:
grandfathers, grandmothers!
The rocks are alive:
relations of all!
The birds of the air
the fishes of the sea
the animals that run
the smallest bugs
we are related!

For hundreds of years
certainly for thousands
Our Native Elders
have taught us
"All My Relations"
means all living things
and the entire Universe
"All Our Relations"
they have said
time and time again.

And here's the good news!
The geneticists
have at last
learned to read the DNA
and lo and behold
they find that the Old American
Elders are spot on!

The white-robes
priests of the new electric monasteries
have discovered
that animals, bacteria,
plants, trees, humans
all share the same
building blocks of DNA
repeated over and over
in different patterns—
same stuff
just arranged uniquely.

But what a great thing!
to learn that the old
Indigenous philosophers
have been right
have seen past differences
have seen through externals
have seen beyond divisions
have penetrated mysteries
to teach us of the
unity of all life—
and without using computers!

But the old wise ones
have talked also
of water
of rocks
of earth
of clouds
of sky
saying:
all my relations
leaving the geneticists
still in the dark!

For DNA does not make life
    having DNA does not make
    one move
    having DNA does not make
    one change
    having DNA does not make
    one "breathe"
    having DNA does not make
    one grow into a mountain
    having DNA does not make
    one erupt
    having DNA does not make
    one unite in congress
    with another!

For surely it is that
    all of us
    have other things
    in common
    known long before DNA
    known long before genes
    and I mean
    those things,
    those structures,
    we call chemical elements
    like
    oxygen
    hydrogen
    you know the rest.

For surely we already share them
    with everything else
    we already know we are the same
    our bodies have nothing not found
    in the earth
    in the water
    in the air

And the Ancient Ones
already have instructed us
of how
we are one with all these things!

And when hydrogen and oxygen combine
in a grand sexual orgy
producing their child water
do they not act?
do they not change?
do they not move?

What could be more alive than water?
Magic water
the greater part of us
alive, are we full of death
of that which is dead?
No, I won't have it said that
my innards are dead
that the salt water core of me
is not alive
and all of my acids
and proteins
and cells
and molecules
all are alive.

To move, indeed, is to be alive.
Uli, motion,
the sacred principle of
ancient Mexico
Uli, motion,
produced first by the
powers of the four directions
who, being in disequilibrium,
produced tension
and the first movement

the beginning of the physical universe
as it would appear.

And indeed the astronomers know
that there could be no
first explosion
no "big bang"
without movement
without motion
and only life moves
it is seen
the dead no not move.

Energy,
yes energy
we all have energy
and in our molecular cores
atomic centers
those ever-moving
electrons
particles
quarks
moving, moving, moving
alive, alive, alive!

Do you doubt still?
a rock alive? You say
it is hard!
it doesn't move of its own accord!
it has no eyes!
it doesn't think!
but rocks do move
put one in a fire
it will get hot won't it?
That means
won't you agree?
that its insides are moving
ever more rapidly?

Rocks are all different!
    That one's not good for a sweat
    because when it gets too
    hot it will shatter!
    It will fly all over the place
    and burn you good!

And what about lava?
    Rocks flowing like water?
    And what about sand
    becoming rocks
    and what about sea shells
    and bones becoming rocks?

So don't kid me my friend,
    rocks change
    rocks move
    rocks flow
    rocks combine
    rocks are powerful friends
    I have many
    big and small
    their processes, at our temperatures,
    are very slow
    but very deep!

I understand because, you see,
    I am part rock!
    I eat rocks
    rocks are part of me
    I couldn't exist without
    the rock in me
    We are all related!

The mad materialists, of course,
    believe in blind faith
    that the elements are like machines
    that we have a mechanistic world

where dead things combine
magically
as if on command
as if commanded by a machine-maker
as if programmed by a
master programmer
now assassinated of course!

But "mechanistic" can only be a metaphor
a metaphor only possible
during the past two centuries
only possible in a factory
where machines are made
and placed and programmed.

Do we live in an auto-matic world
where elements automatically combine
where processes automatically occur?
Well, auto-matic
means self-acting
and nothing self-acts if it is dead
and we are all actors subject
to heat
to cold
to pressure
to attractions
to rejections
to instructions, and perhaps, at our electrical core,
to chance.

And really, a world of machines,
of dead, invariable combinings
is a world which could never by itself change
a static,
frozen,
dead world!

No, it's alive I tell you,
just like the old ones say
they've been there
you know
they've crossed the boundaries
not with computers
but with their
very own beings!

Karanga

Shuffling they come, the old ones long outlawed
Grey-blue their faces, their step hesitant
Trailing maiden-hair hobbles them
They are aglow with phosphorescent lichen
and muddied with clay from subterranean streams

They half turn back, blinking against the glare
Watching for their companions also leaving
the dark.

These were awsome ones
Patterns on the great dark brown bodies
spiralling up to the incandescent eyes—
Potent the bird-men in their time.

Penetrating the earth came the broken call
which these, sure now, answer, walking towards
the blazing city of a thousand needs.

Ochre Lines

skins
drums
liquid beat fluttering under the breast
coursing long journeys
through blue
lifelines
joining body to body
primeval maps
drawn under
the hide
deep
floating dreams past
history
surging forward
upward
through indigo passages
to move on the earth
to filigree into fantastic
gropings over the land
journey marking
red trails
a slow
moving carth vision

FIRE

up up up stay standing up the ground is sacred

Gathering to form a circle. To hold hands. To dance. To talk together each voice cherished; youth, elder, familiar voices and new voices, voices across language, across vast ground stretching and across deep waters caressing as many fishes as stars. Each standing ground in their sacred place. Each an electric blue shimmering strand connecting to the awesome dance around the centre.

and here in our midst   on my allies' ground   ground i stand on that day   how still it was   walking up to the great downed pine across the road   the explosion when it hit the truck   sent dust swirling in slow motion   then the war cries   and the shots coming from across the lake   echoed and joined the sound of birds calling over the rat tat rat tat tat and long long minutes blurring the shouting voices from the camp   and the army's incessant pepperfire   multirounds   overridden by the apc's roar converging on you   encircled   so few of you   so fragile   so fearless they didn't make it   to "carry out orders"   that september day at ts'peten   they couldn't   too many prayers deflected the bullets from spilling death blood on sacred ground   they couldn't shoot through the shadows standing next to the trees   watching out for each movement of our people   watching the dancers   watching those who came to stop the dance   watching the ropes tied to the tree   faint shapes felt only as wind through pines   but they whispered   dance   dance for us   dance for all earth's precious dance hard   the day isn't over   there are those still to break free the sun is burning   red   there is hunger and thirst and the suffering is the dance   stay standing   up   up   up   dance strong   the ground is sacred   and each step is   heard echoing loud   over the barrage of hostility   thudding into and bouncing off   the sacred tree at our centre

Standing ground together is that miraculous dance.
Limlimpt

Not Defeated

We watched you and I
from a distance
Grandfather bent over the paper leaves
knife men with parting sticks standing by.
This day and many others I've
wanted those parting sticks pointed
hard and straight.

We were eating summer pups
buffalo heaped in sour heat
no rabbits, no berries
to fill our dying bellies.
Our warriors crying
beneath the Sundance Tree
falling from barking parted sticks.
Ghost Dancers whistling
bleeding shirts.
We were dying. We were dying.
Dying.

Grandfather talked with Grandmother.
Grandmother said
Riverblood will always be our milk.
Our fires will never die.
Grass will spring in our hearts.
This talk will stain the paper leaves.

Grandfather carried his bending
spirit and joined
the other walk-far eyes.
They shared the pipe.

This is how it came to be
Grandfather drawing suns, moons
lakes, winds and grass in his
feathered hands.

For Blankets and Trinkets

My father dreamt
our winter sleep and lifting wails
was the coming Chinook
not knowing when we traded
our furs we'd hover in bones.
He said our winters would be
pelts of thick sky
no longer weighed down
in buffalo curls.

That year the frog arrived
my heart wrapped
around the thick traders blankets.
My babies pimpled with poison.

Oh little one, I wasn't as fortunate
as your aunt. She was traded
with a man of wonder heart.
I've become a gopher
jumping hole to hole
cutting roots to keep
my teeth dull. I was crazed hunger.
My bones piercing my flesh
arms dried branches too weak
to bury my speckled babies.
My heart, a gooseberry
rolling past my tongue.

I went with the man
with a wooden tail
his grunting and guttural tongue
a grizzly that eats my breast.
I am parched grass
satisfying my thirst
with spirits hidden in his water.

My dance frozen in my feet.
My father's wails long
Buried in winter sleep.

Protect The Island

Across the mid-summer sun
an aluminum boat.
Suddenly aware
I watch it approach
measure distance
in the blink of an eye.

Lifted from a solitude of loons.
I stand.
Protect the island.
It's a lifesaver.
You can't take it with you.
It's a breath of fresh air.

Six vacationers land,
slurring themselves.
Whiskey walk.
I approach. My lungs full and tense.
They call: Where are the fish?
I reply: In the north channel, but they're belly-up.
the rain is vinegar.

Cursing
they say they will write Washington
and Ottawa
and it won't be love letters.
They salute
pile into the boat and shove off.
At the shore trees bow
in the recent wind
offering the greatest applause.

The Green Chief

My wife comes home from work exhausted, throws off her coat, collapses into our old plump easychair and tells me that something has to be done about the traffic. Even though she refuses to drive during rush hour, preferring instead to take the bus, the jam, the noise and stink of it all makes her feel as though she's the one in the driver's seat. Thank goodness she's not is all I can say, both for her and the car, not to mention everybody else on the road. (Imagining her voice a sheet of stilled panic, knuckles white, clutched to the steering wheel, eyes full of twisted expectation as the vehicle lunges to a halt.)

"Didn't someone say that we live in the age of anxiety," I ask as I massage her shoulders, knuckles digging into muscle.

"Age of ignorance," she answers, while she oohs and aahs.

"I wonder if they'll ever invent something to replace them—the cars and trucks, I mean?"

"Not as long as the oil companies have anything to say about it," she concludes matter-of-factly.

"Maybe a few more giant oil spills like the Exxon Valdez, or that one off California, and the public will finally say enough is enough."

"Since when has Mr. & Mrs. Citizen had any say?" she grumbles, the black heat of the street still inside her.

"I was listening to a program the other day on CBC about some Scot who, something like twenty-five years ago, moved to Newfoundland because it was one of the few places where they still used horses... guess he liked horses. The pace, probably."

"Sounds like a smart man," she says and indicates, with her right hand clasped to her left shoulder, that I should massage closer to the left side of spine. Obliging, my knuckle probes deep, releasing a gasp of relief.

"But they're almost all gone now," I feel compelled to add, realizing too late that such a small comment can shatter so much.

"A shame," she says, then, after a moment of silence, "think of it, horses clomping down the road, sleigh rides in winter."

"The fragrance of horse shit," I quietly add, again digging my fingers into the shoulder muscle. "Loosen up."

"Ouch! Easy." She twists. "There's nothing better for roses than horse manure. Where I come from a few of the farmers still use horses. My mother makes sure she carries a plastic bag with when she goes to the market so she can pick some up for her garden."

She's got a point. I've seen her mother's flowerbeds, and I admit they're quite spectacular: gladioli, lilies, geraniums, roses—among others which I don't know the names of. All smelling sweet and shitty.

"So how was your day?" she asks, standing and rolling her shoulders.

"I'm working on a story. I'm not sure where it's heading but it's got to do with Chief Seattle."

"You sure it's even a story?" she laughs, "last time all those notes you took ended up being a four line poem, or was it three?"

I'm not sure how to take this last comment, but she's right. Even in this age of the computer, which might also be termed the age of input diarrhoea, fingers punch away at keyboards like there's no tomorrow, I find myself with the spectacular ability to edit myself into silent oblivion. Like the Invisible Man in that old movie, my words are the bandages which I unwrap, or more particularly either strike or scratch out, until there's nothing left of me. The invisible silent ghost man floating around the room. Instead of a pair of dark sunglasses, all you see is a pen or pencil riding on my invisible ear.

"Chief Seattle? Why him? You're not from the west coast. And besides, remember all that fuss at Enviro-House?"

"Fuss...Don't exaggerate."

"Ohh, that feels good. Thanks, honey," is all she says, unwilling to dwell on the unpleasant, now that she has shed her twist of highway, instead she arches her back-stretches and then pecks me on the cheek.

About a month ago we were downtown and happened to walk into one of those environmental stores that seem to be popping up like mushrooms all over the country. Frankly, she was the one who first noticed the multi-coloured pile of tee-shirts and brought them to my attention, as I busied myself leafing through some expensive magazine which had a feature article on composting.

Something I never really thought you had to read about, but which happened rather naturally. As for the tee-shirts, I think she was thinking of buying one for my birthday. I could tell by the gleam in her eye. And so I thought it best that I head her off at the pass, to use a rather quaint expression.

"Look," she said. "Aren't these pretty?"

"Perfect," I answered flatly, checking out the design, an American eagle swooping off into a sunset above the portrait of a wise stern face. Chief Seattle with his words of wisdom below the picture. It was all there. They hadn't missed a note, except maybe the flaming arrows. Everything we always needed to get ourselves in touch with Mother Earth but were afraid to wear until now, I think I was thinking at the time but didn't say. Or did I?

Needless to say, I never did get that tee-shirt for my birthday and, in fact, never gave a further thought to the old Chief. As for the little "fuss" (to quote my wife) in the store amid the herbal soaps and sponges, tonics and shampoos, rainforest crunch and carob bars, what happened was that I ended up buying the tee-shirt for my wife and trying my best to forget all about it. To put it plainly, it wasn't until I came across a column in yesterday's paper that I dredged up the scene and got to thinking about Chief Seattle again, about what he might or might not have actually said. You see, according to the article, all those things accredited to him he never did actually say.

In other words, the myriad of messages on all those tee-shirts and wall posters are supposedly made-up, fabricated, invented, all that profundity... that... wisdom, such as the "Earth does not belong to man; man belongs to the Earth. What is man without beasts? If all the beasts were gone, men would die from a great loneliness of spirit. For whatever happens to the beasts, soon happens to man. The whiteman treats his mother, the Earth, and his brother, the Sky, as things to be bought, plundered and sold like sheep or bright beads. His appetite will devour the Earth and leave behind only a desert." All those famous and I might add, marketable, quotable quotes concocted by some environmentalist who realized that the message wouldn't fly under his own name; what was needed was (and again I quote) "sentimentalized Indian environmentalism."

This, then, is what I'm relating to my wife, who is now asking me to unzip the back of her skirt so that she can slip into something more comfortable-like jeans and a tee-shirt. I tell her that I find the allegations simply fascinating, my reaction one of scorn and amusement.

"What a scam," I say. "What a ploy, but how can anybody know for sure, unless maybe the ghost writer himself confessed. And then, how do we know he's not just trying to grab the limelight?"

To appropriate or not to appropriate, the question of the day itself usurped, which now becomes to fabricate or not to fabricate. Or better yet, to fib or not fib.

I can see from her furrowed eyebrows that she is taking in all that I'm saying, mulling over it, composting it—if you like—stirring it up, laying the freshness out in her mind.

"Context," she finally says, wiggling out of her skirt, right here in the living room.

"What?"

"Did the article you read mention what was happening in the mid-nineteenth century and even earlier? Repercussions? Legacy?"

"No, why would it?"

"Think about it," she answers, moving to the sofa and peeling off her stockings.

So I do, I mean, while I sit back for a moment and watch her and then, so as not to get sidetracked, I go over to the bookcase and pull out reference books.

One thing for sure, by 1855, London, Queen Victoria opened the Great Exhibition of the Works of Industry of All Nations, now commonly referred to as the first Worlds Fair.

The Industrial Revolution, already begun in the last century with the introduction of the spinning jenny and the steam engine, was booming and expanding business so that unfettered growth had now become a means to an end.

Addressing the cost of the Industrial Age in human terms, Charles Dickens, in England, wrote Bleak House in 1853 and Hard Times in 1854.

By 1867, Canada's ambition to settle the west was national

policy.

In 1790, the United States was comprised of 892,000 square miles, and by 1910, 3,754, 000 and still consuming.

What was to prevent such an expansion? Nothing. Absolutely. Or, as the book I am consulting bluntly states—written in 1955, exactly one hundred years after Chief Seattle's famous or now infamous speech—"Save for a few Indians of Stone Age culture the land in the late eighteenth century was almost empty."

"There you have it, " she says, getting up to go and get her clothes.

"What?"

"That the end justifies the means... always has."

"You mean primitive in one era, wise and witty in another?"

"You got it."

And in a Doris Day singsong voice, I burst out, "Que Sera, Sera... Whatever we'll be we'll be."

"Something like that," she says, leaving the room.

Quotation upon quotation. Truth in Lie. Lies in Truth. And in her trail of late afternoon shadow, my mind flips to another tidbit of information, that during the industrial expansion some of the rivers in those American industrial towns were so dirty that they actually caught fire. All the while the elite, Carnegie, Rockerfeller, Edison, Ford... were wining and dining, celebrating their idea of civilization and success.

And I picture a dark oak room, crystal lit, grey men in tails, with drink in hand, gazing contentedly at the rings of blue smoke they blow from their cigars. Their faces smug and full, their eyes blank, they don't understand what they're looking at, what they're doing.

Then the book I've been reading falls to the floor, and I turn towards the windows, the falling day rising red.

And in the lingering moment of light. Chief Seattle, riding a cross of fire, a river gone mad, stands before me, beckoning me to travel and yet stay where I am, because it is here, here, inside, below the fire, in the calm, the blue, the green, where the connection lies. In beauty. He tells me in perfect silence. "You have heard it before, it is not new, it is as old as we are, they are, all of us. It is survival and beyond."

And I look into his face. It's so bright, sunlight through afternoon rain; it's every face I've ever seen that speaks with words of water that wash over body, mind and spirit, cleanse and free. Fluid, drinkable, timeless.

And with a flourish of his arms he opens wide the blanket of sky that he has, until this moment, kept wrapped tightly round him. And there, inside, is the Earth, mother of us all, spinning blue and green in a cushion of cloud set among stars.

It is at that moment that she enters the room, fresh from changing her clothes, fresh in her womanhood, Chief Seattle now a picture on her tee-shirt blazing a path across her breast, his words a pattern of the present, a flight to here and now. And she with her smile ready to go out into the garden.

Masks of Oka

Of all the images that flooded the press and TV screens during the Oka resistance of 1990, those that had the greatest impact—both positive and negative—were the images of masked warriors behind the barricades. The very fact that the warriors were masked at all seemed to strike a deep-seated chord in reporters, commentators and politicians who were reacting on air to the events of Oka.

Many, like the Minister of Justice, reacted specifically to the masks as proof that the defenders of Oka had something to hide and were criminals of some description. Others, like myself, saw the masks as a kind of theatrical device designed to heighten the media impact of the warriors. After all, anyone who really wanted to know could find out the name of the warriors in a matter of hours. But it was the children who truly grasped the significance of the masks of Oka. They put on masks too.

Like thousands of other Aboriginal observers, and hundreds of thousands of other Canadians, I was glued to a TV screen during most of the Oka resistance. At one point, towards the end of the second weekend after the Canadian army moved in, I heard my five-year-old son, Wanekia, coming down the stairs to the living room. I turned toward him and got quite a jolt.

"That's it," he said to his mother as he came into the room. "If I hear that they have hurt my people or are going to take us off our land, I'm going to fight them and put them in jail."

He had pulled a red ski mask over his head and planted a single feather on one side of it. He was wearing a set of football shoulder pads, a belt stuffed with toy ninja weapons, and a pair of boots, and was carrying a toy machine gun. To be perfectly honest I was delighted with his reaction. I wasn't aware he was paying that much attention to what was going on, but I was glad to see he had picked up the basic message—his people were fighting back.

Over the next several weeks the press featured pictures of masked Indian children at Oka doing similar kinds of things. I heard a lot of reaction to those pictures and, from non-Native people, most of it was negative. The warriors were a "bad example" they said, and the kids were getting the "wrong idea." This reaction often included specific reference to the fact that the warriors and the children were masked. I found myself defending the masks by saying my son now had a better image of his people to grow up on than the image of Indians as stone age stumblebums that I grew up on.

I thought it strange that these same people readily accepted the image of Zorro, or the Lone Ranger, or even Ninja Turtles, as masked heros, but when it was the Indian that put on the mask, "Tonto" suddenly became a criminal. I don't recall a single instance of a news commentator or columnist pointing out that some of the Canadian soldiers had "masked" their faces with camouflage paint.

The more I thought about how people reacted to those masks, the more significant the whole idea of "mask" became. Do we use masks to hide ourselves from others, or do we use them so people will have no doubt who we are? In a bank full of customers, how can you tell the bank robbers from the customers? It's easy. The bad guys are wearing masks. But what if the bank, and its customers, are part of a dictatorial regime of drug dealers that are using the money to oppress and enslave the people, and the bank robbers are freedom fighters who want to end that regime. Suddenly the guys with the masks are the good guys.

Obviously, the idea of "mask" is not as simple as it first appears, even though the impact of "mask" in a given situation is usually quite direct and unmistakable. Most cultures, and most certainly Aboriginal cultures in North American, use masks in ritual or ceremonial contexts. Those masks enable everyday individuals (familiar to others in the group) to become fantastic and powerful spiritual beings in the context of the traditions of any particular ceremony. Are these people "hiding" behind the masks? Or are they using the mask to reveal or embody a traditional or spiritual power or teaching?

In Euro-Canadian culture the overt use of masks is confined to theatre, to Halloween or costume parties, or to criminal behaviour and most often has the idea of "disguise" or hiding. At a psychological level Euro-Canadians, particularly men, are taught to "hide" their true feelings behind a mask of indifference or objectivity. This internalization of the mask then becomes a technique by which we communicate who we are, or at least, who we want others to think we are. These others, in turn, learn to expect to see certain kinds of masks on certain individuals in certain situations. In effect then our very personalities can be described as a kind of mask we present to the world.

In a functional sense, the "mask" becomes the image of whatever role we happen to be taking or "playing" at any given time in our lives. The roles of father, mother, lover, boss, employee, teacher, athlete, etc., each have a kind of "mask" associated with them, that others learn to recognize and react to in predictable ways. By the same token, we, and others, can react very negatively—even violently—when somebody unexpectedly changes their "mask" or refuses to present the mask we expect them to wear. In this situation a particular mask can become, on the one hand, a stereotype, or a kind of psychological prison, and on the other, a technic for announcing to others that we have changed our role.

The masks of Oka were just such an announcement. In a single stark image, the masked warriors of Oka changed the way most Canadians think about Aboriginal peoples, and the way many Aboriginal people think about themselves. That doesn't mean, of course, that all the changes were the same, or that all the changes were either positive or negative. But it does mean that thinking by and about Aboriginal peoples in Canada is forever changed.

Until very recently, the "mask" that most non-Aboriginal Canadians would expect an Indian to wear would involve elements like "drunk", "lazy", "stupid", or "primitive." If an Indian person was not one or more of those things, many Canadians would assume that person wan not an Indian. In fact, within living memory, if an Indian achieved a university degree or became a religious minister or priest, he or she was stripped of their Indian status under the Indian Act. That same Act once defined "person" as "other than an Indian." In an Angus Reid poll taken just before the army withdrawal from Oka, a very different "mask" for Aboriginal people was described by Canadians. The majority (?) of respondents to the poll saw Indians as "hard working," "spiritual" and "environmentally wise." It would seem that Aboriginal people are successfully changing the "mask" that other Canadians expect them to wear.

In 1983, I experienced an incident in an Indian craft store that capsulized the situation of Aboriginal peoples in Canada. I picked up a craft from the Six Nations (Brantford) area and opened the little tag that was attached to it. It had "Made in Occupied Canada" printed under the name of the craftsman. I felt a cold, shuddering chill as I realized that it was not a joke. I have told this story in dozens of university classrooms and conferences over the last seven or eight years as an example of the difference of perception between Aboriginal and non-Aboriginal people in Canada.

Before Oka, the first knee-jerk reaction of most groups to the story was to laugh. Since Oka, the laughing has stopped. If there was ever any doubt about how true the statement on that tag is, the masks of Oka have unmasked the Canadian establishment and eliminated that doubt forever.

the uranium leaking from port radium and rayrock mines is killing us...

The girl with sharp knees sits in her underwear. She is shivering. The bus is cold. The man at the gun store has seagull eyes. Freckles grow on the wrong side of his face. This town has the biggest Canadian flag anywhere. It is always tangled and never waves. For grass this playground has human hair. It never grows on Sundays. The kids that play here are cold and wet. They are playing in their underwear. They are singing with cold tongues. They have only seven fingers to hide with.

Those are rotting clouds. This is the other side of rain. The band plays but there is no sound. i snap my finger but there is no sound.

There is someone running on the highway. There is no one in the field. Nobody owns the cats here. Nobody knows their names.

They are letting the librarian's right eye fuse shut. There is a pencil stabbed thru her bun. She can read "i didn't pop my balloon the grass did" in my library book. She looks into me. One eye is pink. The other is blue.

My father said take the bus. There is yellow tape around my house. A finger is caught in the engine but they only rev it harder. There are cold hands against my back. i want to kiss Pocahontas before she dies at age 21. Someone is stealing the dogs of this town. Doctors hold babies high in black bags. My mother's voice is a dull marble rolling down her mouth, stolen to her lap, not even bouncing, not even once. She has sprayed metal into her hair. i am sitting on a red seat. My hands open with rawhide.

This is the ear i bled from. There is a child walking in the field. He is not wearing runners. He is walking with a black gun. In my girlfriend's fist is a promise. She does not raise herself to meet me. Her socks are always dirty. She is selling me a broken bed so she can lay on plywood. Her feet are always cold. My feet are always cold. Her basement when we kiss is cold. The coffee we drink is cold. The bus driver does not wave goodbye. Why are there only humans on this bus? Why are we wet and cold? Why are we only in our underwear?

i want to run but i have no legs. The tongue that slides from my mouth is blue.

Friday is the loneliest day of the week she says. The blanket she knitted this winter is torn upon us. She laughs at me with blue eyes. She says if you walk in the rain no one can tell you're crying. The soup we drink after if cold. The popcorn we eat after is cold. Someone is crying in the basement. Someone is crying next door.

The dream we have is something on four legs running on pavement towards us. It is running from the highway. It is a dead caribou running on dead legs. i meet its eyes but there are only antlers. In between the antlers is an eye. It too is cold and watching. Its eye is the color of blue.

The plants here have no flowers. The trees themselves are black. Someone is under the bridge. The fish are dying sideways. Rain has started to fall.

The child with the black gun sees my house. He is walking backwards towards me. He swings his head. His eyes are blue. *Can you please sing with me?*

The bus driver does not wave good-bye.

The band is playing but all i hear is galloping.

i snap my finger.

My eyes are blue.

All i can hear is galloping.

The Hope of Wolves

i

You take a child
doused in flames
with steam split skin
a child who knew rape before sleep
and you silence your ears when she cries
YOU!
YOU DID THIS TO ME!
YOU!
and you take it upon yourself to show her the song of trees
when they split the sun
and you give her the peace of sleep
and you point to the place fish bathe
and say this is home to you
this is home
and you tell her to sing to the island where they keep the dogs
that have bitten children
you tell her this
you give her hope
you show her sand
and watch her sniff the air
the way a dog will sniff at fire

ii

Ask her what her
dreams were before contact
was blue a shade or voice?
and she will tell you of a time when she was a blade dancer
and a wave of her hand
could take a whole room down
she will frown and from the sand
she will pull the hot and bleeding heart of her enemy's chief
as he falls shocked and screaming across the sea

iii

Your voice is bathing me you will say
and her mouth will be light that will touch your secret place
I am wolf she will say
and you taught me how
she will smile and hold her hands to the face of moon
not to scratch or mar
but to hold and laugh
and dance
and sing...

(this poem is for JB, MSN, GM, FB, TB, WT and others hurt...)

The Broken Gourd

I.

After the last echo
where fingers of light
soft as *laua'e*
come slowly

toward our aching earth,
a cracked *ipu*
whispers, bloody water
on its broken lip.

II.

Long ago, wise *kanaka*
hauled hand-twined
nets, whole villages shouting
the black flash of fish.

Wahine u'i
trained to the chant
of roiling surf;
na keiki sprouted by the sun
of a blazing sky.

Even *Hina*, tinted
by love, shone gold
across lover's sea.

III.

This night I crawl
into the mossy trunk
of upland winds;
an island's moan

welling grief,
centuries of memory
from my native ‘aina:

Each of slain
by the white claw
of history: lost
genealogies, propertied
missionaries, diseased
haole.

Now, a poisoned *pae'aina*
swarming with foreigners

and dying Hawaiians.

IV.

A common horizon:
smelly shores
under spidery moons.

pockmarked maile vines,
rotting *ulu* groves,
the brittle clack
of broken lava stones.

Out of the east
a damp stench of money
burning at the edges.

Out of the west
the din of divine
violence, triumphal
destruction.

At home the bladed
reverberations of empire.

Another Indigenous People Across The Atlantic

the generations of women
within myself
and yet to come
conjure unspoken words and songs
in a vast dreaming dance
inside our Grandmother's
red womb

Christmas was approaching, but instead of a familiar setting of spruce and evergreen drenched in snow, I saw ripe, abundant mango and plantain flecked with dust from a dry wind which blew from the Sahara. I remember the forest flaunting unfamiliar trees such as the cocoa, palm, niim and a sad, giant tree knowing many woes.

For nine long hours, I had been jostled around in a rickety, old lorry crammed with families, goats and fowl. When night fell, I saw the dark shapes of towering palm trees and of low bushes like great soft eagles, swooping past as we moved toward the African village where I would work as a volunteer.

I was warmly received in a farming village in the forest region of Ghana, West Africa, known as Manso-Nkwanta, which is inhabited by 120 Twi-speaking Ashanti people. I worked with both the community and a Ghanaian voluntary association to help rebuild the foundation for a primary school.

Despite the physical isolation of the village, the lack of running water and electricity, my most lasting connections were made here. I was bowled over by the incredible warmth and generosity of these people in spite of the common problems of malnourished children, lack of proper school facilities, overcrowded homes, poor roads and lack of employment.

By 4 o'clock in the morning, the village buzzed with daily activities. Women prepared meals by fire, swept the rust-hued packed earth around their homes, and tended to crying children. The men would sing in anticipation of a lorry which would take them to a nearby town (3 hours away) for work. They would leave in the darkness before dawn, and return in the evening.

In the village, the traditional division of labour exists whereby men clear and plough the land, while women cook, clean, wash and tend to children. The women also farm and this involves seed selection, harvesting, transporting crops, processing, preservation and marketing food crops. Their average work day is from 4 A.M. until 9 P.M. My next door neighbour, Akua, washed, cleaned, cared for smaller children, slaughtered fowl, attended school and did homework—all in a day's work for a twelve-year-old Ashanti girl. One hot day, I saw a woman walking a steady pace while carrying a forty-five gallon drum on her head. I was in awe of women's physical strength and perseverance gained from hard work, not to mention their incredibly vital energy and intelligence.

On Christmas Day, the women walked in procession with keening voices throughout the village in honour of those who had recently passed into spirit. The entire day was spent in mourning.

On the following day, a great feast was prepared. The Chief (Another Indigenous People Across the Atlantic) poured a libation in honour of his ancestors and the Mother Earth. Then, there began a lively celebration of drumming, dancing and singing; women and men adorned in cloth of every colour. There was no exchange of material gifts in celebration of Christmas.

During my time in Manso-Nkwanta, I stayed with the very hospitable and determined "Queen Mother" known as Nana Nyarko who, like a clan mother, is well-respected by the community. She would often meet with the Elders and Chiefs, and there was always a steady stream of people requiring her attention on village matters. Indeed, she wielded considerable power in the community, yet I wondered what her position must have been before the coming of the white man. I knew that I was witnessing the diminished power of a Queen Mother.

In matrilineal societies, women held significant and highly respected political and religious positions. The Queen Mother was responsible for nominating and deposing chiefs, conducting naming ceremonies and puberty rites, marriage ceremonies and harvest festivals, etc.

I saw an old photograph of an elderly, diminutive Queen Mother named Yaa Asantewa. In 1901, when the Ashanti tradition was threatened, this 61 year old woman declared war against the

British with 40,000-50,000 men under her command. The immense power of the Queen Mother, and of women's roles in general, have eroded considerably during colonial rule.

The most common drum of the Ashanti people is the "talking drum." This drum not only relays current messages to the community, but is also a carrier of culture. During ceremonies, people hear about their history, the battles they fought, what each family-clan is responsible for and legends imbued with moral teachings. The Elders can still interpret the language of the talking drum, but the younger generation is losing this form of communication.

Today, instead of listening to the drum with the ancient voice, the young are moving towards Western television, radio and newspapers as their only sources of information. As they turn from the traditional drum, they lose the knowledge, wisdom and history passed on by their ancestors. Some have even forgotten their mother tongue. Many of the young have migrated to the city of Accra (9 hours away) in search of employment, formal education, and the comforts of modern, urban life.

Upon my arrival in the Ashanti village of Manso-Nkwanta, it seemed that pre-colonial traditions were still at the centre of community life. In the course of time and conversation, I began to realize that many of the ceremonies and festivals have become inextricably entwined with Christianity. However, in spite of the tremendous impact of Christianity, some Ashantis are determined to preserve their rich Indigenous tradition in the face of colonialism.

The Elders are gravely concerned with the increasing alienation of the young from Ashanti tradition. One Elder, with eyes deep and dark, told me that the younger generation is confused. They do not know who to pray to—the ancestors and traditional Gods of the Earth, or to the Christian God in heaven. While these Gods wrestle in the hearts of the young, the souls of the ancestors hunger for want of tending.

I have also heard the young say that "times have changed." Their future no longer lies with ancestors, living Chiefs, the Ashanti, or even the continent of Africa alone. An African writer Achebe (1) surmises: "The white is very clever. He came quietly and peaceably with his religion. We were amused at his foolishness and allowed him to stay. Now he has won our brothers and our clan can no longer act as one. He has put a knife on the things that held us together and we have fallen apart."

From crossing the Atlantic ocean, I came to know another Indigenous people who share a similar struggle in the face of colonialism. I feel honoured to have touched the continent that gave life to these people.

Footnote: 1. Achebe, Chinva Things Fall Apart, (Heinemann Educational Books Ltd.) Nairobi, 1958

Scarlet Requiem

From the window scarlet leaves danced. The air outside crunched cold against the pane inside. The coolness drifted over the top of the vinyl cover on the back of the home-made bench couch he kneeled on. He could feel it. It pricked his nose whenever he pressed it up between the wooden bars that separated the panes of glass. His warm breath against the cool air was vaporous. It clouded his view. It misted the dancing leaves. He could still hear them though, slipping, sliding and whistling their way through their last song before winter put them all to rest on the earth below. No one in the room paid any attention to the leaves. He turned to look in the direction of the murmuring voices. Through a large doorway he could see his aunts leaning forward intently and whispering. The men in the room didn't seem to have anything to do with the kitchen table conversation. Most of them hovered about the old McIary stove or leaned against a doorway or wall. Some of them smoked quietly. One of them sat in a corner of the room Paulie was in. His elbows rested on his knees while his eyes let go a steady stream of tears but he made no sound. Paulie couldn't figure out why neither the dying leaves nor he called anyone to attention. He wasn't sure why this moment was eerie, maybe scary, but he was sure it was. A single leaf cut loose from the herd above and floated, helter skelter, to the pane of glass. It hit the pane at his eye level. It made him start. He jumped away from the window. Like the people in the room, its movement was erratic and urgent looking.

Bits and pieces of words floated around him. They followed the movement of more leaves. These words didn't seem to have much to do with him. Every now and then some tearful woman picked him up, held him, shed a few tears, then deposited him back at the window pane. He accepted these hugs without response, then he resumed his death watch over the sugar maple in the yard. The noise today was unusual, uncomfortable. Maybe it wasn't loud enough. He didn't really know what was wrong with the noise. But it was wrong. Besides there were too many people in the room.

Death's usual reverence was uncomfortable for these

women who looked forward to life. The death of Paulie's mom didn't inspire reverence. She was too young. He heard his one aunt whisper that it was obscene for her to leave so soon. Fearful resignation settled in on the faces of the women who needed death's reverence to feel comfortable, hopeful. The murmurs were steady, the sounds all muffled, the meaning unclear. He turned to look at the moving figures, all large, all just a little edgy. Nothing was smooth. Everyone spoke in soft low tones, but their bodies couldn't lie. They didn't look soft, jerking about stiffly as they were, and weeping ever time they caught sight of him. The stiffness, the tears, the unsuccessful fight for reverence scared him. He returned to the view outside. His hands pressed against the sill's edge with grim determination. His knuckles whitened slightly under the tan brown of his fingers. He had no name for this change in colour. No name for the murmuring bustle behind him. No name for the sound of the wind through the sugar maple or the whisper of leaf after leaf as the wind tore them from the tree. The tree mothered these leaves; he could feel this motherhood and he tried to wonder why she cast them off in the cold wind, but no words took shape in his mind—just feelings.

Feelings of dread. Feelings of cold. Violent feelings grew inside Paulie as the hustle and bustle of people, who failed to find reverence, intensified and they grew stiffer and stiffer with the effort. Sad feelings mingled with cold air and the foggy vapour of his breath clouded the riot of names for the colours deepened his sadness. He had no idea why.

One of the men, his daddy, sat tense in his chair. He said nothing. He never looked at Paulie. Every now and then, one of the other men would touch his shoulder, but the man never moved. All day he sat and stared as he drank cup after cup of coffee. The sound of him sipping coffee seemed to intensify his morose silence.

There was a shift in tension in the room behind him. It made him start and want to guard his back. The voices became crisper, more definitive. Each woman took turns laying out the situation as she saw it. His name came up every now and then. He cringed at the mention of his name in the context of unfamiliar language and unknown decision-making. The old woman in the corner changed his name. He didn't recognize this new name. He thought they stopped talking about him, so he resumed his own death watch over autumn. A wet rag suddenly landed on him from his right side. He wasn't ready for it. It scraped at his face. He twisted, a hand clutched the top of his head and held him still. No sense struggling; the hand was too big, too determined.

"Hold still now," and she cleaned the tears and mucus from his face. The edge in her voice was new. A ball of hot sound swam up from his chest to his face. He was about to let it go.

"Don't cry, now," she cajoled softly, almost sweetly, and he stopped, confused. "Don't cry now?" These words were new; Mommy never said them. A dark whirl set itself in motion in his mind. A whirl of movement, images of some other time he couldn't define. No names for days, nights, weeks—just a generic sense of before. Before it was o.k. to cry. Before, there weren't all these people here, just Mommy, Daddy, and Paulie. Paulie, the name glided about, shrank, grew small and distant.

Panic. He could feel it. It was a memory so close to now. Mommy, something happened to Mommy and in the whirl of images a moment was held, smokey-looking and unclear, but very still. In this moment, mommy was near the door, trying to leave. She didn't look quite right. She leaned against it, slid down the length of its frame, then collapsed. Above her Paulie could see a spider drop toward her. It hung ominously on a single silken thread. She looked so big and so small at the same time. Slowly the spider drifted toward her. It threatened to land on her face. He turned away and caught sight of the view behind him of leaves falling helplessly to the ground. He panicked. Screams came from somewhere inside of him so foreign sounding and full of terror that he wasn't sure who it was that screamed. He ran toward her and grabbed her dress. A hand moved to get him out of the way. The hand jerked at the little boy who could still hear the scream. Another pair of hands pried the boy's fingers loose and the big hand tossed him aside. The images in the room grew fuzzy. Paulie could see a little boy crouched in the corner, mouth open and no sound coming out but he was too unfamiliar with his own face to know it was him. At the recollection of this memory his hand clutched the sill. He tried to help his mind hold onto the memory. It felt important to hold the memory still, to look at it, but it slipped far away in the dark tunnel from where it came.

A decision was made, a decision he had no name for. The feeling of its finality set in. The women rose and began removing things from the shelf. Paulie's hand went up. He reached in the direction of the women who took Mommy's things and put them in boxes. No one paid attention to his hand. What had they decided? The nameless presence of their decision and their current actions overwhelmed him. The panic rose, grew intense. It rested in the centre of the finality which took up all the space but for the small piece of his panic. The finality gained weight. It pressed up against the small boy, pushed him closer to the wall. He could hardly hold his head up. His eyes looked at the floor. He pushed back on the finality. His panic subsided. Push back. It settled the insides to push back.

"Paulie. Get away from that window," and the young woman reached for him. He didn't move. Push back. Hold the sill. Watch the leaves. Let the room have its movement, its scary rhythm, its finality. Paulie will stay put. She couldn't move him by herself. Soon another set of hands helped to loosen his grip and the other swung him upward. He froze. "You're not my mom." It came out rich with threat, full of push back, but the room only laughed its venom. The body of the boy was too small to carry out the threat that lace his voice. They knew it and found his words amusing. He knew it too, but it felt good to say it. She held him up, smiled. Paulie didn't smile back. He glared, just for a moment, then pushed that down inside. It whirled delicately inside—a tiny leaf of red emotion he cast downward to some place deep within his body. It whistled a high pitched scream only Paulie heard as it floated and landed with a quiet whisper somewhere deep inside. She tossed him gently up and down. His eyebrows rose, almost skeptically so; his eyes grew dark, full of threat; it scared the woman, and she stopped. He was aware he had scared her. He made her put him down with just a look—a cold, intense look. He felt power surge inside as he ended his aunt's intrusion this simply.

Paulie tasted this moment of power. He grabbed hold of it hard. He practiced all day until dark dropped over him. He would have forgotten about it, but the next day bloomed the same as the one before... the window, the sugar maple tossing off her leaves, the bustle, the stiff bodies and their incongruously reverent voices, and, eventually, the finality of another decision made, confusing him again and then panic followed. The pushing back rose of its own accord. It came without the need for memory to call it back to life. It came over and over, each time the moment of decision brought the feeling of finality to the room. The colder Paulie's push the more effect it had on the women around him and the more powerful he felt. His cold glare always ended any unwanted intrusion on his person. It changed the way people spoke to him. Sometimes it even altered the way they moved around the room. At first, however, it didn't seem to permanently discourage them. They all took turns trying to solicit some sort of happy response from him. Each by turns were unnerved by the intensity of his cold glare and, finally, they all gave up.

By the third day be became familiar with the sound of the words "Aunt" and "Uncle." He already knew his gramma's and grampa's names. Other words came up that took on familiarity with the repetition of them. "Funeral"... "ceremony"... "after the funeral"... "after the ceremony." Finally, his mommy returned. He giggled and laughed triumphantly when they wheeled her in on the same bed that had taken her away. He knew she would be back. She was sleeping. He made a dash for her. He leaped straight from the bench and landed on the wheeled bed. His hands grabbed her dress and he screamed, "Wake up, Mommy!" Voices barked, hand went out and he rose in the air again.

"Get away from there," and he felt panic again. His scream died in his throat; it moved outside to where the leaves hurled themselves at the earth. What have they done to Mommy? His tongue moved about in his head, searching for the shape of the words. He knew these words, "What have they done to Mommy," but his tongue was unfamiliar with the shape it would have to make to form the words. He looked at the gurney, mouth open, eyes wide and let the panic seize him. His skin grew tight. His muscles press against his bones inside. The skin got tighter still. His lungs let go all their air. Everything was so tight, no air wanted to go back inside. His shoulders hunkered down and his hands formed fists. A knot formed in his gut.

He turned his head one last time to look at his mom. She lay so completely still. She was so still, she looked small, frail, despite her weight. The hands carried him past lines of people—aunts, uncles, older cousins. They reached for his cheek, looked shyly sympathetic at him. Underneath the sympathy, there lay the tightened musculature of faces who struggled for some form of nameless control. Paulie did not believe in the nameless surface of sympathy. He saw the tightness behind the faces. He believed the tightness. He felt it inside himself. Tightness is cold, stiff, like the old sugar maple dropping her leaves all over the place.

One by one, the people all left the house. The man with the huge hands went with the gurney. Paulie stopped his own breath as he watched his daddy take his mommy away. This phantom who came home every weekend and disappeared for most of the time was almost unknown to Paulie. Paulie didn't want his dad to take him mommy away. He couldn't find the words to object and they left.

Paulie had to stay. Funerals were not for babies. He lay on the couch, eyes vacant; he stared at the ceiling for a long time, while the young aunt who volunteered to stay behind with him read stories. She was well-meaning. She wanted to take his mind off the morbidity of his mother's funeral. From the couch, paulie could still see out the window. Below the drone of his aunt's voice, he thought he could hear the sugar maple scream at the leaves, "Get away from there... get away from there... get away..." The sad sound of it whirled about and invaded him in some far away place he was unfamiliar with. It was too far away to make him cry.

He lay so still his aunt worried. She chucked his chin and tried to get some sort of response form him to no avail. He lay there as still as his mom had. It unnerved her. She began to read too fast; her voice got squeaky and went up a pitch higher than usual. She argued this fear into a perverse attachment of blame to Paulie. "Paulie's stubborn. He's spoiled." This helped her voice to finally lose its fear. The others had said something like this earlier whenever he glared at them, so she saw nothing wrong with her line of reasoning. She didn't recover her empathy for Paulie. The fear gone, her tone took on the finality Paulie now loathed.

The story lost all joy for Paulie. A hazy image of a woman, book in hand, rose above the sound of the woman's voice. There were smiles all over her, even her hands seemed to smile as she reached for Paulie. Her image tried to rise above the picture of screaming scarlet leaves. The image of mommy fought for a while with the picture of falling leaves. He could see her mouth move. Her words failed to erase the sound of the leaves who pleaded for their lives. He tried to bury the sound of screaming lease so he could hear his mommy. The screaming would not go away. Mommy's soft voice could not drown the screams and, finally, the image of her lost the fight and the screaming leaves seemed to weep. A lone tear hid behind Paulie's eyes. It tried to escape but failed. For a brief moment Paulie felt sorry for the leaves. His hand went up in the air as though to reach out and comfort them. They were too far away. His hand hung suspended for a second, then fell helplessly to his side. He tried to remember the leaves, the woman, and the sound of her, to hold the images still, but they slipped away.

In the days and weeks that followed people disappeared except for the occasional visit by one or two of them at a time.

Paulie didn't care much for the women who came unless they brought other children with them. They tended to behave as though he were each one of their personal toys. Gramma used these moment to complain about him, called him a handful, and the aunt who was visiting always supported her by bawling Paulie out. Big large fingers were shaken at him for things he couldn't remember doing. During these times, Paulie learned to be inconspicuous. As an aunt arrived he retreated to some corner and busied himself at nothing.

The uncles were easier to take. They accepted his invisibility more readily than did his aunts. Gramma's small complaints were met only by grunts from the men. They never interfered with his upbringing in the same way his aunts did. Wasn't any of their business. No one ever talked about Mommy—not our way, they said. By the time Paulie found the words to ask about his mom, he no longer wanted to know the answer.

Mostly, the house was empty. It felt lonely. There was a deep sadness all about the house. It filled every room. He stopped looking out the window so much. It didn't seem to help. The feeling of sadness grew almost comfortable compared to the wasted hope that lay in searching the window for something he could no longer define.

Daddy came by once in a while in the beginning. He had grown morose and Paulie came to dread his arrival. At the same time, he hoped for an end to his dad's moroseness. He behaved better when his dad came. Maybe this could encourage Dad to be happier. It didn't and slowly Paulie gave up.

He began to forget Mommy. The images grew hazier, less frequent and within weeks they all died. He stopped trying to drag them up. They were too vague and it tired him to do it. Instead he moved about the house of his gramma and searched for familiarity in the lines of his new home. Eventually, the walls took on ordinariness. The rooms became old friends. The sadness and the loneliness became a familiar ambience Paulie identified with. The different smells gramma made when she cooked grew welcome. Fed, he felt some comfort, but most of the time only cold curiosity governed his heart.

Earth grew white. He stared out the window and wistfully watched its whitening. He loved the whitening of each leafless branch. Leafless, the trees lost their scream and the white was so softly melancholy like himself that it was almost a comfort. He watched for something else too. He couldn't quite remember what it was he looked for... Maybe Daddy... Maybe some unnameable feeling.

Winter perished. Spring came and went, then summer took its turn. He matured some. He grew old enough to resent not being allowed to go outside on his own, but he accepted his confinement as part of his general condition of estrangement and sadness.

Daddy doesn't live here. He came to this realizations some time after hot summer days dwindled into cool mornings. The leaves outside began to orchestrate their own death requiem. His visits grew rarer with the intensification of reds over paling green.

Paulie couldn't remember the precise moment he saw it coming. Days merged into other days, memories layered themselves one on top of the other in some crazy fashion like leaves piled one upon the other, suffocating what lay beneath. Then, suddenly; it became clear Daddy wasn't coming back. For some reason Paulie took to wishing for his return. There was a reason beyond his daddy that Paulie could not remember. The moment it was clear he wasn't coming back, Paulie renewed his vigil at the window and stared at it. He stared out the window a lot. He waited for his dad. His dad was somehow connected to memories he couldn't bring up. He couldn't figure out why but he desperately wanted him to come back. He felt the desperation. Inside his mind he whispered "Daddy" with huge intensity as though to will his return. It didn't seem to matter how often he called him or how hard. Daddy never came back at all. Deep shame at this failure to recall his father paralyzed him for a long time. He became listless, withdrew into the world of immediate reality around him, and buried the world of whirling motions inside far from the compelling moments of the here and now. Finally, the words took shape. He had to wait a long time before their intensity subsided enough for him to dare ask his gramma.

"Gramma, Daddy doesn't live here no more?" he asked one day at breakfast. His voice remained nonchalant as he waited for the answer. He pushed hard at the sound of desperation which threatened to come back up. He pushed it back to where it now lived permanently wrapped up in a tiny scream far away from his mouth.

"No," she harumphed. "Now eat your breakfast." Paulie ate in dreadful silence.... Outside the leaves began anew their terrible ceremony. The wind blew and the sugar maple shook all her children mercilessly in the wind. Inside Paulie stared apathetically at the toast while he ate. He gave a cursory glance out the window at the sugar maple shaking off her leaves, then returned to his toast. He didn't remember that once he had felt so sorry for them all.

451 : 49

The borrowed tools we use, the ones we think are going to make things easier but usually end up invoking seemingly infinite difficulty and premature grey hair.	:	The natural implements that we think we can't remember, yet weep for at the graves of our beloved.
The Perrier, Montclair and Vichy that stocks a small space on the refrigerator rack of every environmentally-conscious intellectual.	:	Cool, fresh water gathered at the source. The one that reminds us what the real *On'nigo nohs* is supposed to taste like.
The salt pork and the beef w use to flavour our corn soup, so carefully rinsed after the baking soda process.	:	The so-called savage beasts that the guys who thought they were in charge put on the endangered species list after centuries of bureaucratic rot.
The things that we're taught will work.	:	That which works.
The diseases that teach us to know fear.	:	The plants, the medicines and the know-how. A bundle neatly tucked somewhere.
Insomnia.	:	A power snooze.
Contraception. The ones we asked not to make it.	:	A cry in the night that we delight to and the peeping coo that we too once uttered.
The rebels who conformed, and even the ones	:	The survivors. The ones who

who didn't.		walk the talk
The time we spend getting there	:	Being there.
Conversations wasted on	:	A ceremonial reminder of
complaints about the weather,		who we really are
atmospheric complications		and how we fit in.
and how much time we have felt.		
Languages spoken by the masses	:	Words which make more sense
and all the names		to the earth-toned one who
they decided to call us.		identifies himself
		when addressing the Creator
		and who still refers to himself
		as a human-being.
Borders, boundaries and bingo.	:	Earthquakes, volcanic eruptions,
Bush-like solutions,		floods
the ones that cost a lot of money		and other labour-related
convincing us that		pains
we're doing the right thing		
to balance the books.		suffered by the mother.
Industrial clouds	:	Dew,
and acid rains.		an early morning frost
		and spring break-up.
Soaring oil prices,	:	Our elder brother
hydro bills,		the Sun.
nuclear secrets,		The Gift
and fast-moving atoms		and conversations
to tempt the cold ones		carried on by the Firekeepers
who greed.		
Music to ignite	:	The creature's heartbeat.
jealously		
and other such inflations.		
The clock.	:	The drum.

City

My head aches
from all its recorded thoughts
mindless history
scapes of rolling concrete
My memories
are of other people's memories
now in books
and of other's short spoken words
They are of tall and powerful
WARRIORS
and now 100 years later
(in the city)
slouched near voiceless
near unheard
The City
paternal government
the death of our people
"Now death to D.I.A."
Indian Agent's ghosts
are in my dreams

"Home is where your neighbours are," He said

They're all in the City now
Breeding and dying
Laughing and crying
All of my Clan
inbetween the buildings and the alleys
Looking for themselves
Looking for family
Even looking for our dead
whose graves have been long gone
and robbed

City
Do I look for my family

in your phone books?
Are they even here?
or are they dead?

Do I walk to my Reserve
now empty
with old totems
tall grass
and darkened nights?
Nights so silent
singing and drumming
can be heard
All sounds of the past
when we were
and thrived

Concrete City

wet smog rises into skyline
the working day starts
trails of pushy umbrella people
surrounded by rush traffic
a glitzy high heel
steps on the soiled
trenchcoat (of a nearby street beggar)
his harmonica tune
floats in the air
business suited men
flock into tall
stoneface monster buildings
plastic cheese
and instant coffee giants
dollar signs embedded
into their pupils
the lingering harmonica note
hangs in the damp air
a single echo
of sanity
a solitary reminder
of who the real victims
of the concrete city are

my red face hurts

my red face hurts
and i walk with my head down
to hide the tears

my red face hurts
as i watch my brother die before me
white bullets riddle my body
and i hide my face to cry

my red face hurts
as i watch my father stagger out of neon lit bars
and crumple on piss-stained sidewalks
as hate filled eyes step over him
i hide my shame behind shadows

my red face hurts
as i watch a white man hiding his white sheet
beneath his suit and tie
condemn me because of one man's greed
sentencing me to an early death
my red face hurts as he smiles

my red face hurts
as i see my sister stand on darkened streets
selling her gift to strangers
that use her till she has nothing left to give
and i cry as i pull the needles from her arms

my red face hurts
when i hear the hate on the radio
directed at my hopes and dreams
and another party is born
on the wings of a white horse
and i scream in anger as i watch the door close on me

Cultural Decolonization

What is the nature of cultural decolonization? It is a new focus on the understanding and awareness of Indian/Metis culture and history from an authentic Aboriginal perspective and sensitivity. It is a readjustment of white mainstream culture and history which has served as justification for conquest and continued imperial domination. Moreover it is a reverse interpretation. It shows that conquest and occupation by European imperialists was a step backwards in the evolution of Aboriginal civilization. If our country had not been invaded by European mercenaries 500 years ago, our Indigenous civilization would have been much further advanced and more fully developed in all dimensions: economically, politically, culturally, ecologically and particularly in civilized humanity. The work of decolonizing our culture and history is a monumental task. It wipes from our people's consciousness the sense of colonization and inferiorization. In doing so, we put before our people an image of a historically well organized socio-economic system and a developed civilization. We learn how our ancestors were conquered and how the culture was devastated. Aboriginal civilization has a past that is worth studying. It was a dynamic society, evolving and progressive; not static and archaic. This is one of the greatest white supremacy myths that must be rejected, and made truthful.

Cultural decolonization means perceiving knowledge in terms of a specific place and time as a principle of intellectual inquiry. For Metis, Indians and Inuit the place is Canada, and the time is imperial capitalism. The place provides a perimeter for historical and cultural analysis. It allows our historians and authors to use a critical analysis of British and French colonialism. One of the first tasks of cultural decolonization is to analyze and interpret our history and culture from an Aboriginal perspective. This is one of the important steps in our re-awakening. It is the key to transforming the colonizer's society that continues to dominate us.

Aboriginal centric history—the interpretation of Indian/Metis history from an Aboriginal perspective—has no European heroes. There are only Indian/Metis warriors and the supportive masses. Beginning with the brilliant Iroquois resistance wars which ended in driving out the French mercenaries from Indian territory, to the heroic wars of Pontiac and his warriors who defeated the British, to the liberation wars of the Metis at Red River and Batoche, and finally to the history of our liberation struggles in the 1960's and 70's. The national liberation movement of the 1960's was the first militant re-awakening since 1885 at Batoche, and one of the most outstanding people's struggle in terms of confronting the colonizer and promoting counter-consciousness among our people.

Who will write the Aboriginal centric history and culture. Those Metis, Indian and Inuit persons with an authentic Aboriginal consciousness and sense of nationhood. That is, persons who have been born in and grown up in a reserve or Metis community. Without an Indigenous consciousness it is not possible to write true Indigenous centric history or literature. They must hold a counter-consciousness, as well as social values, attitude and ethic that are integral to the Indian/Metis colonies. Their goals and future must be seen within or associated with our people and communities. Collaborator leaders and associates, government funded elites and mainstream opportunists cannot contribute to Aboriginal culture and history. They are only tourists and exploiters in our homeland.

Those of us who have lived in colonized micro-societies have ben subjected to the suppressive weight of dehumanization and non-intellectual thought imposed by the colonizer. As a result we hold feelings of discontent and challenge; having sensed the obliteration of intellectual activity and the forced "backwardness" in our community. How deeply I felt the eurocentric repression against our Metis culture and history. I lived only fifteen miles from the glory of our ancestors' heroic struggles at Batoche, but that "glory" rung in our ears as a hideous defeat. Anglo superiority stigmatized and smeared us into muteness. At the sound of the last gun, eurocentric historians rushed in to write and publish their distorted myths that flooded the nation. These white supremacy scribes swelled the flow of Aboriginal blood and forced our people into shameful hiding from the odium of their weird and distorted descriptions. Such academic myths are typically used to subjugate the oppressed into deeper colonization and ghettoization. Myths and falsehoods not only structured Metis and Indian culture and history, but at the same time justified brutal military rule. As historians and authors we must repudiate these fabrications and write a genuine account of our ancestors' struggles and victories.

Decolonization and liberation cannot take place without counter-consciousness and a spirit of devotion to the cause of self-determination, justice and equality. There are some excellent Aboriginal centric historical and cultural works emerging from our brilliant Indian/Metis/Inuit scholars, authors and poets. The greatest break-through in the analysis and interpretation in Aboriginal centric history is the work of Ron Bourgeault. In his ground-breaking theories and writings he explores the intentional devastating changes of traditional communal society to European mercantilists for the purpose of exploitation and control. Bourgeault presents a new perspective in Aboriginal centric history, as well as providing a new theoretical basis for emerging Aboriginal intellectuals. Several other outstanding Aboriginal creations from a centric perspective have been produced by Maria Campbell, Jeannette Armstrong, Lee Maracle, Emma Laroque, Duke Redbird and others. Aboriginal centricity is a study of the masses "from below" with a view to the inarticulate and poorly educated people. Therefore, our style of writing must be uncomplicated; a popular, journalists style, and not the academic or esoteric type.

The important factor about these people and their creations is the perspective. They make a clear break from the Euro-Canadian white supremacy interpretation, the typical racists, stereotyped image of Aboriginal to a new factual Aboriginal perspective. They are working from their critical counter-consciousness. Their works could not have been produced without it. Also, they live in close relationships and experiences with Aboriginal communities, which are vital for the Aboriginal creations. In this renaissance period, we must write with and as part of the Aboriginal people; not for them. Explanations to the white mainstream population is not our major concern. Writing and speaking to members of a quasi-apartheid society does not change their attitudes or ideology. That can be done only by changing the structure and institutions of the state. Establishment white historians argue that Indians and Metis have no past worthy of study. To them, we are an illiterate, primitive mass who have no sense of "peoplehood." But, as Aboriginal people, we know differently. We must not only challenge, but must transcend these distorted falsehoods that have stood for so long as legitimate history.

The most ruthless tactic employed by the neocolonial state was to inflict on our people Indian/Metis collaborators, leaders and organizations with powerful generous grants of money that fractured our liberation struggle and crushed our spirited momentum in the 1970's from which it has not yet recovered. This served to abruptly halt our movement towards political emancipation and cultural revitalization. To a large extent, however, these comprador bravadoes have been marginalized and reduced to considerable irrelevance and ineffectuality. Therefore, as Aboriginal artists and intellectuals we should take the opportunity to move forward in terms of authentic culture and history, hopefully without internal conflict. As colonized people, it is inevitable that we will have differing points of view and aims. But that is par for every colony and its peoples. We need only to call to mind the black people of South Africa, Sri Lanka and Somali, it is the imperialist's most powerful parting strategy: to divide and war among ourselves internally,hoping that the colonized will call him back. But his interests have now turned to selling armaments to both sides.

The corporate rulers have structured and perfected a neocolonial state and saddled it on our people; with new suppressive strategies that served to disperse and confuse all progressive activists. Other elites are co-opted in to the middle class mainstream society with jobs that `go nowhere'. It is now the task of Aboriginal intellectuals, authors, academics and activists who possess an Aboriginal consciousness to analyze and understand the "how" of our new form of oppression and powerlessness. The silence of the 1960's liberation struggle was not a defeat, but a temporary diversion. Now, we must sharpen our analytical tools for future challenges and nation building.

There Are No Vanished Tribes

storm clouds migrate in my direction, arms outstretched as if to embrace me in the manner of words. i sit, an anxious mother, waiting for her children to return after a long absence. they come home in the shape of grey blue bodies crawling down the mountains outside a bed i chose as my own. the songs returning home have been contorted through centuries of abuse, lungs clawed at by steel jaws, torn away in their youth then left for dead in clear-cut forests and diverted rivers.

words and song slip off the tongue of crow. she feeds those of us still alive, sliding her beak down our throats, replacing starvation with the voices caught on the breath of millennium. words and song fill my stomach drowning my heart in resistance my mouth wide open they leave in their wake a trail for others yet to come. they have survived and have come home to me, illuminated in translucent light, knowing they have not been numbered amongst the missing. in my belly a ghost dance of tone and rhythm is taking place. only outsiders believe in vanished tribes, between my joints they are still living. they dance within pregnant clouds. they roam inside my house, filling my rooms with conversation and laughter.

i watch as they throw off their cloaks of starvation and disease, discarding half truths and broken promises. they are planning a revolt and scream revolution at the slow rising red moon, chanting, calling me home. their blood is seen roaming across horizons yet to be formed. they call come home, come home, understand the moment is now. they whisper listen to the movement within your ribcage, words, song, vanished tribes crawl out from beneath rocks. they slither into the palm of tomorrow. spitting into the earth they birth revolution. words, song, vanished tribes housed in stones voice slide down my throat. they murmur the moment is now.

storm clouds migrate home
i sit an anxious mother
waiting for her children to return
following their absence;

they return in the shape of words and song
filling my house with conversation and laughter
vanished tribes crawl inside my stomach
where a ghost dance has almost finished

crow has filled my belly;
with the tone and rhythm of revolution
while overhead the moon slowly rises
as blood flows down her cheeks!

Ode to the Horse Powered Engine

"If one were only an Indian, instantly alert, and on a racing horse, leaning against the wind, kept on quivering, jerkily over the quivering ground, until one shed one's spurs, for there needed so spurs, threw away the reins, for there needed no reins, and hardly saw that the land before one was a smoothly shorn heath when horse's neck and head would be already gone."
—The Wish to be a Red Indian, Franz Kafka

1.
Before chrome pistons, crank shafts and cruise control,
there were stallions, palominos and pintos.
Before asphalt, car pool lanes and expressways,
there open plains, prairies and sage bowl landscapes.
Somebody's vision of power was ignited-
a new mode of transport was bred,
and a future designed by genius was born.

2.
We used to live next door to a junkyard
guarded by a German Shepherd named Puppet.
It was strewn with the motor innards of dead cars,
a trash heap of failed metal organs and stale
powerless dreams. On the other side
of us was a field of horses. They stood
all day grazing on buttercups, meadow grass
and the crab apples fallen from nearby trees.
Beauty raced with them. Their bodies were
the carved muscle of a god's extravagant whim,
magnificent packaged flesh of a vision gone to pasture.

3.
I'd like to believe that the Plains Indians
invented horses. That those herds of sprinting
hooves were created by the medicine
of some warrior's nightmare-some
holy man's vision of tomorrow. I'd also
like to believe in Pegasus and Unicorns.

4.
I once dreamed of travelling with a caravan
of mystic gypsies. They didn't own fingers,
but two-forked appendages for hands.
They loved gold, red wine and laughter.
They created fire from their supply of magic
crystals. Nights found them in a furious whirl
of dancing and singing. Their wagons
were pulled by a stock of proud centaurs.
One was fair with the face of a Roman
statue. Another was fiery black
with African features. After everyone
went to sleep—I stole them.

5.
Last March I purchased a car.
The auto dealer wore thick gold
chains and grinned at me with broken
and missing teeth. He sold discarded
engines, snake oil and firewater.
Revving the motor of a Dodge Colt
I heard the roar of 800 horses
trafficking across the dust and ash
arriving to the other side of eternity.
"Got a lot of power, this one!"
he promoted. Next he showed
me a Ford Mustang. Except the engine
refused to turn over. All I could hear
was the echo of drums beating against
the generator. Finally I drove home
in an Escort Pony. We bartered
and made a good trade. The engine
still runs, but I could have had something
more powerful—I could have had a V-8.

6.
Driving to the Park and Ride
on weekday mornings, I am greeted
by herds of horse powered engines
grazing on asphalt in the parking lot.
One morning I find that the herd has vanished,
and are replaced with Zulu trucks
and Masai sports sedans.
On the 6:00 news a coalition
of outraged consumers and civil
rights activist are suing
the auto industry. They win.
I don't know if I should laugh or cry.

7.
Some night I am shaken
to consciousness by
turning dust. hoof
prints lie scattered
across my bed—
and now bare room
of my vision
reveals ghosts of equestrian
soldiers decorated
in sashes of scarlet
and helmets of frozen blue wind.
Their words are electric
forcing my will to surrender
from this nightmare.
Some dreams you never wake up from.

8.
Some saying used to go—
you are what you eat.
Now I hear—
you are what you drive.
How will I explain to my future children,
the definition of irony?

9.
The Monster Truck Rally
is coming to the King Dome.
That same weekend,
the gay rodeo is happening
in Enumclaw. Queers on steers—
the poster read.
I can't decide which to attend,
so I stay home and watch
the 6:00 news. They're
broadcasting a story about crowds
of demonstrators and animal
rights activists opposing the gay rodeo.
One guy complains on camera
that the oppressed are oppressing.
Nobody is picketing the King Dome.

10.
On the Ponderosa, Little Joe
gets in a skirmish with some
horse thieves. Hoss and Adam
throw their two fists in the squabble,
the thieves go to jail and the show
has a happy ending. I switch
channels just in time to watch
Starsky and Hutch apprehend
a gangster for organized grand theft auto.
The show has a happy ending.
I'm still waiting for a happy ending.

The Brother on the Bridge

None of our *ope* knew his name or where he was from, but he must've had one and he must've come from somewhere 'cause he's Maori. Someone said his name was Bruce, but he didn't look like a Bruce. Another suggested Rawiri, someone else said "...Nah, it Wi." Well, whatever his name was and wherever he was from, to me he will always be the Brother on the Bridge. He's a hero this Brother and I wish I had got to meet him, to find out what he was like. Sure, I got to see him... but to find out what he was like... Nah, not even.

Let me describe to you this Cool Black cat and why he's a hero. He's tall without being heavy. Six foot... Six One, lean and cut up to the max, his skin a dark chocolate. He has an obligatory MUM tattoo on his left bicep. Facially, the brother has that *pahau* goatee look. His eyes a deep hazel, the nose aquiline, flared in the nostrils, the lips dark purple and full. And the dreads. A couple of fat ones, some straggly ones but still the *meke*, *tuturu* dreads and the brother was wearing them high and proud in a *Tiki-Tiki*.

So now you know the Brother as well as I do, and in my head, I need to make up his life story. Something tragic or romantic perhaps that will lend credence to his actions that day.

I'd like to think of him holding up the van back in Manutuke or Putiki or whatever *Marae*. I can hear Uncle Boy moaning "Where's this bloody fullah... bloody hell we're running late as it is."

Aunty Girlie is groaning also. "How come he's coming with us anyway, blimmin' nuisance. And he better not smoke any of that Wack-Backy either. And just maybe there's a distant but close cousin who is also aboard the Waitangi bound waka from Putiki or Manutuke or wherever who stands up for the Bro and says "*kia ora* Aunty and Uncle, he's O.I., so he's a little bit of a *hoha, kei te pai tera*, he's got a good heart. "But Uncle Boy is adamant, "I smell any of that Mara-jah-warna... pssssst, he's outta here."

It maybe unfair, but I sort of think of the Brother as a bit of a loser. Well not exactly a loser, but definitely a *hoha* fullah and maybe not entirely trustworthy. Like his imaginary cousin said "So he smokes a bit of Dak, and he's not much of a boozer but if the occasion arises, he's been known to sit around a Keg with the Cuzzies and polish it off, no sweat! There's a Girlfriend, a kid, and another on the way and she's always nagging him about commitment. "The Big C is not cannabis" she yells at him constantly.

On a *tino wera* day, and *Tai Tokerau* will tell you it's like that every day, four hundred more or less, decided to *hikoi* from the bottom *mara*, across the Bridge and up to the Treaty grounds. But not a *hikoi* like ninety-five. The spitting, the *whakapohane*, the *haka*, would be out. *Kia tau te rangimarie. Rangimarie* that was the buzz word. Well, someone was bound to start up "*Ka Mate*" somewhere along the line, but *Te Kawariki* leader *Hone Harawira* reminded us... *Kia tau te rangimarie...* and we did, until we met those Babylon Boys with their helmet visors down and their baton drawn, all in formation at the foot of the Bridge.

The previous day, around 7 P.M., perhaps a van load of Maori from Putiki or Manutuke or wherever stops at a Mobil in Kamo on the outskirts of Whangarei. Uncle Boy has run out of filters and Aunty Girlie needs to go for a mimi. "Who wants a munch? Are you hungry Cuz?" asks the distant but close cousin. "Sweet as Cuz," says the Brother. "I'm just heading over to that park over there to have a... well, you know!"

"Well just be careful Bro, don't let Uncle or Aunty catch you."

"Don't worry Cuz," says the Brother tapping the pockets of his Black Leather jacket "I've got the Clear Eyes in this one and the smellies in this one."

"Well just be careful... and don't be too long."

On a stinking hot day, and *Tai Tokerau* will tell you it's like that every day, four hundred people and thirty crops reached an impasse at the foot of the Waitangi Bridge. Some Senior Seargent was on his loud hailer shouting about some Bull-Shit Law from some Fucked Up Act and why crossing a perfectly good bridge as a paid up citizen of Aotearoa was temporarily not possible. Call me naive, but I truly believed we would reach the Treaty Grounds that day.

"Surely there's no law that stops me from crossing this bridge, officer," I shouted.

"You bunch of Bullies," someone yelled. "Bully Bastards,

Bully Bastards."

"Shit-head fascist Pigs."

And to the Moari cops, the cruelest "*Kupapa*." And as the sun beat down and tempers flared and push turned to shove, and a rock smashed against some cop's helmet, and arms and legs clashed with baton, there was a Brother, stoned as the Venus de Milo standing with three or four hundred spectators on the beach at Waitangi, who came up with an out-of-it idea.

Earlier that morning, here was our van load of Maori from Putiki or Manutuke or wherever, ready to leave Uncle Boys' cousin's place in Moerewa for the final forty minute drive to Waitangi. Aunty Girlie has on her Classic two-piecer, *Hui* Black with a cream blouse. Her finest *harakeke* and *huruhuru kete* safely beside her on the front seat. Uncle boy in his Grey strides and Tweed jacket. The shoes, shiny black, kicking up dry Northland dust as he paces back and forth, a roly stuck on his bottom lip.

"Where the hell is this bloody boy? I told him I wanted to away by nine. Bloody Hell!"

"I told you he was a blimmin' nuisance," Aunty Girlie moans. "Leave him behind Dear, he's been nothing but a *hoha* since we left home. Always disappearing every time we stop. He never talks just grunts and you know... for someone who looks so paru, he smells too nice."

And maybe the close but distant cousin speaks up for him again and says "*Kia* or Aunty and Uncle, *Kei te pai*, he won't be long. I think he's walked up to the shops to get a paper."

But even the cousin is starting to get pissed off with the Brother. More's the chance he's gone up town for some "papers," rather than a "Herald."

For a Brother to leave his treasured leathers on a beach with four hundred strangers, you know it had better be for a damn good reason. Damn good.

How or why no one noticed him sooner is beyond me, but someone shouted out "Hey, who's that over there?"

"Over where?"

"The bridge... the middle of the bridge."

Standing on the top hand rail at the centre of the Waitangi Bridge was our Brother from Putiki or Manutuke or wherever. In all the commotion of the Police and Protestors fracas on the bridge, no one noticed the Brother slip into the water and swim to the middle concrete pillar and by using the criss-cross number eight wiring that encased it, managed to climb the five or six metres to the underside of the bridge. He then must've swing monkey bar style under the bridge before coming up and unto the side. And now, there he stood. Hands on his hips in the classic "hope" position. The Dready hair, proud and high in a *Tiki-Tiki*. The dark we skin shining in the hot Northland sun.

It's an image that will stick in my mind forever. As the crowd on the beach turned their attention to the middle of the bridge, a huge cheer sounded from across the other side of the Estuary.

"Way to go Bro."

"Give 'em heaps Cuz."

And those few Warriors that had defied Police orders not to swim across to the other side started up a stirring rendition of 'Te *Rauparahas'* most famous *haka*, *Ka Mate*.

It encouraged those spectators on this side of the bridge to join in and before you knew it, the protestors that had been in a stand-off with Police for two hours found new resolve in their own struggle and joined in as well. It was a six hundred-strong *Haka* Party and it was dedicated to the Brother on the Bridge. And as Protester and Spectator slapped chest and thigh in unison to stomping feet, the Brother stood precariously on the hand rail, conducting the crowd with a mix of *Haka* and bravado, all the time the crowd cheering him on. Senior Sergeant Loud Hailer barked an order and two Bully Boys were dispatched to deal with this malaprop who had succeeded in getting behind enemy lines. The dummies. Surely they knew they didn't have a hope in hell of capturing him. As the two Bullies closed in on the Brother, he turned his head, gave them the 1 fingered sign of defiance... and with a "Kiss my ass" grin, jumped.

And as the long, black, powerful legs pushed him out safely beyond his assailants, the Brother thought he saw Uncle Boy on the beach. His tweed jacket folded neatly next to a Black Leather one. His sleeves rolled up, he was deep in the throes of his own *Haka*. And who was that next to him in the classic two-piecer, *Hui*

Black with a cream blouse? Was that Aunty Girlie with her arms outstretched, her voice carrying the call of welcome to her as he momentarily reached the zenith of his jump and hung, with perfect timing, the folding of his body to effect the ultimate "Gorilla Bomb."

The effect on the crowd was awesome. The effect on the Protestors even more so, and as they charged the Police at the foot of the Waitangi Bridge, a Brother from Putiki or Manutuke or wherever, idly did the backstroke as the hot Northland sun warmed his body.

Indian Talk: Are You Listening?

Nearly five hundred years ago Cortes landed on the coast of Mexico with four hundred Spanish Freebooters. He sweet-talked a young Mayan girl into serving as an interpreter and informer, and with her help persuaded thousands of Mexican Indian Warriors to join him in conquering Mesoamerica. Gathering other Indians to his cause he succeeded in looting the land and delivering it to The Crown of Spain.

Such is the power of words!

With the continued encroachment on Native American boundaries, it is important to control the tongue.

"As silent as an Indian" is a well known phrase. Everyone knows that the Native American is practically mute. Everyone, that is, except the Native American. For with the Cherokees there is a time to speak and a time to be silent. The time to be silent is when in the presence of strangers. And when nobody is listening anyway. It is not good to talk merely to enjoy the sound of your own voice. The time to speak is when you have something to say.

Among the Cherokees the art of oratory was much prized—right up there on a par with killing enemies in battle and stealing horses. Any feat of bravery was followed by a ceremonial dance, and everyone had a chance to tell the whole story of it—not once, but over and over again if it was exciting enough. In fact, Cherokees are probably the most talkative people on earth. The language is very complex. There are twenty ways to say, "I think it's gonna rain." Folks have been known to spend a whole evening just discussing the details of the language itself. There are different words for your grandparent on your mother's side and the one on your father's side. This is more important than you might think, for, in the old days, one could marry only into those two clans. There are any number of words for your brother—depending on whether he's older or younger than you, and whether you're a boy or a girl.

A verb does not have the usual tense of past, present, future and so on. The Cherokees have a different conception of time—it goes round in a circle instead of in a straight line. One verb form designates whether you personally observed an action, or if you only heard about it from someone else. This has brought about an interesting conversation piece among present-day Cherokees. Many observed the moon-landing on their television screens. The question is: Did we actually see it with our own eyes, or just a photograph that was relayed on to us by someone else? Is it possible that some Sneaky Pete has perpetrated another gigantic hoax?

Much of the Cherokee speaking ability has been lost in translation from one language to another. There was an old Cherokee man hauled into an English-speaking Court of Law. When the Judge (through a Translator) asked him, "Do you beat your Wife?" he started out speaking gently, but as he got into the spirit of the thing, he rose and gesticulated wildly for a quarter of an hour, ending up by slamming his fist on the rail before he at last sat down.

The Translator translated into English: "He says NO."

From the Indian viewpoint, here are some statements from The Drum, a nineteenth century Cherokee Chief:

"White people talk too much and too loudly; they never take time to listen."

"Silence is the language of wisdom."

"In silence we can hear the voices that must be felt with the heart rather than with the ears."

"In silence (The Great Spirit) gives us his most important messages."

Which is remarkably the same as the Judeo-Christian Bible quotation: "Be still and know that I am God." (Psalm 46:10)

Cherokees strive for a balance: half talk and half silence. An interesting conversation between two people is when one person talks only half the time and listens the other half; so that the second person is given equal time. Talking should be a sharing experience, not a monolog.

Only if I spoke with forked tongue would I demand both halves in the Time-Sharing of a conversation. I have filed in my mental computer one of my mother's sage sayings: "Keep your eyes and ears open, and your big mouth shut!"

And: "Speech is silvern; silence is golden!"

However, all seriousness aside, I was brought up on this humorous quip:

WHEN WE TAKE THE COUNTRY BACK FOR THE INDIANS, WE'RE NOT GONNA SHOOT NOBODY—
WE'RE GONNA TALK 'EM TO DEATH!

Beyond the Convent Door

"*Ke chi Okimaw*, he is the King who lives beyond this door and this place is his place." Thus we whisper, children of a lesser order and we savour our heathen noises, "*Mah* (Listen)," and for a few minutes no nun comes and only the wavering light beneath the nuns' chapel door moves and later, between the nuns' patrolling footsteps, we lie in our stiff beds, talking quietly about *Okimaw* and how is it, someone says, that he gave out baskets of bread to the hungry people... when here in his own house he locks it up... "Yes, I saw it too—chains, big ones, and a padlock too. Yes, I do not think he is the real one," and the night's quiet is punctuated with the belly-rumbling of one collective agreement. "Too, he makes us get up early and never even comes, not even when Sister Teresa hit that new girl right on her head with that big steel brush." So we speak sometimes when it is quiet. Then we hear someone crying—probably because they've wet the bed—and won't the nuns like this in the morning but we, the eight and nine-year-olds, know that it's always this way for the new ones. "Don't cry," we say. "When you get big like us you won't be doing that or crying anymore." But we lie. Sometimes, when it almost morning and I've been thinking of God for some time, I cry slowly so no one will hear me and I think it doesn't matter because *Okimaw*, he doesn't really live here.

The Devil's Language

I have since reconsidered Eliot
and the Great White way of writing English
standard that is
the Great White way
has measured, judged and assessed me all my life
by its
lily white words
its picket fence sentences
and manicured paragraphs
one wrong sound and you're shelved in the Native Literature sec-
tion
resistance writing
a mad Indian
unpredictable,
on the war path
Native ethnic protest
the Great White way could silence us all
if we let it
it's had its hand over my mouth since my first day of school
since Dick and Jane, ABC's and fingernail checks
syntactic laws, use the wrong order or
register and you're a dumb Indian
You're either dumb, drunk or violent
my father doesn't read or write
does that make him dumb?
the King's English says so
but he speaks Cree
how many of you speak Cree?
correct Cree not correct English
grammatically correct Cree
is there one?
Is there a Received Pronunciation of Cree,
a Modern Cree Usage?
the Chief's Cree not the King's English

as if violating God the Father and Standard English
is like talking back/wards

as if speaking the devil's language is
talking back
backwards
back words
back to your mother's sound, your mother's tongue, your mother's language
back to that clearing in the bush
in the tall black spruce
near the sound of horses and wind

where you sat on her knee in a canvas tent
and she fed you bannock and tea
and syllables
that echo in your mind now,
now that you can't make the sound
of that voice that rocks you and sings you to sleep
in the devil's language.

about love connections

our self sustained
imprimaturs
acknowledge our
tenuous toeholds on
spiritual science

clown alley still serves
great hamburgers on lombard
street in san francisco
and the spatenhaus in
downtown munich serves the
best wiener schnitzel
on the planet

good memories build layers of
recognition to trade in
for rubber stamp lifetimes

synthetic variables force us
to understand the commonplace
as well as the exceptional
kinda like looking for a
cancer gene in every bowl
of soup ever served

small pox blankets were
never ruled unethical—in fact
were commended by most
authorities over time as
logical cleansers for
savage removal

but the son of mystery
walked among the folk
in that old world

and his main job was
to be the love connection

sex and puritans are so boring
so off the wall and party line at the
same time

who cares if genders
can't figure the real mystery
is some where between bodies
and yet nowhere
buried deep
in mother earth

he came to be the
love connection
he came to authorize
duplicates of himself
NOT temples filled
with memorabilia
to be run by
self appointed big daddies

Untitled

Tonight
is the night
of fire

of fire
sage
and eagle
feathers

tonight
I crawl
through ceremony
sage
and stars

I scream
and scream
again
the names
of those who have
desecrated my body
my soul

I scream at the moon
for revenge
justice

you did not have to go
to a residential school
to suffer hell

I did not go to a residential school
it came to me

but tonight

as I stand
in a forest
in the mountains
I take it all back

one song
one ceremony
one night
at a time

and there is nothing
you can do about it.

Me again

Hello there
it's me again
I come before you
now
in a vision
a dream

this is a warning

I am warning you
that
I am coming
and
this time
I will not be content

to stay in
pemmican/salmon-soaked stories
in teepees
wigwams
winterlodges
and longhouses

THIS MEANS WAR

and this means that
I will invade you
and
your life
and everything you hold
close
to your heart
like never before

but

don't take this all so seriously

because
I am joking
I am the trickster
I come before you now
in the
shape of a dream
consider yourself lucky
this time

because

I could come before
you
in the shape of coyote
a raven
a crow
or even an owl

but

you wouldn't want
to see me
then

I would scare
you
to death
and I know you
wouldn't like that

so beware

I am coming
and I will
take you
this is war
these are the lines
this is how it will
end.

TRIBUTE

words by and for those passed on to the spirit world

Give Us The Stars & The Moonlight
for Mary TallMountain

when you left us we remembered
        your steady words, your strong spirit

your words about the land & people you were taken from
        when you were young

we remembered your spirit
that so often rose up high in the sky
        and carried us over every sharp peak
every deep abyss

you saved us, Mary TallMountain
Mary TallMountain
you saved us with your words & songs & dreams
        about our Native America
your Alaskan, Athabaskan birthplace

Mary, give us this day
give us the stars & the moonlight
        the sunlight fierce, the ocean winds blowing
the shine in your eyes, still present
        in every blinking streetlight
        in every busy storefront window
in this sometimes foggy
        sometimes sunny
vibrant city that was your home for so many years–

Mary,
San Francisco,
your urban tenderloin,
misses you.

Flower Day

when you died
i lay you here
sleep well i said
what else could i do with you

i come now to clean your grave
fresh flowers planted
headstone dusted clean
who else would do it

i hum as i work
i know
that even in death
you need me
at noon
i'll use your grave as a table
and eat
a feast in celebration
a woman
alone

In Memory of Kohkum Madeline

The oblates of mary immaculate
authorized by the god-he
seized her from a winnipeg orphanage
baptized her "MADELINE"

The department of indian affairs
empowered by an all male government
branded her "INDIAN"
registered her "OSOUP"

My brothers, sisters, and i
brainwashed by
christianity and civilization
saw her only in mooshum's shadow
and we called her "KOHKUM PAUL"

1886
they say she came
to old osoup and his arms
a malnourished and sickly girl baby
but they loved her fed her
and nourished her life

1894
at eight years old the old blackrobe
uprooted her again reclaimed her for the god-he
imprisoning her youth shaping her mind
fort qu'appelle indian residential school
she simply became #382

there #382's basic education
combined with domestic and industrious training
produced the appropriate INDIAN FARMER'S WIFE
she learned obedience order respect
for god-he, the father, and husband

like a pawn she was traded
between two old men
properly became mrs farmer's wife
she bore him nine children
lived in his shadow for 75 years

in the dim light sometimes i watched
unbraided fiery red hair falling
hanging protective down
the length of her back

i imagined there were plenty
red haired women in ireland
in the dark i thought her eyes
brown sun kissed
they could melt your soul

1979
finally, her life at an end
as she lay dying in that hospital bed
hanging on to each precious moment
waiting for her to mouth
those mysterious irish words

she didn't disappoint me
the last words she spoke
the language of her people
in her last senile moments
MADELINE O'SOUPE ACOOSE #382 whispered
"*amo anint wapos, minihkwen nihti*"
and motioned for me to sit beside her fire

Southwest Journal: Medicine Eagle's Gathering

(in memory of Chief Reymundo Tigre Perez)

Oyes pues, maestro Tigre, now that you have crossed over the other side, can you tell us what it is like? Is it similar to the stormy times we shared in Detroit, wandering amongst the chaos, searching for the meaning of life in the present tense? Is it the madness of the 1960s with knife held between the teeth swinging from one mast of injustice to another, our written words ambushing the King's representatives at every cove on the shore? Did we do right in risking our lives to immolate Crazy Horse and the Mixteca Indian leader Emiliano Zapata ascending from the mountain top for an occasional raid on the oppressors who held our people captive? The midnight thieves continue to toss stones at our sacred temples, breaking every window then running away without being caught because they know that after all, boys will always be good 'ole boys. From where you can see Tigre, is anyone up there keeping an accurate record of all this?

Just a few miles east of the Kanto celebration dedicated to the well being of the sea creatures, I reconsidered the trophies safely labelled and stored in the crowded automobile, wild desert and mountain sage, red Colorado cedar, earth stones with images running through them, a pair of old gourd rattles from Mayo River country farther south, and a special parrot feather given by the Huichol on the burning desert floor of the Kiva. These objects we took home with us to guide us through the wintry blasts of difficult times. They grant us the authority to speak on behalf of the earth's distress and dismemberment, a genocide against the living creatures of the earth that continues with a renewed frenzy at the scent of money. It was the last time we saw you. We embrace many lessons at Kanto, endured the weather and our own doubts. Our lives were enriched and changed. When authority is carefully passed on it may someday resonate again with the same if not stronger force. This lifetime knows its limitations does it not? A path not taken, a road pursued too far?

St. Vincent Hospital
Congestive Heart Failure
Shown Sunday through Saturday
10:05, 12:35
15:05, 20:05

St. Vincent, *pues vato,*
there is a hole in my heart
where a poem oughta be,
an ache in my soul,
for the loss of innocence.
The Medicine Bundle dangles
over the edge of the bed,
embraces the blood pressure ball—
a black spring bulb draped over it;
027/020 nitro blood thinner
where a poem for life oughta be.

They claim their machines can pump on forever
without being held by hand, if you let them;
until one bright morning without warning,
Death will smile at the foot of the bed,
a macabre jokester playing pinball
with the master control switches,
flicking lit matches at the pure oxygen containers,
wearing dark sun glasses in winter.

Anciano Tigre, following the arrest and subsequent parole by the fascist cardiac police, I was surprised to find my name on the mail still being delivered to the same old house, surrounded by the Tree Spirits who had rescued me. Was this an indication that all was well? Or do you mean to tell me that when we die life really does continue onward and upward without us? Does the U.S. Postal Service also deliver in heaven?

So many foolish questions. So little time to respond. The brief stroll through Santa Fe brokerage houses selling Indian wares and dreams, with slight variations one from the other, did produce a few treasures; a nod of the head in greeting from an Indian homeless person in tattered Levis moving skilfully and stealthily amongst the crowd of wealthy tourist, and the Pueblo Elder living in the city who greeted us at the doorway of the jewelry shop, begging time and money. The Elder said that most people believe that he is crazy from the sun. He said he knew that the lessons of the burning sand are patience and strength. He had wandered the lonely canyons of the Sangre De Cristo Mountains and farther north to Taos searching for his "double," the "other," the Nahual guardian, he said.

Camping in the desolate, dry foothills of the Jemez Mountains having to transport in bathing and drinking water, life grinds down to a crawl before the onslaught of the noon day sun. Wandering among the dry canyon walls makes one appreciate the abundance of water in the northland were it is too often taken for granted. At Sun Dance time, four days among the spontaneous combustion of pinon, cottonwood, juniper and mountain mahogany populations of trees, wondering how they can stand still all day without a whimper in the hundred degree heat. Four nights with the coyote and wild dog songs to Tsi-mayoh in the distance, watching their silhouettes move closer to the campsite when the familiar sounds of the aging evening quieted. Coyote had picked up the scent of Walking Bear, the thick haired out-of-his-environment Husky dog. I wondered if Bear could summon the strength not to dart outside after the intruders. Seven thousand feet above the dry arroyos, the stones there speak of still higher places, stronger winds and more true to life earth revelations in their pristine, simplest forms. The scars are real and the happiness complete in the victor over the challenges of the journey of a full life. It is what separates the *Iyac Tlamacazqui*, the warrior priest, from the simply curious. Maestro, our exploits have been many and the battles won numerous yet always there is one more crossroad, one more raging river luring us to the promises on the other side.

Maestro Tigre, at Chimayo Sanctuario the miniature silver and brass replicas of arms, legs, hearts, abdomens and other body parts filled the showcase at the gift shop. The carved imitations of body parts were used as offerings in prayers to secure a cure. On view were crucifixes from Africa, homemade, brightly painted Christian crosses made of wood and also carved animal representations to be carried on the person for protection. The small wooden, silver and brass animal figurines attracted me the most. These were representations of the animal guardian spirits worn by the Indian people. I chose one that would insure the continued fertility of the creative heart and mind. The store keeper claimed that it was the civilized Spaniards who brought the symbol of the *quincux* and the cross to this continent. I did not mind his ignorance because the inner silence of such truths, tested by the forces of Creation, is stronger than their outward manifestations. Their outward manifestations allow them to be seen by we pitiful Human Beings. The symbols have power only in the truth. it is no wonder that the priest in charge at Chimayo felt compelled to turn to the sole Indian policeman on the church premises to keep an eye on me. It seems that one of the parishioners had turned me in. All that the bumper sticker on our automobile asked was for people to HONOUR INDIAN TREATIES, *como en* Chiapas. It seemed like a reasonable request considering all that had been taken from us. The Indian policeman that was summoned was a young man, visibly embarrassed that the was asked to follow me. We exchanged nods in confirmation over the ridiculous situation. We both understood how deep the scars of history, war and revenge had cut their mark into this vast and complex countryside. We both had our work to do.

That same evening the white column of fragile clouds formed themselves into a crude Indian cross, a *quincux*, the ancient symbol of the four directions, the four elements and the four previous worlds. The red sand cliff overhang in the distance that protected me from a sudden downpour of rain a few days ago shuffled the ice in the cooler with the invisible hand of hot reflected sunlight. The clinking sound of ice being transformed into liquid water, a herons' favourite dining place, became the conduit for the realization that all things truly are connected to one another. Knowledge was contained equally in the majestic rise of Quetzalcoatl as the Morning Star as well as in the scamper of tiny spider legs that hardly left a trace of their passing on the cooling, shifting sand. Sun spots reached with their heavy winds to carry the canyon hummingbird from Cliff Rose to Palo Duro, the lizard from one cactus shadow to another. Automobiles on the curving canyon road above our encampment joined the migration from the steaming city to the cooling lake in the distance. Sharp, piercing mountain shadows slowly dissolved into another crystal clear, cool moonlit night. All was as it should be, and life continued to move ahead as a matter of inches, a moment lost to delay, an opportunity better left alone.

There is one thing I would like to ask of you, Maestro Tigre, please tell me that there are no Indian police up in heaven. Tell me that our people do not contradict one another up there. Tell me, will I have to hide the tequila bottle under my long, yellow, plastic authentic Dick Tracy trench coat to get it through the gates? Pues guy, you will meet me there for one final toast, *que no*? It will be good to see you again in a place where words have no power. We will rest and not be ashamed of being content with watching the Universe unfold before us. We will sit silently and partake of the energy that moves within and around us, that elongates and shrinks us with each harmonic pulsation of warm summer sunlight. We will move as the seed moves to seek its rooting in the womb of our precious Earth Mother, quietly and with much humility.

Assa

I hope you can hear me.
This may be the last time I walk
onto this hill to talk to you.
This sacred ground that holds your bones in silence
is under siege.
The oil companies
want to dig you up and build a road.
Asyoo and I hitch-hiked into town
to stop them.
I tried to translate for Asyoo but
they wouldn't respect a kids voice.
They shoved us out steel doors.
My leg and fingers got caught
and my skin ripped.
I bled on their steps.
Asyoo,
she spit black scuff on their white walls.

Asyoo tells me
her sister, mother, and brother
are here with you.
Why don't they understand
this is our territory.
The Muskeg people's land.
The site where your *haaa* songs echo.

I have never seen you but
your prophecies and medicine songs
swirl in my head.
Asyoo and Amma say you were the last Nache.
I'm proud to be from this bloodline.

We sang your horse song
the one given to you by the spirits.
Did you hear the agony in our voices?

Assa,
where do we go?
What do we do?
Assa,
please help us
I hear their machines coming
down the hill.

Mother

I dedicate this poem to my mother and all the mothers and Grandmothers and Women of all the Red Nations of Turtle Island

mother,
there you were sitting at the head of the table
like always, a place that is sacred to your daughters and sons
smoking sipping on coffee talking and laughing with father
and my brothers in the early hours of the morning when the sun begins to rise

my eyes look to my brothers
dressed in fatigues, ready to protect and defend our people, our land,
ready to sacrifice their lives for our children
they take one last drag and one last sip of coffee with you and father before they go on barricade duties

as I stood by the fridge, tears filled my eyes
I looked at you and saw the heaviness of pain etched around your eyes
I felt your heart pounding to the rhythm of fear
the heaviness of fear, the fear of losing your sons
the fear and pain of not knowing whether this would be the last morning of greeting your sons with love
would this morning ritual be broken?

as my brothers got up and puffed on their last cigarette
their eyes looked to you for comfort
your beauty of love and strength flew like a whirlwind into their hearts
your beauty of love and strength eased their fears of this war
your beauty of love and strength had protected and carried them back home safely each night

Nia'wen:kowa mother, for bringing my brothers home safely each night

A Sister Flies Ahead of Me Now
(For EK (Kim) Caldwell 1954-1997)

I discover you
not unlike the way Columbus
supposed he had discovered us;
you were already there... settled,
imposing, beautiful, shining in the light
of morning.

We sit, reeking of sage,
flying to gather in the Oneida woods.
In the old way of asking, we find
each other sisters in the family circle
of word weavers, of story singers,
of water bearers.

Your smiles collect
on my shoulders and my ears ring
with your words. We are women,
satisfied to sit with our saged-up bodies
and learn each other. We have husbands,
write poems to stay alive, love being brown.
I know you a thousand days by the end
of our five hour flight.

Now you fly overhead;
I cup my eyes, shadow the sun to see you;
yesterday I caught a breath of sage
in the grocery store, thought you might
be there buying oranges or bread for dinner.
I walk past the waft of memory; hear you chuckle.
I buy the oranges and bread myself,
crying and laughing and getting a new poem.

My sage is safe in the Eagle Bag you gave me
when we met. You are there too in the twist
of red cloth, in the pocket of my coat where

my hand can touch your gift. Fire and I send
sparks of prayers to where you fly. You are
a brown, round woman of the air, circling me
and giving me new songs to sing, new words
to weave. So how can I begin to miss you?

Thoughts Right Before Sleep

All the talk
          about understanding
                    the words
                              and what they
                                        signify
not resigning themselves
          to the customary cautionary semantics
                    feeling within
                              the beat of the heart
signifying the heartbeat of humanity
  and life breath
  and the mother of us all

people talkin' the talk more now
          relinquish violence
the new battle cry
no more legacies of hatred
  and petty skirmishes
passed on to generations
already steeped in the confusion
  of those who talk and talk
but continue to evade responsibility
                    claiming no prior experience
                              is reason enough
                    to refuse rebirth
                         into wholeness and love.

*****

when we become caricatures
  living out the soap opera
    competing for the starring role
      in As The Tipi Turns
                    someone always bitching
                      about this one or that one
                        doing it wrong

looking mean in the face at one another
cause this one's mad at that one—again
caught up in the grandiosity of our own paranoia
wearing history like a lead sinker on a weak line

and the work doesn't get done
and the young ones die
the death of those
who will forfeit the lives of others
in an imagined war against the wrong enemy
the ricocheting consequences of ill conceived plans
based on misconception and ignorance of honour
leaving riddled spirits
creating a future full of holes.

*****

the struggles of those
already assimilated
now screaming and raging
about imperialism and exploitation
are perhaps the wails of those arriving late to a funeral.

*****

frustrated static humming on the moccasin telegraph
emotional snipers
tiny razored arrows flying
they wound more deeply
than is believed at first glance.

cheap shots bring their own hangovers
leaving us stranded
in the muddied bottoms
of creeks running dry

*****

lopsided triage
the blind man diagnosing the deaf man
recommending major surgery
the deaf man stares in horrored clarity
his powerlessness to make the blind man see
more terrifying to him
than his own inability to hear.

*****

heard someone say the leaders should fix it
right now
using words like seven generations
most times not feeling in the heart
the understanding of their meaning

they are words repeated in the mind as thoughts
that hurry and distract
forgetting to pray
or maybe never knowing how
thinking is different than praying.

there are those who offer themselves
and their gifts may not include haste
they stand between the past
that has defined them
and the future
the people demand
so often denied the moment of today
whose prayer is needed
to breathe life into the gifts they bring.

Seagull

The sensation of being in flight on a new summer day in the Okanagan Valley was second only to the feeling of a full gut. Which reminded me, I hadn't had my breakfast yet! The craving for food or lack of it was normal for a web-footed sea fowl like myself.

I fluttered my way towards the city to solve the deficiency inside my moaning belly. I landed downtown on top of the Bank of Commerce in Penticton and looked at the street below me. Before I could think further, the smell of food instinctively brought my attention to Main Street. As I looked and found there below me, at the corner of the street, the hotdog stand one of my cousins had told me about. The fresh smell of toasted franks was enough to hypnotize any starving seagull. With that in mind, I bravely flew down to get a closer look to plan my attack.

I landed on a nearby bench trying to look lost as I boldly inched my way closer to the stand. My strategy was, that if I came close enough I could use the strength in my wings to carry me over the grill and, like an eagle, snatch my hotdog and fly away. But, it didn't take me long to find out the hotdog owner must have experienced my kind before. I alertly focused my attention to the sling shot he withdrew from his pocket. It didn't take me long to recognize that the marbles that were being launched from his sling shot were aimed at me. Just when I turned and began to fly away, I felt a direct hit on the side of my head which grounded me to the pavement in a bird crash.

The next thing I could feel was the earth tremble to which brought me to open one eye and notice the hotdog stand owner was running towards me. A sudden irrational fear of being thrown in a city garbage can brought me to my feet.

I quickly began to flap my wings getting ready for takeoff, as my tortured body started down the runway of the city sidewalk. The hotdog stand owner wasn't as slow as I thought. He gave me a boost with the side of his foot that not only contributed to my air travel, but also motivated me in the direction of the heavens as the instincts of survival kept my wings flapping until I came to the top of the Bank of Commerce.

Standing there as a slight breeze blew against my ruffled feathers my head began to ache. Obviously that was not a way to fill an empty stomach. So without delay I readily took off to scout a less dangerous area of being a scavenger. I perched myself on the top of a telephone pole by Parker's Dodge car lot, I looked out below me and felt ashamed. Life had not been fair to me as I looked at my webbed feet. I seen my cousins below me waiting for their daily meal of McDonald's garbage being ushered out the door, anticipating foreign food of any kind to hit the pavement. At first my stomach wanted to join them but then I thought, is this what life is all about. Fighting my family every day for a few pieces of rotten leftovers.

Why are my feet webbed? How come I don't have the claws of an eagle or a hawk? Then I would be able to kill my own food instead of being the local bum I am. The idea of being an eagle made me excited as I took that thought and soared above the town. So as I began to glide through the air I tried to think what it would be like to search for real prey. Rather than the left over throw away food my body had grown accustomed to. Caught up in my own fantasy while flying down Main Street, my eyes zeroed in on a medium sized cat.

My stomach growled as my famished body became alive! So like the macho bird my thoughts had perceived me to be, I swooped down for the kill. The closer to the ground I came the more I began to realize the size of the cat.

I arrived in ill humour and tried to puncture the cat's neck with my webbed feet and at the same time fly away with him. It became apparent that my feet have no muscles in them to control such a hostile animal let alone fly away with him.

My next reaction was to instantly throat him with my strong powerful beak as I quickly attacked the jugular area. Instantly this action of thrusting my fragile pecker into such a thick hide brought tears to my eyes. The cat must have been pretty hungry himself because before I knew it I was at the bottom and the cat's mouth had me by the throat trying to kill me. I couldn't do anything so I started to panic, I was in a fight for my life.

Instead of trying to kill, I was about to eaten by this ferocious feline. I wasn't the eagle I thought I was and if it had not been for a local store owner who came out with his broom and clubbed us both I would have easily become digestive material.

Flying away, the blurred vision from the blow of the broom brought me to face the reality that because of my day dreaming, I had experienced what cat scratch fever was all about. So with that I quickly began to think of a different strategy to fill the emptiness in my stomach. I exhaustedly landed my weary body on a nearby house as I tried to ignore my wounds by the thought of food, which would heal any anguish that I felt. The pain started to set in which made me come to the conclusion that I was a wanna be bird living in a wanna be world. No matter what I did I could never be an eagle. I still admired his ways. How he never lets his hunger change his environment. He would starve before he would bring himself to be the vagrant bird that I am. I guess a wanna be world is what created bums like me.

Webs

Survival, when it is strictly only survival, is an ugly thing. Life is something more than just survival. To be alive is to know splendour and beauty. Living is an artform. I am immersed in art. I am forever spinning art from out of my flesh. My purpose in spinning webs is no longer merely to catch flies to eat. There is much more to it now. Indeed, the concern for food becomes incidental to the act of weaving a web. I love the feeling of being lost in abstractions for days at a time, recalculating the design of a work in progress with every shift in the breeze. Marvelous structures are woven and unwoven in my mind as I release filament and descend. Each web is a surprise, I myself never know what shape it will finally acquire. Every moment of creation is also a moment of re-creation, as the slightest changes in meteorology constantly alter and realign variables in physics and geometry. Supports, piers, brackets and braces demand existence in places that I had not imagined would require them. The weather alters everything.

The finished product, as I have already said is always a surprise. When I complete a web, I stand back into one of its corners and contemplate it, marvelling at the results of a genius that has spontaneously responded to every shift in the elements. I am not boasting. All spiders are possessed when engaged in the act of weaving. We enter a trance and dance with creation. The genius is never ours. We disappear from the world of petite and enter into pure abstraction. It is never out of egotism that we marvel at our webs. We know that we were only instruments and that the web is a product of something much greater than ourselves.

I never like it when a fly lands on my work too soon after its completion. I need time to concentrate, on the undisturbed web. We believe that in contemplating webs the fullness of appreciation eventually blooms into realizations. Ideally, each web should yield a truth. But life being what it is—so full of chaos and so contrary to design—it is rare that any series of webs will yield their true potential to their creators. More likely than not a fly will crash into the web soon after its completion. How disturbing such moments are! How profoundly disturbing! On the one hand, there is the thrill of catching the next meal and on the other hand there is this extreme sense of violation as a part of oneself is rent to threads by the thrashings of a fly.

These moments are disturbing because they overwhelm us with those eternal questions. What if life, if it is not to be in the knowing of wonders? Why, then does life interrupt itself? Why must the process of knowing be rudely dashed by matters of appetite? Why are not the worlds of appetite and abstraction in harmony? In other words, why does it so rarely happen that a web will remain undisturbed after its completion until it has yielded wisdom to the weaver? Ideally, a fly should land only after that golden moment. This happens by chance every now and again but it is really quite rare. Imagine how wise all arachnids could be!

Perhaps, however, we are not meant to know more than we should. There is a popular horror story told amongst us a of a certain spider who once tried a most unusual experiment. He decided to construct three webs in a row. He planned to build the outside ones first and the inside one last. This way he figured the outside webs would shelter the inside one.

The webs to the front and the back of the inside web would stop all the flies coming in from both directions. The central web would remain undisturbed and he could contemplate on this web for as long as he pleased. This he did. And when he had completed the project, he set himself on the corner of the inside web and observed. He studied the fascinating weave at his leisure. He sat there for hours and hours and great mysteries were gradually revealed to him. The wonders, however, that the web disclosed eventually trapped him just as surely as webs entangle flies.

He became totally consumed by the outpouring of knowing and he forgot himself. He forgot that he was a spider. He forgot that he had eight legs and a breast full of filament. All the knowing of himself vaporized. Just as he thought he was about to crack the riddle of the universe, a swallow came by and plucked him form his reveries.

I can never forget that story. And sometimes I can't help but think that webs are unnatural. If knowing can only come by fits and starts, then webs are illusions. This artform generates a false sense of completion and harmony. It deceptively suggests to us that it contains the all. In truth, knowing is not so neat and compartmental. Knowing is more like dew. It is everywhere, but it only gathers into little drops that plop off boughs one by one. Yet webs are not altogether deceptive. After all, they elevate the act of survival. Somehow webs prevent life from ever degenerating into ugliness.

Mountains I Remember

I loved the Kootenays and was content there
midst the towering peaks
sculpted by erosion
knowing even they would be levelled
as all are humbled eventually

Through time such redundance must be spoken
and memories preserved in rocks
fade under a system of weather patterns
so unpredictable that we are amazed it works

The goats know these things
showing it in their stares
Circumspect and vigilant they cruise
over each mountain path
limber and sure as dancers

Later we missed the ocean
maybe because we'd known it longer
wishing for the place where life began
billions of years ago

Still I recall looking down
sensing order even in things
I feared the most
While under the earth's surface
constant turmoil lurks
earthquakes and volcanoes
occur in clearly defined paths
and I understood that a matrix of patterns
exists throughout the earth
connecting all that is

Feeling a part of
not separate from
I trusted in those mountains
loving more than I could remember
and fearing less and less